JONATHAN FALLA

The Physician of Sanlúcar is Jonathan Falla's fourth novel, after *Blue Poppies, Poor Mercy* and *Glenfarron*. Jamaican-born Falla lives in Scotland where he is Director of Studies for the St Andrew's Creative Writing Summer School. He has won a Creative Scotland Award, a PEN story prize and other awards for his fiction, drama and film writing.

See www.jonathanfalla.co.uk.

First published in the UK in 2013 by Aurora Metro Books
67 Grove Avenue, Twickenham, TW1 4HX
www.aurorametro.com info@aurorametro.com

The Physician of Sanlúcar © 2013 Jonathan Falla

With thanks to: Neil Gregory, Richard Turk, Jack Timney, Alex Chambers,
Fay Allum, Juliet Peacock, Sarah Strupinski.

10 9 8 7 6 5 4 3 2 1

The author gratefully acknowledges a Creative Scotland Award received for
the work on this book from the Scottish Arts Council.

Cover design: Alice Marwick/www.alice-marwick.co.uk

Printed by Ashford Colour Press Ltd, Gosport, Hants UK

ISBN: 978-1-906582-38-8

THE PHYSICIAN OF SANLÚCAR

JONATHAN FALLA

AURORA METRO BOOKS

In memory of my mother Sheila

(1915-2012)

Extract from

SKETCHES OF THE PATAGONIAN SEABOARD
'SHEETS FROM A SAILOR'S STORY'
by
Captain Huw Asbury Prothero

But of all the cheeky escapades I saw during my Patagonian years, few surpassed the *Dafne* business, both for audacious planning and for the mystery of its outcome, for none can swear he knows the fate of *Dafne*. It was a tale of gold, but where is that gold today? As thoroughly lost as Blaenau Ffestiniog in a rainy mist. The misfortunes of *Dafne,* however, I can illuminate, for in this drama I myself played a walk-on part.

In late 1913, even on the distant Chilean seaboard we knew that war was coming. We were far from Europe, and this might mean that we'd be left in peace, but it might mean our fate would be decided we knew not where.

Now: war demands gold, and Kaiser Bill knew that Chile had gold aplenty. The numbers of German colonists could only facilitate matters. Their agents set to work. At mineshafts among the cacti of the Elqui valley, or by the icy pannings on Tierra del Fuego, records were falsified, consignments diverted. Agents of the Anglo-South Chilean Syndicate were suborned; one was garrotted in an Antofagasta bordello. An ingot here, a bag of dust there: little by little, the Germans put bullion aside. Along the Chilean coast we heard rumour: something was up. We were not fooled. I was in from

Patagonia with my ship's engineer purchasing parts when I caught wind of trouble. Miss Dinah Morris, a smart young lady presiding over a seaman's lodgings at Valparaíso, fixed me with a stern dark eye one morning and confided:

'Captain Huw, there's something up, now mark my words.'

I knew better than to contradict Miss Morris; one's evening cutlet was liable to be served lukewarm. War broke out that very day.

Stockpiling was, however, only half the Kaiser's problem; to pay for howitzers, his gold must be shipped to Europe. But how? British cruisers would pounce. Hence the extraordinary role prepared for *Dafne*.

On the coast, we were all acquainted with this grubby little tramp, but nobody thought twice when she quietly absented herself. It turned out that *Dafne* had been taken to a small shipyard way up north; there she underwent a refit entirely to do with speed. Her hold was halved by new twin boilers, their capacity far in excess of your average coaster. Her triple-expansion engine was enhanced, her cylinder compression vastly increased, her working pressures upped to levels that, in retrospect, may have been rash. She was transformed, save in her looks – for when *Dafne* reappeared among us, she was outwardly as rusty as old barbed wire. *Dafne's* new commander was Gunther Hase, a Chilean but with Hamburg family roots, very competent and affable, who lodged not infrequently at Miss Morris's boarding house. His crew was drawn from the German community – names we all knew, men with whom we'd drained a bottle – and Hase now received very specific instructions.

For a short spell, they pottered up and down making a show of touting for cargo like the rest of us. We were then surprised to hear – for she really was a grubby little thing – that *Dafne* was engaged by the German navy as a 'fast collier'; her hold (excluding one new, locked and puzzling compartment) was filled with coal. To our astonishment, she was assigned to the elite Pacific squadron commanded by the celebrated Vice-Admiral Graf Maximilian von Spee in his fine cruiser *Scharnhorst*. Well!

The hostilities had us rattled by then: might not the substantial German population in Chile turn against us few Britons? Even civilian captains like me, serving under the neutral Chilean flag, did not sleep easy. Next we learned that British warships had rounded Cape Horn and were steaming up the coast.

'Captain Huw!' averred Miss Morris, 'there's going to be an awful scrap, and what will it mean for us?'

It was Dinah Morris who heard talk of a secretive vessel in the German fleet, and concluded that this must be *Dafne*.

Here, yours truly plays his hand in the game, for it was to me that Miss Morris confided her suspicions. Why was *Dafne's* coal cargo so reduced? What was in the locked compartment? Why was her crew entirely German? Why was absolutely no-one allowed on board? And why was the obliging Gunther Hase behaving so out of character, so uncivil? I confess I poo-poohed such doubts, but Miss Morris intimated that my continued welcome depended on my doing her the courtesy. She insisted that I contact our nation's representatives about *Dafne*. I did so; they took not a blind bit of notice.

I hastened back to my own command at Punta Arenas; I had no intention of being caught in the spray when shells flew over the sea!

Well, a scrap there was indeed.

It was a warm Sunday; our naval gunners could not see the Germans in the evening haze. British ships were silhouetted against the setting sun: perfect targets. *Good Hope* sank with all but five of her crew. *Monmouth* took forty direct hits; filled with roaring hellfires, she was seen to turn towards the Germans...

'In the dusk,' said Miss Morris, 'the horizon itself seemed to burn. There was a low growling over the sea, like a bear in pain.'

German casualties were three wounded and no dead – not one. Sixteen hundred British sailors perished. Our boys wore patented new lifesavers, inflatable rubber rings about the throat to hold their chins above the water. As, one by one, they jumped into the sea, their necks were snapped.

The Germans steamed south, around Cape Horn and on to the Falkland Islands. Spee was to lure the British aside while *Dafne,* packed with oversized boilers, her powerful new engines, ample coal and gold bullion, would sprint for the Bay of Biscay, the gold to be transferred to German submarines and slipped into Kiel. They had no idea that a vengeful British squadron had reached the Falklands first; too late, the Germans turned and fled, pursued by faster and more powerful ships. They fought like furies, disciplined gunflashes rippling up and down the *Scharnhorst,* the *Dresden* and the *Gneisenau* – but fine gunnery could not save them. Spee went down with his flagship; the sea was icy and few Germans were saved. The British comforted the enemy officers, dressed them in cobbled-together uniforms and invited them to dine, everyone keen to be civil.

But here was a mystery: what of *Dafne* and her cargo? Now the tale takes a strange turn, for little *Dafne* never again appears in maritime records. One British officer had seen a small collier burst from the shelter of the Falklands 'as though Old Nick were at her heels', and turn towards mainland Argentina. Was that *Dafne?* Neither ship nor gold nor the good Captain Hase were ever seen again in a South American port – officially. We drank a sombre toast to Hase, a proper gentleman. But the story of *Dafne* was not done yet. The sequel came at Bahía Sanlúcar, a remote anchorage at which I made regular calls as master of the mail packet *Luisa Menendez.* This drama was played out in the early days of 1915, and a principle player was a close acquaintance of mine from Punta Arenas, Dr Matthieu Macanan.

One

THE STEAM CHEST
1905

If we go back a little.

There was a timber box in the centre of a timber room, and the room had the sweet reek of sweat. The box was the size of a large tea chest, but built of un-planed lumber planks, and through the imperfect seams were seeping wisps of steam. On top of the chest was a man's head. The neck was mounted in a collar of leather flaps between which oozed tiny plumes of vapour.

The head was running wet. Sweat dripped from thick whips of red hair, drops beading the entire face which was a lurid blotchy pink like a child's thoroughly spanked bottom. The eyes were open, and they blinked and peered about anxiously. As the sweat coursed off the forehead down over the lashes, the eyes searched about for escape routes. But escape from the box would be difficult, because the front opening was closed with a large steel hasp.

'I cannae mair,' gasped the man in the box.

'You undertook for the full treatment,' replied another, watching. 'We cannot contemplate half measures.'

'Ye maun let me oot!'

'Four more minutes,' insisted his tormentor. A youngish man, this, tall and with a long stride and a handsome but rather melancholy thin face, to which he now raised a mask of padded white cotton. He knelt beside the chest; there was a small annexe jutting out at floor level, made from galvanized sheeting. A plume of steam escaped as he opened a tin door. He stirred a little coal brazier with a poker, unstopping a brown glass jar and pouring a dash of liquid into a pot over the heat, followed by water from a tin mug.

As he poured, he turned his masked face away from the fumes.

'Oh, dear God!' wailed the captive.

'Three minutes,' returned his captor, voice muffled by the mask, and with no hint of sympathy. 'You do wish the contagion to be eliminated?'

The physician moved to a nearby stool, glancing as he went at a cream-coloured tin clock on a shelf. The prisoner strained to see the clock, but it was behind him.

'Doctor,' he wheezed, 'I am punished enough...'

'But not cured. I'll not waste mercury on ditherers. And you have three more treatments to come.'

He fingered his face mask, and his victim noticed.

'If it is safe, why the mask?'

'I'm not in your condition,' the doctor parried.

Only when the clock permitted did he return to the firebox, inspecting the little suspended pot: the elixir was consumed. He went to the window, opening it wide, then stepped to the outside door, throwing that open also so that the winds tore through the room. At last, he parted the front doors of the box and the two halves of the lid; whimpering, the prisoner attempted to stand from the bench inside, took one faltering step forward, then collapsed onto the bare floorboards. His naked body was as red as a gourmet's lobster.

'Doctor,' he shrieked, 'the cold! For pity's sake...'

The doctor took from a wooden peg a blanket of soft grey guanaco wool, and draped it around the bare shoulders with surprising gentleness. The crouching man croaked:

'Oh, dear Lord, pity a poor sinner who has paid a heavy price in full.'

'You've yet to pay me,' remarked the other.

Two more came to Dr Macanan that morning. There were new whores in town; word was out, the sailors had hurried ashore, the farmers trotting eagerly in from the distant *estancias*. Not that the whores of Patagonia were celebrated for anything other than rock bottom prices, being *mestizo* slags from Buenos Aires worn out by city trade – or so their clients grumbled unkindly to Dr Macanan. Still (these gentlemen observed), an old whore was better than no whore. So the men rode into Punta Arenas and visited the merry-houses, one-storey timber dwellings with net-curtained windows and a low fence around the wind-blown garden, and with a great number of small rooms at the back where a pidgin of Spanish, Gaelic and German was exchanged to an orchestration of bedsprings. A month later, the farmers would return to town with a burning in their waterworks, with swollen testicles, and with ulcers on the penis, fingers or lips. They would hurry past the stone palace of the Chilean governor and the neo-classical residences of Hispano-German merchant-princes, through neighbourhoods where the dirt streets had no names nor the houses any numbers, out to the shacks and traders' yards at the edge of Punta Arenas.

Clutching pencilled directions given them by friends, they eventually located the wooden building – clad in galvanised tin plate – which they sincerely hoped was the French doctor's clinic. They crept round the back and slipped up the outer stair, cursing the arthritic knees that had started to grieve them at much the same time as their pee turned to fire. They tapped at the top door quietly to avoid alerting the neighbours, and because they were frightened of Dr Macanan – who, it was rumoured, would tell you the truth.

The visitors were Russians and Spaniards, Welsh and Croats, Swedes, Chileans and Americans, and not a few Scots, sheep men from Wester Ross, from Sutherland, and from the Hebrides. The Scots pronounced the doctor's name 'McCannon', and Dr Macanan from Montpelier was sometimes faced with a man mumbling confidences to him in Gaelic. The shepherds had come to Patagonia for the £40 a year (own dogs provided), and because they had heard that it was much like the Isle of Lewis but on a grand scale; for every acre of ground on the Western Isles, there were 300 acres of Patagonian grassland, smooth and uninterrupted. It was a place where you could see the earth curving. When gales whipped across the broad inland seas – Seno Otway and Seno Skyring – the water rose into standing sheets. The winds were cousin to those of Lewis but far harsher; the open sky was more exhilaratingly vast; the sheep grazed grass like Lewis sheep, but the pastures were so huge that the shepherds were told to buy a telescope for watching their flocks. The only bother was the odd savage, the dearth of women, and the distance to town. Also, the mutton was darker and tougher, and the venereal diseases were astonishing.

In his examination room, the French physician would tell each mortified visitor to urinate into a glass jar. He would then sit the jar on the windowsill, study the floating threads of mucous, and murmur darkly:

'These are blenorrhoeal filaments.'

The blushing sheep man commonly stammered some rigmarole of excuses, which the doctor would cut short.

'I suppose you got these quite innocently? Perhaps by urinating upwind?'

His patients appreciated this withering tone; they took it as indicating Dr Macanan's clinical resolve, and they hoped it would speed the cure. Dr Macanan would now peer at the blenorrhoeal filaments, tapping at the glass with a fingernail, and asking:

'Is there pus?'

The shepherd would admit that there was pus. The doctor would command him to drop his trousers (extraordinary Patagonian garments seemingly made of sailcloth stitched with fencing wire). With a wooden stick, Dr Macanan would lift the delinquent member, frowning at the purulent tears of guilt it wept.

'I feared as much,' he would whisper.

Dr Macanan delved into the urethra with a cotton bud; this unfailingly produced yelps, and a bleb of yellow goo. The stained bud he would carry to a small table, where he would soak it with drops of seventy per cent spirit. He would take his victim by the wrist and, with a scalpel, lift a flap of skin on the forearm, putting a yellow smudge onto the bleeding underfat. If the patient tried to draw his arm away, Dr Macanan would fix him with pale grey eyes.

'I am inoculating you with your own killed gonococci. Do you understand?'

The shepherd would mouth weakly, 'Yes, yes,' and be still.

After which he'd be told his sentence: doses of cubebs pepper in liquorice. Also, copious liquids by mouth, especially sheep's milk (no shortage there). Regular bowel movements were essential; the rectum must be unloaded to reduce pressure on the seminal vesicles. No alcohol (O, dear Lord...). Highly spiced dishes to be avoided (not that Lewis men were keen on those). And, needless to say (but it must be said repeatedly), complete continence.

For those with a weeping ulcer on the glans, the news was worse: syphilis.

'What can be done?' they would whisper.

'Mercury,' they'd be told, and they'd pale.

'Is there no danger?'

'Plenty, in unskilled hands.'

But the patient could rest assured that he'd be treated by the safest, most modern and most effective method available: transdermal absorption of mercuric vapours, in the steam box of Dr Macanan's own devising.

Having little choice, the patient nodded his consent. After which he would be told the price.

So the Chilean sailor, the Hebridean shepherd, the German miner or Argentine gaucho would all slink away from Dr Macanan's rooms, terrified by their diseases, the treatment thereof, and by the French doctor. Macanan was never physically harsh, but awe was part of the treatment. Chilly reproof was expected; patients would feel themselves unshriven were the doctor not to look down his long nose in censure.

More observant visitors wondered if this manner came quite easily. They sensed a distractedness in Dr Macanan, a gravity beyond his years. They wondered if his aloofness was a tad forced; the doctor's considerate hands did not match his icy disapproval, his soft grey eyes belied his stern words, and his reputation was gentler than he himself knew. But Macanan deterred his clientele from prying into his opinions, or into his professional life. He was not a man for the open country; he rarely left town, and would not go out to visit the farms. Why was that? The only reason anyone could offer was that Dr Macanan was reputedly afraid of horses.

*

Dr Macanan's neighbours were aware of the class of disease in which he specialised. The landlord (downstairs) was an Estonian ironmonger who specialised also: in picks, sieves and barrows for the gold prospectors. He had supplied the hardware – screws and hinges, hasps and brackets – for the construction of the doctor's steam box. He could hardly dislike Macanan; his French tenant paid the rent promptly, and was a model of courtesy whose appearance was always neat, his clothes as modestly grey as his eyes, his shave impeccable, his crisply waved dark hair kept short and orderly. The ironmonger's wife, who had aspirations, would have been thrilled to include a physician in their 'circle'. But Macanan was unforthcoming, and attempts to get to know him, to engage him in conversation about Europe and about his past, always failed. Dr Macanan fended off such approaches, and retreated to his clinic. The suggestion that he might take his meals with the Estonian family met with polite refusal: his hours were irregular, he explained; it suited him to walk out to a nearby eating house.

The ironmonger's daughter Tilly was employed in 'doing' for Dr Macanan, cleaning his private rooms, and she reported to her parents on the neat rows of books to be found upstairs; some of them were doctoring books, with pictures that made Tilly gasp and blush and peek again. Others were songs or poems, or something of the sort (Tilly could not read, though she did sums nicely). It was all most intriguing – as were the implements and blades in their wooden chest, the locked cabinets of frosted jars, and the more personal items too: the bottle of vetiver cologne (sparingly used), the razor and strop, the electro-plated fob watch, the tortoiseshell shoe horn, the boots that had a faint hot smell, the linen basket's contents slightly stained, the bed with its impression of the doctor's body that Tilly sometimes found still warm when she went in first thing to wipe.

The trader and his wife respected the doctor, for Macanan would treat all aches and ailments at very reasonable prices and even with some success – this in a land where it was considered good physic for a broken limb to disembowel two puppies and bind them on either side of the break, something the Estonian wife had never thought quite nice. Dr Macanan was, the couple understood, a real doctor, one with a solid income, though the trader's wife clucked and shook her head reprovingly at the shifty invalids who came asking for the clinic.

'I don't know,' she remarked to her husband, 'how he can abide such people.'

'Well, dearest,' replied the ironmonger, 'he answers a sore need.'

She smiled bleakly. When she saw further shocked white faces descending the staircase after treatment, she tutted once again, remarking with more sympathy:

'Poor smitten souls! That Dr Macanan is heartless.'

But her husband had noted that the poor smitten souls seldom failed to return for further steaming.

'Macanan has a heart,' he said.

Which gave his wife a notion: a young man who had a heart must want that heart caressed. He must want the play of female fancy in his home, and her legs parting in his bed. Tilly was young also, and personable save for the hairy brown mole upon her neck. In fact, Tilly was downright pretty. She smelled good, too, meaty but not rank, a smell that spoke of human richness. She had thick black hair that could be washed, she had a bust that was generous without being fatty, a wiggle to her hips and an appealing cheek.

'Oh, you are so provoking!' the mother chided her daughter over nothing at all in the family parlour. Then mother raised her eyes to regard the ceiling with a great expression of shrewdness.

'Still,' she remarked knowingly, 'men like to be provoked. Just a little, now and then. By a comely girl.'

Open-mouthed, Tilly followed her mother's gaze to the ceiling: above them, a man's firm tread could be heard going about his professional business. She looked again at her mother to find the latter staring at her with lips pursed in calculation. Her mother took Tilly by both wrists, and murmured:

'Not too far, and not too quick.'

So Tilly went upstairs to do her duty, and found Dr Macanan sitting at his desk writing in a red buckram journal.

'What a lot of writing you do,' said Tilly. 'You ever write about us?'

The doctor glanced up at her, surprised.

'Like, our family an' all? Mind, we ain't got no babies, more's pity. You like babies? I wish I had babies.'

Dr Macanan said nothing, but continued to peer at her. Goodness, thought Tilly: he was manly! For a tiny instant, Tilly imagined that she saw a tender yearning in those soft grey eyes – then it was gone.

'I'll fetch your coffee, then,' said the girl with a little pout.

Tilly was wearing a short-sleeved blouse anyway, but she now declared it to be an unseasonably hot day and she further unbuttoned the already low neck. Dr Macanan looked down steadfastly at his work. She brought the coffee, coming to the left side of the table; in order to place the cup by his right hand, she must lean across in front of him so that her bosom was directly in his line of sight; his view was now straight into her cleavage. Her black tresses (today with the Patagonian dust and the sebum rinsed out) she allowed to brush his cheek.

'There's your coffee, then.'

He didn't speak. Slowly, Tilly straightened and looked down at him, at that crisp wavy hair, at that fragile reserve that she would crack!

'Don't let it get cold,' she urged.

The scent of her (not unlike a rump steak marinaded in vinegar, *alerce* honey and chillies) lingered about the table.

'Thank you, Tilly,' said Dr Macanan in a quiet, distant voice, and the girl felt a flush of success...

Except that he would not look at her again. He picked up his pen once more, studied the page, paused.

'Will that be all?' she breathed.

'All? Oh, yes.'

He recommenced writing.

Tilly was undeterred – or at least, her mother was undeterred. She took her daughter by the wrists once more.

'Open him up, girl! Boil him open like a mussel.'

In the days following, Tilly pressed home her attack. She minced, she pouted, she risked a little petulant huff; as the December heat built, she damn near stripped off in front of Dr Macanan. She let him glimpse and smell her deep dark armpits one day, then became lady-like the next. Noticing one afternoon how engrossed he was in a volume of verse, Tilly contrived to let him catch her turning the pages of one of his anthologies; as he entered the room, she blushed like an inquisitive, awe-struck innocent (though she had the book upside down). She was hoping that he'd exclaim, 'Oh! Do you love verses too?' and pat a chair next to his, to invite her to sit and read with him.

But he never did. And if Tilly was brutally honest with herself, Dr Macanan now appeared barely to register her presence. He continued with his writing and his reading, absorbed.

'Thank you,' was all he ever said.

At the end of a month, the Estonian ironmonger found his daughter sobbing with vexation in the kitchen, and her mother scowling at the girl, and they would not tell him what was the matter.

*

Meanwhile, the procession of shifty men continued to climb the doctor's outside stair. One December afternoon, windstill and as warm as it ever is on the Strait of Magellan, the ironmonger was startled to find a rather different figure rapping at his door: a priest.

Beneath the man's cassock of brown wool, the battered toes and sandals of a missionary brother showed. The newcomer was a burly man, his skin dark and his hair cropped short; there was incongruity between his vocation and his prize-fighter physique. Even standing still, he had an energy that might break things. The ironmonger wondered what the priest would look like, naked and lobster red, after a good steaming in the box.

The visitor spoke with an accent the ironmonger could not locate: south-eastern Europe? Dalmatian, or Bulgarian? They came from all over to Punta Arenas. Directing him up the wooden stairs, the tradesman gawped as the timbers shook under the brother's bounding energy. From the top, the priest glowered back down until the door opened.

Brother Ferenc Zsolt (he was in fact Hungarian) entered Dr Macanan's clinic with mingled revulsion and curiosity. As he introduced himself, he circled the room touching the brown poison bottles, the urine jars, the battered microscope, and the steam box with its aperture for the neck. He poked at the leather flaps.

'A Turkish bath, Doctor?'

'For administering mercury,' replied Dr Macanan, 'in the form of vapour.'

'It requires repeated doses, yes? I know about your speciality, you see.'

Macanan replied: 'Four sessions in the steam chest, yes. On alternate days.'

'So patients attend over seven days in total?'

'That is correct. Repeated small doses are safer.'

Brother Ferenc smiled: 'Safety is perhaps not the first consideration in the minds of the men you treat.'

But Dr Macanan did not smile. He looked out of the window to the edge of town and beyond.

'Out on the sheep runs, life must be intolerably lonely.'

Brother Ferenc wondered at him; the doctor's own life seemed hardly convivial. It was said he did not get about, and he was hardly made for the open pampas. Even here in Punta Arenas, Macanan cut a lonely figure. He was well-made indeed, but smiled sparingly, and had few friends. Solitary figures were hardly unusual in Patagonia: humanity was so thinly spread. But Dr Macanan seemed as isolated in Punta Arenas as any shepherd on a sheep run, and was quite as reserved.

'Well, well,' said the visitor, looking again round the room. 'No certificates on the wall? Every doctor has certificates on the wall.'

'It is not a legal requirement. I studied in Montpelier.'

'Not Paris?'

'Montpelier is one of the oldest medical schools in the world,' answered Macanan. 'It was founded in the 13th century.'

'And you studied there how long?'

But Macanan was not in the mood for interrogation.

'Was there something I might do for you?' he asked.

Brother Ferenc, momentarily thwarted, regarded him a moment, then changed tack.

'Certainly,' said Ferenc, suddenly brusque. 'I am not concerned with Scotch shepherds and Argentine gauchos. It is the natives that interest me, Fuegian Indians. Have you visited Tierra del Fuego?'

'No.'

'Would that appeal to you?'

'If there was good reason.'

'Very pressing reason: you can hardly imagine the extent of contagion.'

'Amongst the natives? How did that happen?'

Ferenc did not reply; he was inspecting with prurient horror a kidney dish containing urethral dilators.

'You have expertise that we need.'

'Surely not,' returned Dr Macanan.

'Please, have your laugh,' said the priest, irritated.

'I wouldn't dream of it. But I don't see how I could help.'

Ferenc looked pointedly at the steam chest. 'Is that portable?'

'Possibly. But I am not used to travel.'

'Well, good heavens, the travel will all be arranged; I shall accompany you myself. There will be guides and every assistance, and you will be comfortably lodged at the Paloma Sagrada mission. Doctor, you are desperately needed.'

Macanan was silent for a long moment. At last he said:

'Nonetheless, it would depend.'

'On what?'

'The available transport.'

'Transport?' The priest was bewildered; what transport was there ever in Patagonia? 'Horses will carry your equipment.'

'But for myself?'

'For you? Forgive me, but travel on Tierra del Fuego is, of course, on horseback...'

A farcical possibility struck Ferenc: Dr Macanan wanted a carriage.

'Doctor, please understand, there are no roads. The horses will be our own, from the mission, and I will ensure they are the very best...'

'I do not ride. On horses. I do not do it.'

Dr Macanan examined his instruments, refusing to meet Brother Ferenc's penetrating eye. Ferenc stared at him incredulous: how did the man get about? Hot air balloon?

'I can arrange for mules,' he offered. 'Mules are quite different; mules are quiet, utterly dependable.'

The doctor looked again over the shingled rooftops to the beech woods on the hills. His silence had the obduracy of a mule.

'Your mount,' said Ferenc tentatively, dreading to imply any insult, 'can be led by another rider, in front...'

*

After Brother Ferenc departed, Dr Macanan stood studying the mercury chest, as if considering whether it was friend or foe. He remained very still for some moments – then, abruptly, he turned aside, put on a woollen jacket and stepped out of his clinic, descending the wooden stairs. He wandered the lanes as though in search of food. But though there were inns that would have served him fish and potatoes, or soup and *empanadas*, Macanan did not stop and walked on round the corner where he encountered a syphilitic, wavering and wobbling across the road. The bridge of the man's nose had collapsed, his face was vividly blotched.

He was a former seed merchant, and had once been led to Dr Macanan by a neighbour who urged, 'Is there nothing you can do?' There was nothing; it was far too late; there was degeneration in every part of body and soul. The syphilitic now saw Macanan, peered at the doctor without recognition, dribbled, and drifted away.

Two
BEAUTY MADE TO DANCE

In January 1906, Dr Macanan crossed the Strait of Magellan by the regular service, a small steamer of the Chilean government.

As the boat worked its way eastward, waves of mechanical throbbing rhythmically shook the glasses and the bottles of brandy and pisco in the smoky little saloon. Macanan preferred to stand out on deck, gazing at the opposing shores, both now distant. Behind him, Punta Arenas was a smudge against the background of wooded hills from which the town's poor quality coal was extracted. Before him, Tierra del Fuego was, as so often, veiled in its rains. When the clouds shifted and the sun flashed, he glimpsed the peaks that filled the heart of the island, with their skirts of dripping evergreen beech. He had never imagined wanting to go there. But wanting to go had not often been the reason he had moved anywhere. Needing to leave, more usually. Needing to be gone.

Of Tierra del Fuego, he knew very little. The Estonian hardware merchant, who supplied all the prospectors, had assured him that the rocks were so magnetic that an iron nail would cling to a boulder; that the centre of the island consisted of nothing but crags and frozen bogs; that the glaciers on the south side hung near vertical, down to the sea. Why would anyone live there? What was the mentality of the natives? How was he to communicate and persuade? He had taken the steam chest apart, he had agreed to its being crated up and transported on mules to remote missions, but it did not seem possible that any savage would agree to sit inside and be steamed.

He stood on the foredeck in the knocking wind, considering

another trivial but persisting problem: what to do about Tilly. Macanan was more observant than the Estonians give him credit for: he had realised immediately what the plot must be. Nonetheless, he liked the family and hardly blamed them; in a town as remote as Punta Arenas, one must capitalise on everything one had, daughters included. He didn't wish to fall out...

'Dr Macanan, is it not?'

He looked round: a stocky, rubicund little man faced him, whom he had seen bustling about the deck ordering the crew to tidy this, stow that.

'Captain...' began Macanan, ignorant of the name.

'Prothero, Huw Prothero,' said the other, proffering a cheery paw. 'You'll be enjoying the blow? Getting rid of the cobwebs?'

'I confess,' said Macanan, 'that I've never before crossed the Strait.'

'It's not something to do by way of a Sunday outing, see,' laughed Captain Prothero.

'Is it so dangerous, the crossing?'

'Oh, we've to keep our wits about us. There's plenty rusted hulks on the foreshore. I'm thinking to write a history of the wrecks; it would make a fearsome read. The currents have a tremendous rip, and often it's too deep for anchorage. There's a grandeur there, mind. Wouldn't you say there was a grandeur?' He gestured towards Tierra del Fuego.

Macanan said, 'I can hardly see it in the spray. Is it grand close to?'

'Close to, there's not a deal to see,' beamed the Welshman, 'unless you've a taste for blizzards, or cannibals in canoes.'

'A taste for cannibals...' wondered Macanan aloud.

Captain Prothero guffawed:

'Hah, yes, very good! They may get a taste for you.'

'Is it true about the cannibals?'

'I've no idea; they've eaten no part of me. I see savages wandering the beach often enough, naked and shivering, poor creatures.'

'You know the territory well, I expect.'

'I've chuffed up and down the Chilean coast much of my career, and I've commanded this little tub three years – but not much longer. I'm appointed Master of a new Argentine service to Bahía Blanca, the mail packet *Luisa Menendez,* starting next month.'

'My congratulations.'

Huw Prothero beamed at him, entirely affable.

'Well, well, I must keep us from running ashore in the meantime; mustn't add to the wrecks. Good day, Doctor. We'll be there in an hour.'

He stomped away to the stern, barking at his Chilean hands who humoured him with as little effort as possible.

The steamer slopped towards the Fuegian side and the settlement at Porvenir. Macanan found himself on the jetty in a salt breeze that pushed and worried at him, never quite letting him relax. He cursed himself for agreeing to this.

'Think,' Brother Ferenc had urged, 'of the misery of the Fuegians. Think of the time you give to Europeans, men who knowingly bring their misery upon themselves. Compare these to the simple natives who succumb to civilisation – your civilisation and mine, Doctor. Their society is rotted by other men's pox. Think what you – you alone – can do for them.'

This last appeal had almost backfired. Macanan was less sure of his skills than Ferenc imagined.

He had searched for good reasons not to come to Tierra del Fuego, but it was too late. He was confronted by a terrifying string of quadrupeds, and the moment when he must climb onto an animal's back.

'Oh, come now!' The priest was there on the quay, laughing. 'It's no dragon; it's a mule, stolid and dull.'

There wasn't a single wagon, only sullen mules and ponies, and a gaucho in a felt hat and leather chaps. Dr Macanan never learned whether the man was a professional working for hire, or a Believer in the service of the Brothers. Glowering at his mule (which ignored him), Macanan climbed aboard; he was uncomfortable and stiff from the moment his thighs splayed out in the ridiculous way that saddles enforce. Bystanders grinned at the discomfiture of the clever gentleman with his trim dress, his well-shaven chin and his vanity miffed by a mule, but they misunderstood: it was not vanity distressing Macanan: it was fear, pure and simple. He'd have ridden in a frock of turkey feathers if it would keep his mount docile.

When the doctor was as settled as could be, the gaucho tucked the reins out of trouble, took up a lead rope and set off, dragging Macanan after him. Just one thing made Macanan smile: he had wondered whether Ferenc, in his awkward woollen cassock, might ride side-saddle. But before mounting his pony, the priest had hitched his skirts up about his waist revealing a pair of stout britches and long riding boots; he rode with his cassock in a roll about his hips.

Thus they left Porvenir: Brother Ferenc, then the gaucho leading a visibly queasy Doctor Macanan and, behind the doctor, a train of six pack animals. On two of these, bundled in oilcloth, rode the sections of the steam chest.

They moved north along a foreshore track, crossing a coastal plain of tussocky grass, still green in mid-summer. There were a few desiccated cartwheel ruts, but Macanan never saw a cart. Streams meandered to the sea by cuts in the grassland, showing a thick black underlay of matted roots.

Then, a sight Macanan did not understand: a ship, a two-masted schooner with an auxiliary stack, sitting at anchor one hundred yards offshore. The ship's rigging appeared to be draped with marine detritus, like a wreck risen from the depths; there were lumps of something suspended from the spars, dozens of large lumps.

'Meat,' said Ferenc. 'Carcasses for sale. There's prospectors panning a river beyond that headland.'

Later, there was a colony of penguins, stubby birds with proud but pleasing faces, shepherding their young about the turf. The parents had tired pink rims to their eyes, but the juveniles wore sweet, playful ruffs of brown. As Macanan rode past, they took little notice but stretched out their young wings and dipped this way and that, like novice tightrope walkers.

'*Pingüinos*,' smiled Ferenc.

'Charming,' replied Macanan politely.

'The English pirate Drake and his men killed 20,000,' said the priest.

'Sailors must eat.'

'You know how penguins choose their mates? The males must find a pretty stone to drop at their lady love's feet. If it's a nice stone, she may agree to watch him dig a hole in the sand bank. Then she inspects the hole. If it will not make a nice house, she will walk away.'

'Very sensible.'

'Yes, it's important to make a good home if you are to get your girl. I wonder about those European ladies who come to join their husbands in Punta Arenas. If they could have imagined the place they are fetched to, would they have left home?'

On they rode, the gaucho leading the way, the flat-packed steam chest creaking on the mules' flanks, an ache in the doctor's spine, and his loathing and mistrust of the animals undiminished. They reached Gente Grande Bay, where there should be 'large people' though Macanan saw no one. They traversed a broad sweep of pasture and glimpsed a distant profusion of white flecks Macanan decided were sheep, though they looked like maggots. They rode among low grassy knolls like a sea-swell in the coastal plain. Now the mountains edged towards the water. There by a stream they camped; this struck Macanan as odd because, not more than two miles away, he saw a ranch house: surely the rules of hospitality in a harsh land would have got them a bed? There should be, among the corrals and pens, an abundance of sheds and bunk houses where they could lodge. He could see men coming and going on horseback. But Brother Ferenc seemingly wanted nothing to do with the ranch. It was as though he could not see it, and the taciturn gaucho – who set about preparing tents, fire and dinner – did not look that way at all.

The next morning they continued, Ferenc with his cassock once again hitched up like rolled skirts, Macanan jigging in the saddle with a sore spine, aching groin muscles and churning gut. Another ranch lay before them. Surely they must call there: to deliver letters, to hear the gossip. But as they descended the grass slopes, Brother Ferenc reacted to the ranch as though to a repelling magnet. He made staccato indications to the gaucho, who took the string of mules in a broad sweep inland.

'Why do we not visit?' Macanan called into the breeze.

'Visiting is delay,' returned Ferenc, spurring ahead. He seemed in no hurry to speak to anyone they saw. They passed another large flock of sheep, observed by unsmiling men on horseback with rifles in cases slung from their saddles.

'Can you not train Fuegians as shepherds?' Macanan asked.

'They would eat the sheep.' Ferenc twisted to speak to him. 'They are in a bad condition, Doctor, and not just medically. They are surplus to the modern age; they get in the way of gold panning and ranching. We have gathered together some 250, to receive the Gospel. At Paloma Sagrada, we give them employment on the loom, or in metalwork. It is rudimentary, but it is all they can manage. You shall see.'

So Macanan held his peace.

Now they rode in the face of a wind that with splintered fingernails scratched up the waters of the Strait. Past other bays, other headlands. On the second day, the mountains drew closer to the sea; the rocks and woods sometimes advanced right to the water's edge, so that the procession must pick its way between slimy boulders, or follow wet, winding tracks through the sword grass and undershrub, watching for low branches. Elsewhere was nothing but open prairie, flat as a board.

They came to a river which hurtled down a cliff, then swilled across 500 yards of grass. On the foreshore were shanties of rough-hewn timber little better than driftwood. Beyond these, Macanan saw men standing by stilted troughs into which they poured buckets of river water. They stared into the swill – and sluiced in another bucketful.

Macanan turned to speak to Ferenc, but the Brother had pulled his pony towards the cliff to ford the river as far from the camp as possible.

Macanan, following, glanced back towards the shanties and saw, in a space between the huts, a woman. She was a native, dark skinned and with lank black hair, and she was stark naked, crouched on the dirt with a rope about her neck, looped over a tall post. The prospectors were ignoring her for now, though one of their dogs, ambling past, cocked a leg against the post. The woman was motionless, as though awaiting execution; Macanan wondered what sort of execution that would be.

Ahead of him, Ferenc was hastening away to the river crossing.

You know well – thought Macanan – how contagion came here.

The gaucho hauled the string of mules after Ferenc. They continued in silence, hours further.

And there at last was the mission of Paloma Sagrada, the dove of the Holy Spirit.

It was on an island – or not exactly an island: a promontory with a gravel causeway, only the wind was thumping the sea into the gravel, creating a foam that rendered this causeway invisible. The promontory was a rocky excrescence from the flat shoreline, with a fringe of pines giving an illusion of shelter from the blasts driving into the Strait off the Atlantic.

They splashed across the gravel. There was a child, a native child. It was, Macanan decided, a girl; he knew this not from the face or the stack of coarse rust-coloured hair, but from the sacking smock. She had shoes. Many children in Punta Arenas did not have shoes, and scuffled cheerfully through the dust barefoot. But this walking mop had small boots without laces. The girl was crouched, staring fixedly into a rivulet among the pebbles. As he approached on his mule, Macanan thought she was either defecating or building a little dam – but she was poking at something with a stick. The girl heard the plod and clop of the mules; she saw the caravan approaching, and fled to the nearest trees.

Macanan looked down; the girl had been investigating the split abdomen of something dead, a thing of macerated brown fur and blue loops of gut: an otter perhaps. He had no wish to inspect it. Macanan's only thought was to get off the mule as soon as possible.

Among the pines, the church stood, dominant and red. The walls were timber framed panels bolted together, and at the east end he passed an apse with glazed lancet windows. He supposed it had all been prefabricated in Punta Arenas and shipped here. The roof was of corrugated steel thickly daubed with red oxide paint. Nearby stood a belfry: two stripped tree-trunks with a cross-bar tying the top, from which an iron bell swung in the bitter wind. Beyond the church were three houses – plain, prefabricated, red – and beyond those, several larger buildings: a store, a school, a workshop. It was neat and orderly. It was all enclosed in a tall picket fence.

But along the waterfront were very different structures: shanties thrown together from driftwood, forest cuttings and mission waste. There was a shambles of decaying boats, boxes, ladders, and frames for drying fish or hides. There were wigwams with guanaco skins in pale foxy colours draped over sticks. The wigwams resembled bonfires more than habitations. Macanan saw people creeping in and out, wrapped in scraps of fur, thick canvas breeks, and caps of fox skin.

He dreaded a scampering crowd of children, shouting, pointing, giggling and thieving – but nothing of the sort happened. Figures appeared in doorways, or stood up from logs or benches and stared at the doctor, monk and gaucho, but there was no mobbing, no shrill cheek, only an expressionless gaze that slipped away if he met it.

To Macanan, the entire community seemed shifty.

*

'We leave in the morning,' Ferenc said.

Riding again.

Macanan, rebuilding his steam chest in a lean-to behind the school, objected: they'd just got here. Weren't the Fuegians to be brought to him? But Brother Ferenc would not let him off. The natives must see the doctor in the flesh, or they would not believe in his existence.

At which, Macanan felt a new dread: what if the Fuegians turned him down entirely? How absurd and improbable it appeared: he was supposed to visit the savages at home, ask to inspect their genitals, pick out the ulcerous and the dripping, and invite the owners to the mission to be steamed. But Ferenc gruffly assured him that the poor remnants of the tribe would turn up, that they would submit to treatment.

They knew all about the mission, Macanan had no doubt. They'd have heard of the workshops, where their women sat under the heavy gaze of bespectacled Romanian nuns, spinning, carding, weaving, and longing to walk outside. The women wove coarse cloth, to make nothing more than those same clothes in which they sat spinning, carding, and weaving. The men, peeking from the tree line, were more reluctant: they knew that women who'd gone in before had contracted heaving coughs and died. Why did the women not leave? Because of the sea or the priests? Because of the horsemen?

Ferenc insisted that Macanan must come to the native camps.

At nine the next morning they set out once more, Macanan

chewing his lip in misery, Brother Ferenc solid in the saddle more like a dragoon than a priest, with their gaucho and a guide from the mission but without the pack train. The tide was in, and the causeway gleamed with brine. They were halfway across when Macanan noticed the solitary horseman coming towards them, leading a packhorse over which was corded a single sheep. Ferenc had seen him also, and there was a stiffening, a tension. They drew close, the newcomer clearly set on speaking with Ferenc. Under a broad hat of acid green, Macanan saw the spider-veined cheeks of a drinker, and sparkling if watery eyes.

'Welcome back, Brother!'

A Scot by his voice, which was surprisingly scratchy, as though worn threadbare by exposure to Fuegian winds. Ferenc barely nodded. The man looked Macanan up and down so intently that he bristled under the stare.

'Is this the doctor, now? Don't be surprised: we heard you were coming. You're to rid the island of pox!'

Macanan said he'd be looking into the matter.

'Good, so, the savages will be delighted. Ferenc here will have told them all about you. The savages like to know about a man, as do we all. Can't abide a secretive fellow. And when do you expect to be back?'

'We cannot tell,' said Brother Ferenc.

'Well, I'll keep a look out for you. I've heard interesting things about you, Doctor.'

'That cannot be,' replied Macanan. The other smiled vaguely at him with those watery but steady eyes, and murmured:

'Dr Matthieu Macanan...'

Macanan turned pale.

'We must get on,' insisted Ferenc.

He tightened his rein, and his pony kicked the shallow water, making to pass by. But the other addressed Macanan, who was watching him as though he were a snake.

'Brother Ferenc has not introduced me, you notice? My name's Lovell – you'll not forget it. I've meat here for the mission.'

The sheep regarded Macanan dully.

'It's a gift,' smiled Lovell. 'One a month. Can't have the Brothers and Sisters going hungry – nor their natives, of course. That wouldn't do, would it? The natives wouldn't stay were it not for food.'

'There are other nourishments.' Ferenc spurred his pony past Lovell with the gaucho following and Macanan in tow.

'Good day to you,' cried Lovell as Macanan went by. 'Happy hunting.'

They left the peninsula, turning north again along the shore. The sky was milky, the wind ruffling the sea into a seersucker. Macanan tugged at his collar and scarf, trying to seal his throat against the cold. After nearly a decade of residence, the cold Patagonian winds still defeated him. He saw a pair of guanacos who started at their coming. He glimpsed how the wind stirred the guanacos' necks as though the animals were pulling their collars up against the wind, revealing the creamy under-fur.

The riders moved inland, passing up a gully onto a trail that led them into the trees. Around much of the Fuegian coast, guanacos with their long yellow teeth clipped the evergreen beeches, nipping any saplings caught in the open. But where the rocks reached the sea and the slopes became steeper, the trees took control.

On they went, rising to higher ground, in and out of copses of evergreen beech. Macanan had little notion of where they were going; he let himself be led, while he brooded on the man Lovell, and on what he could say to the Fuegians they might encounter, who might or might not allow a complete stranger to examine their pudenda. If the natives said, 'Certainly not,' what would Macanan and Ferenc do then?

He noted that it had grown yet colder; although there were flickers of sun, still the wind swirled through the woods, penetrating his defences, draining his energy. Not far above them on the mountain, the snow fed hundreds of streams and upland marshes, and poured chilled air upon them. The ground was sodden, their mounts plashing across moss and tiny ferns in a fine wet spray. And then, without warning, they came upon the Fuegians.

There were huts in a clearing: two huts, built of birch stacked into a tepee. The huts looked miserable, scant protection against the cold; there was no attempt to bind the boughs together, or to cover the gaps. Moving about were half a dozen people, several of whom (Macanan could hardly credit this) were naked. Others had cloaks of heavy fur, white-edged and shaggy, but they seemed careless of these and let them hang to the ground, or hoiked them onto one or other shoulder arbitrarily – until it dawned on Macanan that the natives kept their cloaks to the windward side. Only the babies were well wrapped.

There was a man seated on a jumble of skins, his arms and chest naked; he was intent on making an arrow. He held a stick a yard long, peeled and scraped white, and he was squinting down its length to gauge its straightness. Sprawling on the grass, three youths watched him. They heard the mules; in an instant they were on their feet. There was a bow in the doorway of the hut; Macanan saw the arrow-maker glance at this, but the Fuegians made no move.

Ferenc had stopped some thirty paces from them, and was speaking to them in their own language. The priest slipped off his pony, passing the reins to the gaucho. Macanan thumped down awkwardly, but Ferenc paid no attention; he kept up a stream of introduction and enquiry, giving the Fuegians only time for brief answers before a new question. The Fuegians seemed cowed by this performance – as was Macanan, by Ferenc's facility and fluency in a weird tongue.

Macanan could follow none of it. Colder by the minute, he shuffled his feet in the wet heather, hoping that his boots were watertight. He concentrated on the Fuegians: the two women with infants were, he decided, surprisingly handsome, tall and disdainful. The baby of one peeked over her shoulder, out of the fur. The women's hair was thick and black, centrally parted to frame humorous eyes and strong noses, while each had white chalk highlights on their cheeks.

Were these people as healthy as they looked, or riddled with insidious disease? Macanan kept changing his mind. At first glance he thought they looked miserable – but he altered his opinion; they were sleek and strong. He studied them, searching for ulceration, collapsed noses, blotched skin, stiff and awkward gait: the stigmata of syphilis. The groins: he needed to see the groins, broken and erupted. The nakedness should make it easier.

But the light was not helping; the sunlight coming through the birch trees around the clearing, and the scudding shadows of the leaves and the small clouds, all made shifting patterns on the skin. If only he could achieve a diagnosis from here, standing well back. But he could see no avoiding the moment when Ferenc would wave him forward to inspect the Fuegians intimately. At which, Macanan predicted, one of the natives would lift a stave of wood and strike him dead.

He saw Ferenc gesturing, and the Fuegians eyeing him. Macanan stood straighter, trying for a manner both dignified and benevolent. Ferenc had that manner. Ferenc was indicating Macanan, but not summoning him: the doctor was an exhibit, and the Fuegians were scrutinising him. The natives nudged each other, murmuring. There was negotiation. The Fuegians were replying.

Of a sudden, the discussion ended; Ferenc turned away from the Fuegians and walked back to his pony, taking the reins. The Fuegians lost interest; the hunter worked again on his arrow, the youths watched him. The women suckled their babies and talked among themselves. This, Macanan understood, was dismissal, the failure he'd expected. It would be the same with other natives. In a few days, he would trail off to Punta Arenas. All a waste of time.

But Brother Ferenc, mounting his pony, was smiling at him and gesturing that Macanan should remount also; before he knew it, the gaucho had lifted him into the saddle and the cavalcade was returning the way they had come.

'The illness is obvious, no?' called Ferenc over his shoulder.

'But they didn't agree...'

'They agreed,' said Ferenc with an air of closure, 'because I offered them food. Didn't you look at them, Doctor? They're starving.'

*

Next day, two native women arrived at the Paloma Sagrada. They appeared in the morning outside the kitchen, dressed in shabby skins: a gesture to mission prudery. Macanan, coming from the bunkhouse, saw Brother Ferenc striding across the compound in his virile way, calling to them. Macanan took a few steps forward, but the native women saw him. They pointed him out to Ferenc, who looked round and called encouragingly:

'Well, Doctor, they say they have come just for you!'

Which sent a chill through Macanan.

Ferenc, however, ushered the women straight into the refectory. Macanan drifted that way, stepping onto the porch. Inside, there were long scrubbed tables. Already, the two women in their skins were seated; Ferenc placed a tin bowl in front of each, with alloy spoons. The women peered into their bowls; one of them picked out a gobbet of porridge in her fingers. At once a nun appeared, jabbering crossly, pushing a spoon into her fist. The women began to eat, gobbling, scalding their mouths.

'First I want them to eat well,' said Ferenc, stopping Macanan at the door, 'then to go back and fetch their people, to bring in the men. We get no shortage of women; these must bring the men.'

Afterwards, Macanan saw him march the women away to the mainland; he also saw, across the plain, horsemen of the distant ranch observing.

Macanan went back to his mercury chest, checking his supplies for the twentieth time.

'Patience,' said Ferenc.

In the afternoon, led in by the first women, fifteen Fuegians came.

It was, Macanan saw, the family they had encountered in the forest, plus another group. He recognised the hunter who had been making arrows, and the two handsome women with small babies buried in their furs. He saw them survey the mission compound, taking in houses and workshops, stores, church and belfry: structures that Macanan was sure they had studied often enough from a distance. They did indeed have hungry eyes; the first two women waved towards the dining hall, and the newcomers turned that way as though on rails. Macanan glanced towards the workshop where two dozen Fuegian women were, just now, spinning wool under the direction of the Sisters, unaware of the new arrivals since, as in a Victorian school, all windows were set high to allow light in but no view out.

Ferenc was there, and other priests, circling about the Fuegians like sheepdogs. They told Macanan to stand apart; it would be better that the doctor wait at his 'clinic', with the steam chest in the lean-to next door. There he would be in all his professional pomp, and the Fuegians would be brought to him. Macanan felt the small comfort of having no control: it could not all be his fault, what happened.

Again he reviewed his preparations: the wooden benches; the writing table; the record cards; the notebook for his observations; the examination cubicle contrived with a screen of woollen blankets (what would natives expect by way of privacy, once they'd been disrobed of their furs?); the sticks (for lifting the penis to view); the glass jar brought on the off-chance he might persuade Fuegians to urinate, so that he might look for blennorrhoeal filaments. Through the door of the lean-to, he saw the steam chest like a torture cabinet, with his leather case containing the mercury, a stack of fuel for the firebox, and a pitcher of hot water for the steam.

A stir behind him: Brother Ferenc was bringing a first few Fuegians led by the hunter. A nun came hurrying from the workshops to assist, wiping her hands on her apron. Ferenc gestured the men to leave weapons outside: one carried a spear with a barbed tip of white bone; another had a bow and a leather quiver of arrows. *Leave them by the door. You don't bring weapons into a clinic.* The Fuegians glanced at each other. *You are not hunting here.* The men shrugged, passing weapons back to friends outside. Their feet, that had never walked on a floor, slithered across the smooth planed beech. They sat, unfussed, peering at everything.

The hunter regarded Macanan with clear dispassionate eyes. The others – a tall woman, and two men – seemed to accept that this exchange was significant. The hunter's face revealed nothing; he expected nothing, feared nothing, presupposed nothing. That cannot be, thought Macanan: he must have terrors and prejudices to match my own. But I cannot see them. He gives me no help.

Macanan came forward, looked straight at the Fuegian hunter, and gave him a simple smile and a nod. The man considered this a moment, then stood up. This felt to Macanan like acceptance. The doctor indicated the examination bay. The Fuegian came closer, Brother Ferenc behind him. The Fuegian sat on the edge of the plain wooden couch.

'Please tell him,' said Macanan, 'that we wish him and his people to be strong, for hunting and for protecting their families.'

Ferenc relayed this. The Fuegian made no response, but continued to scrutinise Macanan.

'Please say that I think some of his people may have a tiny creature in their skin. This is doing them harm.'

The Fuegian murmured something.

'He asks,' returned Ferenc, 'do you mean, like fire-ants?'

'Much smaller,' said Macanan, 'not something that he can see. But more dangerous to him. Could you ask him to...'

The Fuegian stood and opened out his fur cloak: he was naked except for a penis sheath of thin leather with cords tied at his back. Before anyone could speak, the man had removed this also.

And stood impassive, with the doctor peering at the speckle of red papules that littered his trunk. Macanan approached with an apologetic shrug, stooping before the Fuegian and holding out a twig stripped of its bark with which he lifted the penis; across one side of the glans was a broad ulcer. This had been weeping a yellow fluid like thin oil, now dried into ragged crusts; the exposed flesh looked granulated, as though sprinkled with red sand. The ulcer was healing.

Macanan straightened.

How could he say: This is not good? In a Fuegian's life, what would that mean? That the man was in pain? Clearly he was not. That the sore would get worse? But superficially it was getting better. That he could not hunt, and was in danger of starving? Obviously not so. That, in ten years' time, his brain would soften and he would become a madman? He wouldn't know what this was about, and certainly wouldn't believe that some future addled head was linked to a sore penis years before. The lives of these people must leave many dreadful scars; why should he fret about an ulcer?

The Fuegian was speaking to Ferenc in indignation.

'He wishes this imperfection taken from him, the marks taken off him. He asks, what will you be doing, to make him perfect?'

So there it is, thought Macanan: vanity, in these of all people. (Why should he think, 'of all people'? Well, he did.)

He held out a hand invitingly: *Come this way.* The Fuegian snatched up his fur cloak, and they went through the narrow door, down two steps into the lean-to annexe. Ferenc began explaining that the treatment was in this wooden chest, the smoke that the doctor would make inside it. Macanan tapped Ferenc on the arm, holding out a glass vial of quicksilver; the Fuegian turned it over and over, eyeing the slippery silver, saying nothing. Ferenc spoke of the four sessions of mercury steaming; of the seven days attendance; of the shelter offered here at the mission. And all the food they could eat.

To which the Fuegian responded with a question:

'He says, will there be a cure, after four steamings?'

Oh, such certainties! But havering would not do on Tierra del Fuego.

'Yes,' said Macanan.

He had already lit the brazier within the box, heating the water. Intrigued, the Fuegian hunter came closer. Macanan thought: We've lured them here. I am the bait.

The hunter was prowling round the steam chest, lifting the lid, pointing at the seat within, firing queries at Ferenc. Macanan had no idea of the answers the priest was giving. Blinding with improvised science, he supposed.

'A few moments,' Macanan said, 'to get steam up. You may sit him inside.'

He returned to the other natives next door. Courteously, he held out his hand to one of the women.

She stood up, and Macanan was startled: she was statuesque. She carried her rich, creamy fur cloak high over one shoulder; the other arm was bare and brown, and held across her chest. She resembled some splendid Roman lady, and Macanan suddenly thought her marvellous. She was lovely; she was desirable. She held her head high and scrutinised the doctor with amused tolerance. Her eyes were clear and piercing; at any moment, he thought, she will ask me to justify what I do; she will ask for details of the infectious organism or the precise action of the mercury.

But the Fuegian woman held her peace and Macanan's eye. He thought: for some reason, she trusts me – and he wished she would not, for that made it his fault again.

'Please, come here,' he signed. The stolid Sister Marta in her black shrouds grasped the Fuegian by the elbow to propel her forward. The native woman glanced down in mild reproof, removed the nun's hand from her arm and stilled her with a serene look. The Sister stopped in bewilderment, her eyes pleading with Macanan: *Doctor, the savages – what should I do?*

Macanan celebrated: Oh, splendid!

So that, when the Fuegian woman stepped forward by herself, Macanan was half in love with this wonderful fur-clad lady. He beamed at her, and she beamed back and he thought: we are complicit.

But he had to ask to see this woman naked: did she know that? Among themselves the Fuegians often went naked – but here, with foreigners? The nun was there as chaperone, but would that be understood? Macanan was particularly loth to offend this woman – to affront her beauty.

At a loss for what to do, he remembered the second woman who had entered with her. Even as he looked for her, this other woman stood and marched across the room, her bare feet slapping on the beech boards.

Macanan, relieved, said: 'Wait one moment, please.'

He returned to the annexe; the head of the Fuegian hunter now protruded from the top of the steam chest with a foolish grin, like a conjurer's stooge about to be sawn in half. Coils of steam were seeping out.

'All ready, I think,' said Brother Ferenc.

Macanan crouched, unstopped a brown glass bottle and, with a brass measure, added a tincture to the boiling water. He drew out a shutter, so that mercuric steam swirled over the man's body.

'Ten minutes,' Macanan said to Ferenc. 'Do you have a watch?'

Back to the women waiting for him with that disconcerting patience. The taller one, statuesque and beautiful, again held his eye so that he felt diminished by her. He hesitated, spellbound – and had to pinch himself into action. He gestured, and the nun patted the wooden couch with a brisk, 'Jump up here'. The Fuegian murmured to her companion. Wary now, she regarded the couch uncertainly, until the nun took her by the shoulder, turned her until her buttocks were against the edge, and attempted to press the woman's shoulders back.

The Fuegian brushed this off. With her steady gaze, she regarded Dr Macanan a moment longer – then lay back upon the couch, letting her fur fall aside.

Macanan's stomach turned.

Across the woman's abdomen was a dense array of red pustules, with a weeping, flaking crust from near her breasts to her waist. From her navel downwards, this crust became large plaques like white fungus, but slimy. The woman raised one knee and let it fall aside so as to reveal her crotch, and the plaques of half-dried slime around her pudenda. Her feet too: even her feet, there was a rash all across the soles. These bare feet had walked all across the floor, pasting their contagion. Macanan swallowed hard.

She was observing him. He was gawping; he must recover his professional poise. He looked to the table where his pencil and notebook lay ready...

But before he could write, there was a disturbance. From the annexe he heard voices raised, the argument spiralling into a shouting contest. The waiting Fuegians got to their feet, staring towards the door of the lean-to, towards the fuss. The woman on the couch swung her heels down, and gathered her cloak about her. Macanan saw the Fuegians outside the window catch onto the argument; these now crowded through the clinic door, and the wooden chamber filled with loud stamping and the pungency of furs.

Then a rattling commotion began in the annexe. The hunter was struggling to get out of the box, while Ferenc held him in with one massive hand on the door. The Fuegian shouted, fired by panic and outrage. His face ran with sweat from steam and anger; he began kicking at the inside of the chest. It won't withstand that, thought Macanan...

But at his back the natives were shouting to the hunter who yelled back louder still. Ferenc kept talking, urging the man to calm down, stay still, be confident, think of the cure – but the hunter was ignoring him, was summoning rescue. The crowd bundled in, seven of them piling into the tiny lean-to. They pulled Ferenc aside and sent the big priest staggering; they released their kinsman. The Fuegians all stormed back through the clinic, and outside. They roared with rage, and Macanan had a hideous sense that they were offended not by Ferenc but by him. He wanted to call out: *None of this was my idea!* Macanan took two steps after the natives, and a man spat at him.

Those outside seized their weapons and marched off across the mission compound. At the high windows of the workshop, faces strained to see; they must be standing on the tables. From the doorways, women in mission shawls stared until the sisters hustled them inside. Chattering with fury, shaking fists at anyone who dared follow or plead, the natives streamed out across the causeway.

The departure was observed by five riders: sheep men with rifles resting across their saddles, who waited facing the causeway some seventy yards from the foreshore. Macanan, hurrying after, saw that the horsemen were disciplined, evenly spaced, motionless: like cavalry. He recognised the man at the left end of the row, who wore a hat of a peculiar bright green. Lovell green.

The ranch men watched the Fuegians leaving, gaining the mainland, heading for their forests. Brother Ferenc was trailing after, the powerful priest with his scheme in tatters, calling to the primitives, bellowing pleas and commands. Then one of the Fuegians turned, raised a wooden spear with a white harpoon tip, and flung it at Ferenc. The weapon did no harm: it struck the heavy folds of Ferenc's robe and fell wobbling to the ground. The Fuegians fled.

But before they could go ten steps, there was a *crack* across the wide sky. Someone fell: not the man who had flung the spear; another collapsed onto the turf. A second *crack* came from the line of horsemen; all these men now had their rifles raised. The knot of Fuegians – one with a shattered, haemorrhaging forearm – began to run along the foreshore over the tussocky grass, between the horsemen and the sea.

The shots came quickly, the line of horses walking forward while the men fired with control, speed and purpose. Natives fell: four, five, or more. Others were discarding their cloaks to run faster. The horsemen kicked their animals to follow at an easy trot, still shooting. Macanan saw one fugitive dodge left and right, jumping down a bank to scamper through a stream, but struck in the back and thrown into the fast-running water. He saw a mother thrown so violently by the impact of a bullet that her baby rolled several yards from her. He saw a rider spur his horse that way, dismount and seize the infant; for an appalled moment Macanan thought he would butcher it there and then – but the horseman stuck the child under his arm and started walking back towards the mission, a figure of mercy.

From the causeway onto the foreshore came Brother Ferenc waving his arms, shouting at the riders. They heard – Macanan was sure – but they turned their faces away. They were rescuing Ferenc, weren't they? They were saving him from savages who had tried to spear him.

There was only one left: a tall figure in a cloak, statuesque and with long hair pulled about by the wind. She stopped fleeing and turned to face the oncoming horsemen, standing in their path, disdainful. Then she saw Macanan on the causeway; she gazed at him steadily, proudly, as though she regarded him as the more significant. The moment was frozen. The riders hesitated among the corpses, and it seemed to Macanan that the woman's disregard almost stopped them. There came a last shout from Ferenc – more a screech – and one of the ranchers glanced his way.

But a moment later, they shot the woman also: two bullets together threw her in an elegant half turn, like a dancer pirouetting, before she fell onto the grass. Nearby, Brother Ferenc continued to shriek at the horsemen. From the causeway, the doctor stared, white-faced and trembling.

Less than an hour later, while the nuns clucked over the baby, Dr Macanan set out for Porvenir, in company with the taciturn gaucho only. He had swept up his few instruments and the bottles of tincture of mercury, and stuffed all these into a leather bag, but he had abandoned the steam chest; he had not waited for that, he had left it here. This puzzled the gaucho since there was, at the mission, no longer anyone needing treatment. But the doctor was not discussing it. Teetering on the edge of nausea, Macanan dragged himself unassisted onto a mule, and departed without a word of farewell.

*

Two days later, Dr Macanan waited for the steamer to Punta Arenas. He was standing on the Porvenir waterfront by the cluster of tin-roofed sheds and dwellings that passed for a town on Tierra del

Fuego. He was motionless, save that his tall frame was pushed at by the wind, and his coat flapped. He was staring across the Strait, but saw nothing of what was in front of him.

'Penny for 'em, Doctor?'

Startled at the Scotch voice, he looked round and saw with dismay the stocky red-faced Lovell scrutinising him.

'Deep in thought, I see,' said the ranch man in his wind-shredded tones. 'And I've an idea you'll be thinking of savages. Have you not met enough for a lifetime? They came flocking to see you.'

Macanan scowled, but Lovell grinned at him.

'They only came because of you, eh, Doctor? Ferenc could not catch them without you.'

Lovell spat.

'Savage is the word for them, Doctor, and a savage is a man who drags all humanity down. In the sum and average of things, we are all brought lower by savages. Aren't I right?'

Macanan stared at him in disgust. Lovell's eye lit upon two or three packing cases discarded on the mud.

'You see those? Those boxes? Let me tell you something, let me tell you how savage your Fuegians are. They cannot cook, did you know? Not the wit to boil an egg. Now, those boxes: your Fuegians find them as flotsam on the beach, you see. Your Fuegians go hunting for *cururos*, little digging rats, and they pack a hundred or more rats into a wooden box. Then they leave the whole thing to rot over the winter, and in the spring they cut lumps out of it, like cheese. To eat, Doctor – to eat. Now, is that not the most revolting thing? Come on, agree with me: it turns a man's stomach. That's what savages do: they turn your stomach.'

Lovell edged closer, and Macanan caught rum on his breath.

'The thing is, Doctor, I wonder if you're not pondering something else: a conversation or two, back in Punta Arenas – am I wrong? You'll be needing conversation when you get home, won't you? Not with savages, but with civilised men.'

Dr Macanan said nothing. Lovell persisted:

'Who might those interlocutors be, then? I suppose there's a number of folk you'd consider; a medical man like you will have access, eh?

Few doors closed to Matthieu Macanan. You'd get the attention of the authorities, or maybe gentlemen of the press. Possibly even the police. Isn't that right?'

Still Macanan was silent, but he made to move past Lovell in a wide circle as though to avoid contagion.

'Consider just one thing, Doctor – if that is what you really are.'

Macanan did not look at Lovell. He stopped, surveying a point on the dirt road some few yards off.

Lovell – that scratchy little voice – spoke to his back.

'The thing is, when folk hear unhappy news, they tend to ask about the body as brings that news. What sort of fellow is it, they say, that bears bad tidings? What sort of man would spread distressing reports? Who is he, and how does he know those things? Was he perhaps part of the business himself? Did he receive money to go to Tierra del Fuego, trading on his qualifications, drawing the savages in?'

Lovell came to stand alongside Macanan, as though to share his profound scrutiny of that point in the dirt four paces before them.

'These people wondering, these doubters, they might discover things about the teller of nasty tales. They might hear a story – from seafarers and such riffraff – of folk who'd studied doctoring but had not played fair – all sorts of nonsense. Of folk obliged to depart from their university town.'

At last, Macanan looked down his long nose at Lovell.

'Stories get about, you know,' Lovell smiled, 'with the boats, and all the newcomers. I've heard such talk in Buenos Aires.'

He glanced out to sea.

'And look now, there's the steamer. That's very good, you'll be home in Punta Arenas shortly. Have a good journey – Doctor.'

He walked away. Macanan did nothing to stop him, just as he had not stopped the shootings. In later life, he would often think back on all the things he did not do at this instant. He did not lay a hand on Lovell's shoulder, spin him round and drive a fist into his face. He did not shout, 'Murderer!' Nor did he call to the retreating back: 'Threaten as you like, Lovell, but I will go to the authorities.' He did none of this.

He would excuse himself that he'd been in shock – like an adulterer claiming that he'd fornicated only when drunk. But shock and drink are excuses like any other. With each moment watching Lovell walk away, the immediate impact receded and the excuse grew thinner; the opportunity faded, and he had done nothing.

So he stood, and a clamour of thoughts and feelings pressed in on him. As he glared after Lovell, he thought of another figure, a Fuegian woman fleeing along a foreshore, proud and beautiful but disgustingly diseased, now pursued and exterminated. For several fatal seconds, all resolution was clouded by this image.

Macanan started back into the present, and saw a second chance. Lovell was still in sight, making for the bar. The steamer was closing rapidly with the jetty: Macanan could go aboard, or not. If he did not board – if, instead, he set out after Lovell, or went to the little police station to lay a complaint – then the packet boat would go without him, and it would not came again for two or three days. Macanan would have to find uncomfortable lodging in a tiny settlement where Lovell had many friends. Best, surely, to head for Punta Arenas, make his report there...

So he boarded the boat.

By the time he reached home, Macanan had thought of many other things. He recalled the power and influence of Lovell's employer, one of the great Chilean-German merchant houses. He imagined the counter-attacks that would follow his accusation; he thought of his career shattered, his clientele scared off, perhaps his life endangered. He knew that his enemy's money would ensure that he would have a struggle to be believed, and he told himself that Brother Ferenc and his confraternity must know of many more atrocities, yet they had managed nothing. Nonetheless, he was so outraged, so grossly outraged in every corner of his humanity, that he could surely have found the strength to act. All this Macanan might have faced: abuse, financial ruin, physical danger, legal obstruction, all of it...

But he did not.

Some ten days later, the steam chest was returned to him, with no word from Brother Ferenc. Dr Macanan re-opened his practice as before, but had few exchanges with anyone. Not even the ironmonger downstairs, nor his wife nor Tilly, no one could get a decent sentence out of him; only occasionally was Macanan seen taking a brandy with Captain Huw Prothero who was newly appointed Master of the Argentine mail packet *Luisa Menendez,* and who was happy to spread a map upon a table in a bar and recount tales of the coast. Apart from those conversations, Macanan grew increasingly taciturn, and his patients found him ever more distant. Until, one day, without explanation, he closed the clinic, settled his rent with the ironmonger, paid off Tilly and set out for the north, leaving his peculiar reputation behind him.

Three
THE CAVE OF HANDS

There were two silver foxes, with white tips to their silver-grey tails. They were dog and bitch, and now there'd be orphans somewhere. The female was killed by the gaucho's *bolas,* her ribs staved in by a stone ball on a leather thong that whipped around her breast, then slammed into her flank and her heart.

The dog scampered from them onto the lake ice where the horses could not follow, thinking that he had escaped – but the crust on the brackish water was thin, and fifty yards out it gave way beneath the fox; he dropped into the bitter cold below and could not haul himself onto the ice that always crumbled under his paws. They saw him thrashing and floundering.

Macanan said to the gaucho:

'Shoot him, please.'

'Señor,' the man replied, thinking of his ammunition, 'he dies anyway.'

But the gaucho took his orders, and shot the fox. He was rather surprised; it was almost the only instruction he'd had from this peculiar employer who could be decisive on behalf of foxes, it seemed, but rarely for himself.

They rode at an ambling pace; some trotting would suit the horses, but Señor Macanan would not tolerate anything more than a walk. The ground rose and fell like a petrified sea littered with volcanic debris. Here and there rolled a desiccated ball of shrub, nudged this way and that by the wind but never going far. Perhaps there was a seed in the centre of the twigs – but what a grim landscape in which to take root. You'd not thank your parents for that start in life.

The gaucho noted everything in passing: where there was firewood, where there was game, and where they passed into new terrain. Señor Macanan did not appear to see anything.

'Keep your eyes open for meat, Señor.'

The guide was a scrawny man with bat ears that projected through his lank black hair like semaphore flags. He was finding Macanan hard going: withdrawn, seldom speaking, always brooding. The Frenchman was an appalling rider, and sat stiffly upright in the saddle, his long legs dangling uselessly. He was obviously frightened of the horses, tolerating them only because he must – an attitude which to the gaucho was incomprehensible. The horses took liberties. Señor Macanan did nothing to kick on his mount, so that the gaucho was obliged to ride up and give the animal a hefty smack on the rump, or to take a lead rein for hours on end, pulling Macanan behind him. The señor let the horse take him, unquestioning; only, he glanced sometimes over his shoulder, though the landscape behind them was the same as the landscape before them, and quite as empty.

On the trail, Señor Macanan simply did as he was told. When the gaucho said it was time to change mounts, Macanan let his animal drift to a stop, and waited as if frozen, until the gaucho cut a new animal out of the little *tropilla,* their troop, and brought it to his client; only then would Macanan dismount, back away from the horses and watch while the saddle was moved across. He deferred to the gaucho in all matters except one: they must always move on, long fatiguing days of riding; they must not rest – as though there was something coming slowly but inexorably after them that they must shake off. The gaucho was born to ride, but the Frenchman must be suffering; he had seen Macanan cursorily inspect red weals on the inside of his calves, where the stirrup leather pinched and gnawed, but nothing had been said. The gaucho noted how stiffly his employer moved when they dismounted each evening, and how poorly the man slept on the hard ground. Surely, he must be tormented by exhaustion. But never a word.

It was disturbing, this silence, this passivity. True: Macanan had engaged the gaucho to make decisions for him on the road. But the endless mute submission to suffering – to the gaucho, it seemed unwholesome. It smacked of mortification of the flesh. The gaucho had nothing against this, if it was what the señor wanted, but he had no desire to be mortified likewise; he very much hoped he hadn't taken work with a saint. Señor Macanan seemed to exist in a distant world, his thoughts far away, his handsome face full of melancholy brought from some other country.

'Señor,' the gaucho had grinned at Macanan back in Punta Arenas, 'you want to go to Sanlúcar at such a season? What for?'

'I wish to see it.'

'Señor, of course, I'll take you anywhere you pay to go – but Sanlúcar... You know about this place?'

'A seafaring friend has described it to me.'

'There's nothing there!'

'I wish to see it.'

The gaucho's job – Macanan had made clear – was to get him to Sanlúcar without asking questions. This educated gentleman seemed resolved to remove himself as far as possible from all friendly civilisation, which was fine and dandy, the gentleman's lookout entirely, just as long as Señor Macanan didn't expect to be dragged or carried in body or soul. For that was what could happen on these stony plains where the night frosts were so bitter and there was no shelter; people and horses dropped their heads and gave up. The gaucho had seen guanaco give up.

'I tell you something, Señor,' he said to Macanan. 'Me and some friends, we were out for a few days' hunting and we got caught in the snow. We rode into a valley and there's this herd of guanacos, two dozen maybe. They'd gone into the valley to take shelter but they were so damn cold they couldn't move, didn't try to escape, not one step.'

He looked at the señor expecting the prompting question: So what happened? But Macanan, plodding steadily, said nothing.

'We shot every one of them,' supplied the gaucho, peering at him.

Macanan said nothing at all.

Let the señor not give up. Let him keep silent if he must, but let him keep coming. The gaucho had decided that if he made any working decision, and if the Frenchman said nothing to contradict him, he could assume consent.

So now he was scanning ahead for shelter, though there was nothing but the sharp black scoriae jumbled among pebbles on ground that was almost white. When the wind shoved, the stones shifted on the ground. The last marshes and shrubs were nearly a week behind them. It was barely spring, and the rain could turn to hail in an instant; whatever seed lay in this dirt was keeping its head down.

The gaucho looked north, up ahead, but there was no relief. He looked to his right, but there was nothing between them and the Atlantic Ocean except more rubble and salt pans. He looked left, inland to the far Andes cordillera, and from time to time he even looked behind them, south, as though there might be some refuge they'd passed without noticing.

On they rode, Señor Macanan preferring to be led. It had begun to rain again, the same steady, cold spring rain, hour on hour. They rode in silence beneath their capes and broad hats, hauling the pack animals. The horses hung their heads.

Then there was a district of thin grazing, a haze of grass which made the horses twitch with interest, peer about and tug at the reins. They stopped five minutes in every hour, to let the animals rest and feed.

Rivers had gouged their way across the plain.

'Here, Señor, I think.'

They halted above a ravine. Below them, grey clouded water rippled towards the Atlantic. There were clumps of gorse, even a few tiny yellow flowers, quite a little garden. There was prickly pear, there was *calafate,* and a thorn bush like a sloe. But the gaucho was intent on the river. He leaned forward in his saddle and peered down at the current: the water had a malevolent energy under its turbid grey surface.

'What are you staring at?' asked Señor Macanan.

The gaucho sat upright

'This water, Señor. This grey colour is snow-melt from the mountains. The rivers may fill soon and we could be caught between them. Tomorrow we must move quickly.'

He glanced at Macanan; he knew he was saying they must ride faster. 'Look, Señor: that is ice.'

A large fragment was floating past, the size of a sheep's carcass and a similar dirty grey. It swayed and wallowed like a drunk. Another lump followed.

Macanan and the gaucho looked west to the faint outline of the Andes.

'So,' the gaucho shrugged, pointing to a gravel promontory above the river, 'we sleep there. Out of the wind, but clear of the water.'

They dismounted – Señor Macanan with obvious relief – and the gaucho urged the *tropilla* of horses down a gully, hobbling the animals on a patch of grazing well above the current. On the promontory, they pitched the brown tent, its fabric heavy with three days of rain. They searched for fuel. There was driftwood from the distant forests, but everything was wet, the bark soft and the wood oozy. So instead they must tear and tug at stubborn, deep-rooted thorn bushes, making a heap of thorn wood and guanaco dung which burned with a pale lethargic flame but which smouldered a long while. They had, for their supper, two enormous rhea eggs, and another stolen from the nest of a black-necked swan; they made a hole in the top of each, stirred the contents to a smooth yellow with a stick, then stood the eggs in the ashes to bake, eating them with coffee and dry biscuit. They carried the last morsels of a puma that the gaucho had shot and roasted, but this they kept for breakfast.

They were out of the wind, but cold air poured down the ravine, so that their damp clothes became colder and colder, while the fire refused to burn vigorously enough either to heat them or cheer them. The temperature of the clear sky fell quickly. They made hot maté to drink, which gave a brief warmth but did nothing to make Señor Macanan communicative. Almost before it was dark, he crawled into the tent and wrapped himself in a fur cape.

The gaucho checked the hobbling on the five horses, then sat a few minutes smoking a cigarette, looking up at the stars, wondering at their stillness, wondering if the wind ever affected the position of the heavens. Then he too lay down, for a moment feeling the cold in his protuberant ears. Exhausted by minding a client who took so little notice for himself, the gaucho fell into an unaccustomed deep slumber.

*

Some hours later, Macanan half-woke. He was stiff with cold; outside there was a hard frost, which he sensed on his face. The ground below him was as cold as it was hard. He was also hungry; baked swans' eggs alone was not enough. He was weakened, less resistant. But just now there was something else. He lay hoping that his brain would decide either to sleep again or to surface properly. Close by, the gaucho in his own heap of furs snored gently. But there were sounds outside that Macanan did not understand, a steady low hiss and an irregular thumping.

He sat up beneath his fur, then hauled himself to the entrance of the tent. Nothing seemed to be in the right position. He unlaced the stiff ties – then understood what was wrong with the tent: two of the guy ropes, saturated and then frozen, had snapped. He looked out, blinking urgently and turning his head this way and that to see better from the corner of his eye. There was no moon; the fire had died to nothing but fading cinders, and only the dimmest gleam came off something else. The gleam was hardly a pace in front of him, and the sound was there before his face. He saw a curious twitching, and thought the darkness itself was pulsing until he understood that there was a dry bush just by the tent that was no longer dry, but was swishing back and forth in water.

He pushed back into the tent, reaching for the gaucho and shoving at the first bit he found.

'Wake up,' he growled. 'There's a flood.'

A shadow sat up in front of him.

'A flood!' Macanan shouted.

They stood before the tent, for a moment mesmerised by darkness that rushed about them.

'The horses,' whispered the gaucho.

The horses had been hobbled halfway down the ravine, on longer grass.

Macanan took one step forward, and his stockinged foot touched icy water.

'Oh Lord...'

He turned towards the tent and tripped, falling heavily against the canvas, feeling a guy rope snap under him. He scrabbled his way inside, seizing his two leather bags, hauling everything outside and colliding with the gaucho who remained stock still.

'Forget the animals! Nothing we can do. Save the tent, for God's sake!'

But the gaucho did not move, for without horses he was nothing. He stared into the dark where the animals had been.

Macanan reached for him, seized him by the shoulders and shook violently.

'We're flooding here, right here, you see? The water's rising. For the love of God: the tent and bags, or we're lost too.'

He thrust leather satchels and fur capes onto the gaucho, propelling him away from the water, away from his drowned horses. Stunned, the gaucho climbed the gully, while Macanan groped around the tent freeing ropes. The canvas subsided, and he shouted to the gaucho for help, but the man was pitiful and useless. Macanan grasped the flaxen cloth that was stiff with frost, hauling it away from the water and up the gully, dragging it behind him like a bride with an impossibly heavy train. The gaucho returned, at last stirred out of his shock, but now merely rushed up and down the rapidly shrinking ledge, crying:

'Did you see the horses? What has happened to them?'

He was like a trapped dog rushing back and forth. He cared for nothing but his *tropilla*. Macanan called to him:

'Help me, damn you!'

The tent snagged on rocks or bushes. Macanan slithered back down the gully grabbing at parts of the canvas, pulling, trying to find the catch. He gave a heave – and heard the canvas rip.

'O mon Dieu...'

He heard a splashing, and oaths. The gaucho came to him babbling.

'The water is cold, Señor, the water is coming.'

Their ledge above the stream was awash. The fireplace was overrun, the cinders hissing feeble defiance before being swirled downstream. At the foot of the gully, where the two men crouched, the first chill slops were creeping upwards.

Macanan grabbed again at the ruin of their tent.

'Señor,' sobbed the gaucho, 'we can do nothing, we cannot see.'

They climbed the gully, down which they had urged their animals the evening before, and up which they now dragged the heap of saddle bags and clothing. Where the gully opened onto the pampas, there was nothing but volcanic rubble and an occasional dry twist of twig – no shelter at all. The wind poured over them in the darkness.

To the east, towards the ocean, the sky was lighter but overcast, and Macanan could see in silhouette the gaucho hugging himself, shivering and chattering. They scrabbled at the heap of stuff to find their fur capes, then crept a few feet back down into the gully, crouching just below the lip to escape the wind, hoping that the water would not reach them.

There they stayed, cowering in a rocky corner, only they didn't huddle together for warmth, for they were still strangers. There were foxes howling, gathering closer. The gaucho muttered that the foxes would steal and eat anything of leather, any horse gear, saddles even, and he fussed about gathering these close – as though they still had horses. When the light came towards them on the gale, they stood in their capes and saw that the world was changed. Where there had been a ravine with a stream trickling, there was now a grey-brown deluge on which ragged dirty ice jostled to the sea. Where there had been horses, there was snow-melt and silt. Of the *tropilla*, there was no trace. They'd been hobbled; they could not have swum or saved themselves. That's what the thumping had been, in the darkness: panicking horses, trying to free their feet.

So Macanan and his guide gazed at the river, at the ice wallowing past. They had saddlebags but no animals to saddle. They had a heap of stuff but no means to carry it. They had everything for survival, but only if they stayed just here, where they would in due course die.

'Well?' demanded Macanan. 'What's best to do?'

But his gaucho was broken, deprived of his horses. His eyes were inanely wide, his lips were pressed together, his face screwed tight to hold back tears. He was shrinking from their troubles. He was useless.

So Macanan took charge.

He gripped the gaucho's shoulder.

'We go on, you understand? There's no choice. What about

settlements? Are there any settlements?'

The gaucho mouthed something.

'Speak up!' commanded Macanan.

'Maybe an Indian camp,' the gaucho mumbled. 'They come sometimes, not every year. Half a day north.'

He gestured across the water before pulling his cape tight around himself and staring at his feet.

'Look,' said Macanan, pointing downstream.

There was a pony, just one. It was a little mare called a *picaza*, black with a white star. It was a quarter of a mile from them, standing with its back to the wind peering at the water,.

The sight of a horse restored some life to the gaucho. It took him, nonetheless, a full hour to catch the pony. A remnant of hobbling cord was still tied to one leg, but the animal was reluctant to let him approach. But at last it recognised the man and permitted him.

'Which way are we going?' the gaucho asked Macanan, as if this had not been clearly stated.

Macanan pointed across the river.

'To find your Indians.'

'Señor, they may not be there this year,' said the gaucho, but he was ignored.

They lit a small fire of thorn brush in the gully, warming themselves and drinking a mug that lent a flicker of strength.

'Oh, Señor!' exclaimed the gaucho, fishing in his satchel as though remembering that he had the keys to a nearby luxury home. He produced a fold of cotton rag from which he took pieces of fatty roast puma meat, passing half to Macanan.

The black mare watched as they chewed and sipped. They filled one pair of saddlebags with the barest essentials, and put these across the mare, then tied onto her also two smaller bags such that they themselves could carry, walking. Lastly they tied on the fur capes, rolled tight. Mid-morning, they were ready.

'Maybe the animal will not swim again,' havered the gaucho.

'It will swim towards you,' Macanan said. 'You cross first.'

The gaucho looked at the water before them, an expanse of grey liquid ice. He turned and looked south across the empty pebble plains...

'One pony cannot carry us both,' said Macanan. 'If we go south, it could be a week before we see a soul. We must find Indians, and buy another horse.'

The river boiled past in whirls created by the spurs and outcrops now underwater. The far bank was only sixty paces from them, but every yard looked appalling. Up and down the riverbank, there was the same shale edge crumbling into the rush. The mare peered in disbelief.

Still they lingered.

'There's bushes there to grab,' pointed Macanan.

'For the horse?' asked the gaucho, more in anguish than sarcasm.

A peppery sleet was taunting them.

'Find a gully for the horse to climb,' Macanan said.

He reached down and unlaced his boots, tying them to his belt; the gaucho followed suit. They stood on the stony shore.

'Go on,' Macanan gestured.

The other stepped down to the edge of the appalling water. It seemed he would just stand there, so they might remain all day, waiting; perhaps he could not swim. But the gaucho crouched and launched himself. He struck out, his head held out of the stream like a dog. The currents grabbed and hauled him about; sometimes he'd be facing upstream as though swimming to the Andes, only to be spun towards the Atlantic.

And then he was at the far bank, fifty paces downstream, grappling with that clump of bushes that Macanan had indicated. The gaucho hauled himself out and stamped up and down in an agony of cold, clapping his hands about his sides.

Peering at the man on the far side, it occurred to Macanan that one pony could carry him alone, without the gaucho, back to the south and to Punta Arenas. He'd have the guanaco cloaks for warmth, with the hunting rifle and the little food remaining in the bags. The gaucho would doubtless try to swim back after him, but was exhausted and would in all probability disappear. He'd be swept away, or he'd never make the south, not on foot, with nothing, and his corpse would soon be eaten. Macanan could perhaps do it.

The reverse was also true: if the black mare crossed the flood, the gaucho might mount and vanish northward, heading perhaps for Comodoro Rivadavia, or for Bahía Blanca, far away, where he could say what he liked about the death of Señor Macanan, his employer.

So the two men regarded each other. The gaucho began jogging up and down the bank, looking for some slope where the mare might find a footing and scramble ashore. He stopped by a small indent, examined it, and seemed to think it good, waving and gesticulating, as though Señor Macanan should mutter instructions in the animal's ear: *Over there, for God's sake.*

Macanan tugged on the mare's halter; they went to the gully, the pony's eyes swivelling while it stamped at the crumbling slope in protest. But Macanan gave it no time to think, slapping and thumping at its rump, shouting, pushing. The ground, invisible in the grey swill, dropped away faster than the pony expected, and it found itself swimming with the strength of panic towards the gaucho, who yelled: *Here! Here!*

But the pony, seeing the shouting man on the bank, would not swim towards him, and she veered away downstream. The little mare attempted to turn back towards Macanan's side, the southern shore, but the current would not let her. She twisted frantically; they saw, just above the water, her head swinging left and right. Each time she turned her body across the flood, the stream flung her back, while her thrashing hooves propelled her rapidly downriver. The glacial water was stiffening her muscles; the weight of saddle bags and furs bore down on her, and with every flailing yard her strength diminished and the banks receded. The gaucho and Matthieu Macanan watched her nose straining out of the water to breathe as she carried away their prospect of survival, taking everything.

Until she disappeared around a bend.

Which left the two men still facing each other across a snow-melt flood, in a mean little sleet, without property or reasonable hope.

Macanan stood by the water. At that moment, he saw that the gaucho, in spite of having just crossed this flood, was also shuffling towards the edge.

He's going to swim back. He will say it's his job to look after me. But he wants to go south.

Matthieu Macanan thought of waving his arms, of shouting: Stay there! But the gaucho would ignore him, or pretend to misunderstand, and launch into the water regardless. So Macanan must pre-empt the other, before there was the ludicrous spectacle of two semi-glacial men swimming past each other, or even arguing and struggling mid-stream. He must swim first.

Before the gaucho could step into the river, Macanan plunged forward, rushing down the gully in the hoof prints of the mare and straight into the stream that made him cry out against the cold. He struck out without looking at the gaucho, for he must have the greater conviction, if the other came against him. Had he looked up, he'd have seen the gaucho raise a hand in protest.

Macanan, who could not manage a horse to save his life, was the better swimmer. Though the flood chilled him, swirled him and tried to trick him with currents that crossed one above the other, nonetheless in a minute he was hauling himself up the far bank, upstream of where the gaucho had floundered ashore.

He stood on the bank, with the river already forgotten behind him, and with the gaucho, half frozen, jigging about nearby. Without a word, they both sat on the ground, pulled on their boots with stiff fingers that could barely tie. When they stood again, they shivered so much they seemed to be shaking the water off like dogs.

Macanan peered through eyes that would not focus, dimmed by cold. He glimpsed the gaucho before him: the man appeared to be shrinking even as he watched, the fight bleeding out of him into the grit. Macanan reached out a clumsy hand, grasping at the gaucho's shoulder.

'What is your name?'

The gaucho gazed back in mute bewilderment at the doctor who had hired him weeks ago. Macanan shook his shoulder.

'Tell me! What is your name?'

'Félix, señor.'

'No going back, Félix.'

The gaucho said nothing.

'Do you understand me?' Macanan shouted at the shrivelling figure, over the noise of the wind and their own trembling that made their ears rattle. 'There's no going back. Have to find horses, find people and food. Have to go north.'

He pointed to the bleak expanse beyond them. Félix the gaucho's head wobbled with what might have been agreement, or hypothermia. Macanan turned him by the shoulder to face north.

'Come, Félix.'

They began to walk.

The wind was at their backs; it drove them ahead. Some days past, they had seen rheas – the little Patagonian ostriches – running before the breeze with their wings outstretched like sails. Likewise Macanan now felt the wind behind him. He was happy to be out of the hated saddle. He moved quickly.

There were occasional patches of grazing: thus there was a chance of Tehuelche Indians camped somewhere, with food and fire. Shortly after leaving the river, they crested a low ridge, and saw a herd of wild horses grazing. The two men gazed at these unattainable animals a moment – then Macanan marched forward, and the gaucho staggered after.

Again they crossed a sterile plateau of grey-brown grit, littered with yellow pebbles. From time to time, as though a colour-brush had been drawn over it, the ground beneath them turned blue-black with the wreckage of old lava. If they took their eyes off the ground, within moments they twisted an ankle.

They were bowled northwards by the wind, faces lowered like old prospectors racing towards a glimpse of gold on the ground. The gaucho ached for a rein in his hand, and he looked resentfully at the gawky figure striding unsteadily away in front of him. He could not keep up.

'Señor...,' Félix the gaucho bleated.

But Macanan sped on.

Hour after hour the air rushed past them, so that their clothes were soon dry but stiffly cold, and their ears ached with the incessant noise. The wind could drive them along, but it could not feed them. Famished, they wobbled across the next ravine, dragging themselves up the far side. There they gazed over a pebble tract that seemed to have no end.

'Does it get better?' asked Macanan.

The gaucho waved wearily over the expanse, saying nothing but glancing eloquently behind him: they should have gone south.

They looked for signs of an Indian encampment: there was nothing, only phosphor and salt lakes ringed by a mile-wide crust of white sodium. In the centre of one lake, they saw five guanacos standing up to their knees in the saline. There was not an animal within reach, not a berry to eat.

In the distance was a low ridge.

'Maybe we'll see something from there,' said Félix.

On they went, with sore feet and wrenched ankles, light-headed, the wind still at their backs under a sky now heavy with cloud. They came to the ridge and staggered up the slope – and the landscape beyond was as sterile as the landscape behind them.

They stumbled down the far side as the clouds turned black. Macanan saw that the gaucho had begun to lurch, to wobble on his feet. He saw the gaucho look at him, saw alarm in Félix' eyes.

'What is it?' called Macanan.

'Señor, are you not well?'

'I?'

'You do not look so good, Señor.'

Macanan himself was lurching and wobbling more than the other. Standing face to face, the two men studied one another, swaying, dismayed, incredulous, biffed and deafened by the gale. They shuffled in a risible, teetering dance, as though they might suddenly totter into each others' arms. With an effort, they both turned to face north once more, and proceeded only because their upper bodies were falling forwards in a near-faint, and their feet were trying to catch up.

It began to snow; they were so cold they could hardly feel its touch on their faces. The flakes grew larger, were driven into their eyes.

At dusk, they stood on the lip of the next ravine.

'Look there,' said Macanan, rubbing at his eyes to be sure. There was a shadow in the slope opposite, a cave's dark orifice.

'Take shelter,' Macanan coughed weakly, 'out of the weather.'

He waved his hand, which felt ten times its proper weight, at some lifeless shrubs.

'Bushes, look. Make a fire.'

There was a scree tail of sandy dirt leading to the mouth of the cave. As they crept up it, the ground slipped beneath them, a tease and a torment. When they finally reached the lip, they lay prone, peering into the dark interior. It was a place, surely, that pumas inhabited, and vipers. The two men felt the chill in the ground beneath their chests and bellies; there was no reason to imagine any warmth inside the cave. But they'd be out of the wind and snow.

To one side of the cave mouth was a thicket of what might have been gorse or broom, now parched black. It would burn wonderfully. They crawled to it, and began ripping off branches which, though quite dead, still clung on. They exhausted themselves in making a heap of burnable brushwood. They dragged it to the mouth of the cave.

Felix the gaucho looked expectantly at Señor Macanan.

'But I have nothing to light it,' said Macanan, because everything had been loaded onto the pony to swim the river.

For half a minute they studied each other, with snow catching on their eyelashes. Had we the strength, thought Macanan, we'd be laughing uncontrollably.

They pushed passed the thorn heap and into the cave, where they collapsed on the floor of coarse sand. There they lay, and slept, shivering. They could have hugged each other for warmth, but did not, for they still did not know one another.

*

Light woke Matthieu Macanan. There was sunlight at the cave entrance, probing tentatively like a wary soldier. Chilled to rigid, he lay waiting for the sun to touch him, though when this came it was insufficient to loosen his distress, or to warm his starvation. He lay on the floor of the cave unable to move even his head, nor lift a hand or arm, let alone walk to safety. He felt like some Gulliver, lashed to the ground with a thousand tiny cords of defeat. But the shelter of the cave was sweet to him. He had a curious moment of hallucinatory hearing: it seemed to him that there were horses coming from the south, ridden hard, and that bitter voices were calling his name, voices acrid with spite, come to drag him back to his guilt, and the last tiny electrical impulses in his muscles flickered with a farcical suggestion that he might fight the pursuers in the cave mouth – but they missed him, they did not notice Macanan and Félix in the cave; they rode by, and were only in his imagination anyway.

He lay still on the sand. He was so overwhelmed by finality that he believed his flesh had already begun to decay, even before death. The pragmatic life was packing its bags to leave his body, impatient for his soul to acknowledge the obvious and clear out.

An absolute cold drew over him, deeper than snow, ice and wind. This surely was death. The chill spread out from his core. He examined this notion with resignation – with relief – as time passed. He did not twitch a limb, was scarcely breathing or circulating his blood, but lay still on his back.

He wondered if Félix the gaucho would stir or speak. But the man might have been dead already, or in a deep, unconscious sleep; his horses gone, he had nothing to wake for. Matthieu Macanan thought of gaucho stories: one, of a *tropilla* of horses caught in a snow drift so deep that they could not escape, but only walked in a circle until they had formed a perfectly round hole, in which they all lay down and died. Each place on earth had its ways of dying.

He lay still and listened to the outside world, but could distinguish nothing but a continual rush that might be the wind, or an artefact of his inner ear. With a realisation that he was not yet altogether dead, he began to pay some attention to what he could see. He registered that the light had moved around the cave – not direct sunlight, but the silicate glare of the stony ground outside, coupled perhaps with reflection off the river. Once his eyes had accommodated, he could see quite well. He could see the texture of the rock precisely. He could see tiny crystals; he could see flakes that for a thousand years had been poised to detach themselves; he saw grains that had been loosened by flood or wind, and now hung on a spider's thread, or from some fibre of primitive plant life, or from nothing – and had perhaps hung so for a millennium.

And then he saw hands. Scores of hands, reaching out to him.

At first, he saw just the one, but when he established what it was, then they were everywhere, clear as could be. They were painted – no, but in negative, so the hand shape appeared pale, surrounded with dark ochre shading, in places near black. The outlines were clear, right down between the outspread fingers, all around the thumb and wrists. How had it been done: pigment blown through a reed? There were fat, chubby hands, and there were thin, elegant hands like a pianist's; there were childish hands, feminine hands, and some hefty like a hunter's – a hunter who could fell a puma with his fist, thought Matthieu Macanan. Or a sabre-tooth tiger, or a milodon, or some long-extinct bear. They were surely very ancient.

Yet they spread above him in such vivid proximity that he believed they might touch him. The haziest delineation was around the wrists, the sharpest at the fingertips, and so the latter seemed nearer, as though they reached down, feeling for him. It was tender, a caress; some entire tribe was placing hands upon him. He felt now not lifeless but quite relaxed, not desiring to move, only to have those hands upon him. Matthieu Macanan lay prostrate, and out of unmeasurable time the people of the cave reached down to bless him, to bless his entire body. In reward for his effort in coming, they offered him a chance of forgiveness.

There was a sudden change in the light in the cave entrance: a darkening, a movement of shadows. There were new sounds, voices speaking words he could not follow, a language he'd never heard. There were new hands upon him, warm immediate hands, easing him out towards the daylight.

There were faces, dark and angular, smiling with curiosity, kindly and welcoming, and it seemed clear to him that they were saying:

'You have come. You have come, and earned your rest.'

In the face of this, Matthieu Macanan passed out.

'THE DECLINE OF THE NATIVE'

from

SKETCHES OF THE PATAGONIAN SEABOARD

by

Huw Asbury Prothero

Little by little, the remotest coast of Patagonia has been opened to commerce, but it has not been plain sailing. It took me years to persuade my employers – the owners of *Luisa Menendez* – to permit me to call at smaller, isolated harbours such as Montero or Bahía Sanlúcar. They havered, citing the difficult shoreline, the risks and delays.

'Wait and see!' was their refrain, 'and when demand is there…'

I would have left the matter, but Miss Dinah Morris – of Puerto Montt and latterly a guest house proprietrix in Punta Arenas – upbraided me, saying that it was the business of navigators to lead the way, not to wait on trade. This I put to my directors, and at last good sense prevailed. Thus I discovered the poignant remnants of native culture that persisted in that isolated district where, from 1907 to 1915, dwelt Dr Matthieu Macanan.

It grieves me, the record of seafarers with regard to the natives of Patagonia. A man must be proud of his profession, but a sailor contemplates this history with shame. I only protest that Welshmen played little part in it.

In the year 1520, Ferdinand Magellan's ships bumped over a sand bar into a fine natural harbour. I know the spot: even today I find that terrain particularly bleak and wind-blasted, but there is fresh water and abundant meat, especially guanacos and ostriches. A group of Patagonians approached Magellan, clad in fur cloaks. Iberian and native, curious and restrained, traded in nails and trinkets and got on well. Further south, at the Strait, the crew of Sir Francis Drake had a more rudimentary policy: when those fine English mariners met with aboriginals, they murdered them with sword and musket.

On Tierra del Fuego, ranching and gold panning did for the tribes. When cattle and sheep appeared, the natives speared these as they would any other meaty beast, and so European gentlemen (some of my acquaintance) went out in heavily armed parties; they would hack off ears as trophies, for they'd be paid for each kill. Children they sold to the missions.

And the women? I blush, but Miss Morris (dauntless enquirer!) insisted on hearing all. Most native women would be dragged into camp for recreational duties. These ladies were, to our eyes, unspeakably dirty, so the well-equipped cavalier would carry a scrubbing brush in his pack; women would be shorn and soaped in the river, then abused. When the gentlemen moved on, the girls had their throats cut. Miss Morris learned from one of her lodgers of a fellow who had found two squaws hiding under a bush. He had slaughtered both and departed, leaving a babe in the arms of its dying mother. Dinah's informant had thought it a fine joke, till she threw him out.

When I came to Patagonia in 1896 as a callow youth out of Penarth, South Wales, there were still a few hundred natives on Tierra del Fuego. Today they are gone, quite extinct. On the mainland, sheep swarmed like grubs over the hunting grounds, while the natives succumbed to disease, degradation and starvation.

Miss Morris, in earlier days, ran a guesthouse in Santiago de Chile, where from time to time I stayed. One afternoon, an exotic figure appeared at the door requesting lodging. I let him in. He was a dark-skinned fellow who spoke a stilted antique Spanish very courteously. He introduced himself as Orkeka, *cacique* or elder of the upper Río Zurdo. Dinah served his dinner, while instructing me to engage him in conversation. His people, incensed by the depredations of ranchers, had sent him to Santiago to demand their land rights. Each day he would trudge off to the law courts and ministries to submit his petitions, but investors had got there first, had tickled palms with silver; the matter was closed against anything Orkeka could say. Each evening, he would return to the boarding house sunk in gloom, growing daily more taciturn, pushing his food aside untouched. Whilst in the city, Orkeka developed a rash that looked more fearsome than the warlike old chief himself. Dinah sent me for a doctor but, before help could come, Orkeka slipped away. The contagion will have accompanied him back to the Río Zurdo, and doubtless spread like fire through his community. We heard no more of him.

Later, strong drink got among the aboriginals, a seed of decay deliberately sown by persons casting a covetous eye upon the land's imagined riches. The natives were famed for their skill in hunting with the *bolas,* heavy balls bound up with long cords, used to bring down the running ostrich and other game. These *bolas* were made of common stone, or occasionally of iron, but a rumour spread that, inside the leather casings, the ball was sometimes solid gold. It will be readily imagined what sort of predators came flocking, and soon groups of natives were killed in ambushes and drunken brawls.

The gentle, guileless natives were easily 'fleeced' by sheep men. They needed some official tribune for their interests. None such existed.

My directors finally agreed to *Luisa Menendez* making calls by Dr Macanan's home at Sanlúcar, a very remote region where he laboured for many years. I enquired of my friend if he did not feel himself in danger from the justified resentment the natives must surely bear towards any foreigner. Were we not, in their eyes, all tarred with the same brush? The doctor answered: yes, it was so – but what cowardice, to skulk behind a fear of retribution! Dr Macanan's position was simple: the white barbarians were coming, and would bring ruin to the natives; all that a decent man could do was be there and stand by them.

I feared he'd be swept aside; such was the record of civilisation in Patagonia.

Four
THE DOVE
1914

She lay fingertips upon her husband's wrist, near the blood that oozed from his torn finger. On the back of his hand, the crimson had dried into flakes, like so much mud.

'He caught it in the motor,' she said.

She was pale, from seeing her man bleed. But her colouring was pale anyway, her eyebrows blonde, her hair white-gold.

'Not *in* the motor, Silke,' the husband babbled in shock, as though it mattered traumatologically. 'I dropped the... you see, I dropped it...'

The young man – whose name was Theo Kahn – sat helpless on a stool staring at Matthieu Macanan, in utter incredulity at finding a doctor in this place.

'The cloth is dirty,' the woman Silke murmured, her voice softly accented. 'It was all I had.'

The cloth on which the injured hand rested was indeed dirty, and oily, but it was a fine creamy linen nonetheless. Matthieu Macanan wondered where she had got it. He imagined the undergarment beneath her long woollen skirt, rent into strips.

'No matter,' he said. 'I shall dress this and strap it.' He turned to the unlit stove where a covered jug of boiled water stood, now lukewarm. 'I do not use stitches where I can avoid them. One sews in contamination.'

The woman surveyed the walls of logs sealed with ochre mud, and the roof of old iron sheets.

'Silke,' said young Theo, 'there's another stool, look.'

'Forgive me, Mrs Kahn – yes.'

As Matthieu positioned the bloodied hand over an earthenware bowl, the young woman went to this stool; he was minutely aware of the low thud of her boot heels on the boards, the little scrape as she turned around, the rustle of her clothing as she settled tidily. He was also aware of something else: his hard-won isolation was besieged.

'You are German?' he enquired.

'Austrian. From Carlsfelden, by Linz.'

To Matthieu, Linz was the name of a cake and also of a symphony. When did he last hear a symphony…

He was finding it a distraction, having her observe while he swilled boiled water over the wounded hand. Her presence made his hands shake even as, with a scalpel blade, he eased the white flaps of skin back into place. Grow up, he told himself: you know how women stare.

'You will come and see the *Taube*, please?' said Theo Kahn. 'You've not seen it yet?'

'I've been upriver three weeks; I only arrived home last night.'

'Then come! You will be amazed. You will honour us, Doctor – a man of science.'

'I don't claim that,' Matthieu murmured.

'But I cannot believe you,' insisted Theo. 'A man of science, of course.'

He peered at Matthieu as though fearing that his invitation might be snubbed.

'A cultivated man,' he gushed, 'a French scholar who has travelled, who understands...'

'I have never seen such a thing,' said Matthieu. 'I have heard of them, but none has reached Patagonia.'

The young Austrian beamed.

'None has reached Patagonia,' he echoed in ecstasy, 'until now... until here!'

He took a sharp breath, flaring his nostrils against a jag of pain. Matthieu waited for him to relax, then said:

'I shall be most interested.'

He heard the terseness in his own voice, and the irony: that of all the ramshackle clinics in all the backwaters of the world, these people had chosen Sanlúcar...

'There,' he was brusque. 'That must not be disturbed for five days.'

His patient peered mournfully at the finger, now strapped tightly to its neighbour.

'This will not make it easy to work on the motor.'

'I can hold things for you,' his wife said.

'Yes, yes,' he gave Matthieu a coy grin: 'You already do, of course.'

Matthieu winced, fastidious.

The woman was piqued.

'There is much that I could do, if you would let me.'

But her husband let it pass.

Matthieu watched them walk along the bluff towards the tiny settlement of a few dozen souls that looked out over the bay. He felt again a niggling resentment; he had come a great distance to insulate himself, and with success for a few years. He did not like to be broken in upon.

But he told himself: he was not to be obsessive. There had been intrusions since the *Luisa Menendez* had first delivered a few callers and communications; Matthieu had controlled his misanthropy, and had tried to be minimally civil. These Kahns were surely no more threatening? In the distance, Matthieu saw Silke Kahn take her husband's wrist while looking into his eyes: perhaps she suspected a faint or collapse coming on, for Theo had faltered in his walk. She got him restarted, and passed her hand though his arm as they proceeded, her skirts swaying around her boots. It was the first time, Matthieu realised, that he had seen a couple arm-in-arm at Bahía Sanlúcar; possibly it was the first time this had ever occurred. Soon the Kahns were silhouettes in the morning light that came off the bay and off the silver sea beyond the spit, light that was reflected by salt crystals on the soil, making the dirt shine and the air shimmer. They vanished among the shacks where they had taken lodging.

If 'taking lodging' was not too absurd a notion here. Matthieu gazed a moment at the dozen cabins, the one *boliche* or bar-cum-store, and the sheds of the traders in guanaco fur, ostrich feathers, and the very little wool that this region as yet produced. He thought of the Austrian woman, Silke, and the looks she'd be getting from the handful of men hereabouts, men who saw a woman once a year, and then only in the merry-houses of Punta Arenas. He thought of her husband, his soft manner and his notions, among the coarse herdsmen, the louse-infested hardcases whose answer to any imagined slight was to whip an eighteen-inch blade from their belts. Then he thought of the woman again. Silke. He said the name under his breath: Silke.

Matthieu, suddenly conscious of dirt, went back indoors to clear up, laying the dust with a little river water and sweeping it with a coarse broom out through the door, re-arranging the contents of his roughly-made wall-cupboard, even lifting a jar or two to wipe underneath – until he stopped himself. Moments ago, the Austrian couple had surveyed his premises, peering at the lumber walls, the packed clay in the joints, the rough fittings, wondering if this doctor was really a civilised man. And now he was wanting to impress the visitors after they had departed: what childishness was that? He tried to see himself as they might: the fastidious Dr Macanan with his neat professional manners, sweeping and dusting premises little better than a shanty. Risible behaviour! One moment he begrudged the newcomers' intrusion, the next he was all house-proud vanity.

He called for the boy who looked after his mules. His mules! Now, there was a change – but Matthieu had as little to do with the animals as possible. He took up his leather saddlebag, glanced over the contents, hitched it across his animal, reluctantly hauled himself aboard by stepping from a driftwood log, and departed for the Indian encampment two hours away. His long legs flapped as uselessly as ever, his stooped shoulders and long face just as ungainly. The boy Lipi rode before him, hauling the doctor on a lead rein. Matthieu had by no means overcome his fears.

*

It was late afternoon before Matthieu and Lipi returned to Bahía Sanlúcar. The river wound to and fro, cutting its perverse way across the dirt plain, and from the bluff one looked down onto miniature sheltered pastures within its bends. Although in summer the river was reduced to a gravelly trickle, near the water the grass was still green and fresh, and dusted with colour: white and red orchids, and pink cowslips. The waxy young leaves of the *calafate* shrubs were spangled with lemon yellow flowers, and flocks of tiny swallows with glittering blue wings zipped after insects.

As they neared the bay and the settlement, the trail cut across a bend in the river, and passed among certain peculiar bumps and protuberances in the ground. There was little to see; you could easily – if you were daydreaming, or fretting about something – miss these markings altogether. Look closely, and you might make out the shapes of buildings, of enclosures, fragments of mud brick and collapsed walls. There was once a Spanish township here, part of an attempt to colonise the coast long ago, abandoned when the colonists had starved and lost their minds with isolation. Passing through the ruins, Matthieu would recall that he had aspired to that seclusion. Now, he supposed, he must allow the world to touch him, little by little.

The mules stopped outside Matthieu's own door. He considered its plain boards. He slid off the saddle, telling the boy to turn the animal loose in its corral, where it shuffled round to put its rump to the grit in the wind. Matthieu placed his medical bag just inside the door, then walked into the settlement to the store of Rahman the Turk where the Austrians stayed.

He heard Theo calling:

'Silke? Are you ready? Silke?'

Kahn sounded anxious to be away somewhere.

'Herr Kahn?'

The Austrian had not heard Matthieu coming, and gawped at him.

'Oh, Doctor! Heavens, please forgive me... Silke?'

This call was directed at the open door of the storeroom. The iron roof shifted in a gust of wind, groaning on its nails.

'Here I am.'

Mrs Kahn appeared in the doorway, fiddling with a clip in her wispy white-gold hair. Seeing Matthieu, she made her fingers more decisive with the clip.

'Oh, you've come,' she smiled at him.

'Herr Kahn was insistent,' replied Matthieu.

She nodded.

'We are just going back to work. We're nearly done, in fact. Will you inspect with us?'

A few hundred paces from the rear of Rahman the Turk's property, a strange shelter had been constructed. It had no roof, but consisted of fencing some nine or ten feet high, not solid but made of heaped thorn laced with cords and tied between tall poles. Matthieu stared in astonishment. He'd been upriver with a distant group of Tehuelche Indians a mere three weeks, and this had all happened in his absence. Where had Kahn obtained the poles? From Rahman perhaps, but who had hauled them in? No trees grew in this district of rocks and salt.

'It is a windbreak,' said Theo, 'from these dreadful gales that might tip the whole thing over. Later I will build something permanent.'

Matthieu saw that the front could be opened out by unfastening two poles and dragging the corded thorns aside. There was an L-shaped entrance passage, so the wind could not blow straight through. Matthieu must avoid snagging his shirt.

Theo exclaimed:

'See here, Doctor. It is *eine Taube*.'

It almost filled the thorn compound, but only at the nose did the oily bulk of the motor seem imposing; the two great blades of the propeller were like opposed scimitars. The rest was so lightly made – so like a bird – that it seemed to have little mass or weight. Both wings and tail were tensioned by a web of steel wire, slung from a modest pylon over the cockpit. The wings were long and curved, the trailing edge stiffened with battens that bulged slightly under the fabric, like quills or long pennons. The end of each wing spread out, as though the bird was sunning its plumes. The tail fanned prettily.

'*Eine Taube,*' echoed Silke. 'In Spanish, *paloma* – a dove.'

'What do you think, Doctor?' said eager young Theo. 'An Ettrich-Rumpler *Taube*. The motor is a 99 horsepower Mercedes.'

'I really know nothing of these things,' Matthieu murmured, but Theo did not notice.

The 99 horsepower Mercedes was painted red, with a sheen and scent of mineral oil. Its solidity was at odds with the slender wires, the frail cloth, the quills. Matthieu thought of ninety-nine winged mules soaring over Patagonia.

'And it flies?' he whispered.

'It flew here,' Theo laughed.

'Not over the Atlantic!'

'No, no, we brought it from Bremen to Argentina by ship, of course. But from Comodoro Rivadavia, I have flown it.'

'But where could you land?' exclaimed the doctor, looking at the wire-spoked wheels like a perambulator's, then glancing at the boulders littering the landscape.

'I dealt with that,' said Mrs Kahn.

'Silke came on *Luisa Menendez*,' smiled Theo, delighted by how well everything was going. 'She paid gauchos to clear a patch of ground.'

Matthieu regarded the woman in astonishment. While he had been away, Captain Prothero had delivered a woman travelling alone with money, who had proceeded to organise a work gang in Bahía Sanlúcar. Well, there were plenty of single women in Punta Arenas; they had been his raison d'être. But very different women. And not here!

Not in Bahía Sanlúcar.

He walked on round the aircraft, almost lost for words. Everything he said showed him up as utterly ignorant.

'How do you find your way?' he asked, 'in the air?'

'Aha!' Theo smiled, 'that is not such a silly question.' (Matthieu was relieved.) 'Of course, I carry a compass and a map, but from a thousand metres, the old Earth looks different.'

'I'm sure,' breathed Matthieu.

'So different!' Theo enthused, embarking on a lecture. 'Important highways marked red upon the map are, from above, nothing but grey scratches. Woods are not the bright green of the cartographer, but brown, even black. Cloud shadows are most deceptive; they fox you into seeing gigantic land formations that are not there at all. If the motor is vibrating, the compass can spin like a top, and in mist or cloud it is easy to lose your sense of direction altogether – which, when one direction might take you straight out over the Atlantic, is a dangerous...'

'Oh!' exclaimed Matthieu, pointing.

'Ah, yes.'

There was a rip in the fabric covering the body of the Dove.

Theo fingered it, glancing at his wife.

'That,' she said, 'is what I must mend before Theo can fly again.'

Matthieu placed a hand on the fabric. He drummed his fingers on it, and the cloth was taut and resonant. It was linen – cousin to that rag he'd thought came from her skirts – and it had been soused in cellulose, and was translucent.

Silke smiled:

'When the *Taube* is flying, the light shines straight through it. When we climb above 400 metres, from the ground we can be heard but hardly seen.'

'*You* fly, Mrs Kahn?'

'The *Taube* can carry two,' she said. 'There are two seats. Come and see. Theo, where is the ladder?'

There was a ladder of driftwood, knocked up in haste. Theo placed this carefully against the aircraft's flank, and invited Matthieu.

'You're a man of science, Doctor. You will enjoy this.'

Again, it sounded like a plea.

From the top step, Matthieu peered down into the cockpit. The wooden seats had green leather pads, slightly scuffed. There was a stick with a round ring handle of iron covered in leather, which must rise up between your knees. Lower down, he glimpsed piping and a little brass tap, which he supposed must carry the fuel. Jutting from the dashboard was a compass, a gauge or two that he did not understand, and a short vertical glass half-filled with pink fluid.

'That's the pitot tube,' Theo called up to him, guessing what Matthieu was looking at. 'It shows the airspeed – that is how fast you are flying. There is a nozzle facing forwards, and the air pressure is shown by the rising fluid.'

Matthieu could grasp that, at least. He fired a few questions in what he hoped was a shrewd, appraising tone, then felt self-conscious and foolish, and came down the ladder.

He said, 'You propose to fly out together? Man and wife!' As though that was an improper joke.

But Theo would not rise to any bait.

'Doctor, you must understand what we're about. It will be a mail service. Imagine that – here in Patagonia! It is scarcely begun in England;

it is not dreamed of in Imperial Austria, not even in Carlsfelden. In the USA they talk of it... but I shall do it here: Bahía Blanca to Rivadavia and Punta Arenas. Do you know what they have found at Rivadavia? Oil, oil in the ground, when they were only looking for water. Imagine the business there! I shall carry mail, packages, anything light that would take weeks by sea. People will pay handsomely. I can bring you medicines. I can bring your professional mail.'

Matthieu did not receive professional mail. His medicines came on *Luisa Menendez*. He did not wish anything else to be addressed to him.

'Why,' he said in incomprehension, 'stop in Bahía Sanlúcar? There's no one here.'

'Fuel, Doctor. I have installed an auxiliary tank, and I can fly 180 miles in one hop, but then I must land. This will be one of my depots and postal drops.'

Again, Matthieu did not know what to say. He gazed at the fragile body of the Dove, tightly varnished in cellulose, and he visualised the space inside packed with letters and little parcels. Packages of gold dust, he thought with a faint shiver, from the Chilean prospectors. Land titles, and legal rights to oil. He imagined Silke Kahn seated inside, suspended by wires in the doped translucent linen. Would she wear a hat? Did one wear a bonnet in a Dove? He thought of her holding down her skirts in the wind. Surely the incessant gales of Patagonia would tear a fragile bird to shreds. He placed one hand upon the fuselage and felt it twitch slightly, so that for a moment he believed it to be alive and trembling – until he noticed the wind pushing through the fence of thorn.

Silke Kahn was watching him.

'When I have mended that tear, you shall see Theo fly.'

She returned his look with a steadiness that he decided was too steady, for surely she was anxious for her husband sailing about in the clouds; her calm was but a foil to his absurd Teutonic death wish. Matthieu thought again of her coming ashore in Bahía Sanlúcar, sent with money to get gauchos to prepare a landing strip. Sent in advance of a Dove with sunlight in its wings. Put ashore with a tin of motor spirits. Set down on the beach by a steamer's cutter that promptly turned tail, without waiting to see if she'd be violated there and then on the beach. But she'd managed. How was this possible?

She had managed; she'd had no choice.

Still she held his look. He was not used to it.

*

Matthieu Macanan was not the sole inhabitant of his house. There was a family living under the floorboards.

They were snakes: Patagonian lanceheads, pretty little vipers with turned-up noses like freckled schoolgirls. They are the southernmost species of viper, and not common even in Patagonia. Mostly they live in the grass tussocks along the coast, but this particular family had taken up residence beneath Matthieu's house, where he often heard them slithering and hissing. When he first realised what they were, it made him uneasy. He would glance nervously at the ground when stepping outside, and regarded the earth closet with caution. At one period the sounds ceased, and he felt relief that they had gone – but then he realised that it was winter, and the lanceheads were sleeping in a family knot. In the spring, they awoke.

He had often wondered what to do about his snakes but, short of tearing up his floor, he was at a loss. Besides, he was averse to killing. He had grown used to them. He lay at night listening to the curious discussions that went on under his floorboards. First there would be a slippery rustling as the family awakened and rearranged itself. Then there would be dialogue: a long, slowly-building hiss, answered by others from different positions below the boards. Next, there would come little clicking sounds, persisting for a minute or so, as though of a clockwork motor. After that, renewed hissings died away like a soft release of steam, or occasionally gathered into a petty argument. In the darkness, in his fur bed when he lay wakeful, Matthieu found the sound of the lanceheads quite companionable. He'd been afraid for his feet when he got up to urinate, so he had ensured that there were no gaps between the boards and no open knotholes. But, that done – with the demarcation lines clear – he had accepted the snakes' presence. He had no business disturbing them. He had no business disturbing anything here.

*

Silke Kahn returned to his 'surgery'; he called it that with reluctance, given its mud-plastered timber, its spiders and its un-planed furnishings which, scrub them as he might, always had a dull gloss from oily guanaco fur. She came to visit, and he had hoped for this. His vanity revived; from dawn he had been sweeping and dusting, tidying his few surgical instruments away into their cases. He threw open the window, then closed it hurriedly, because the wind re-coated with grit everything that he had just cleaned. He wiped all the surfaces with a wet rag – and mocked himself. He looked out of the window facing the bluff and saw her coming, and wiped some more.

When she entered, it seemed to Matthieu that she occupied no space. In his surgery, he sometimes had half a dozen Tehuelche Indians jabbering while one of them wailed and friends stripped off the man's britches to reveal a broken leg. Or there might be a youth who had been chasing a rhea, who had swung his *bolas* ineptly and caught himself a clip round the temples with the stone ball, and who would stagger through Matthieu's door with blood matting his hair, to collapse on the floor. Or a mother with mewling small fry who would squirt the boards with diarrhoea and pry into everything dangerous. All these would take up a great deal of room. But Silke Kahn placed herself with such finesse as to fill, it seemed, no volume at all.

'You'll forgive me taking up your time?' she began, though there was no one else present.

'I hope,' he responded, 'that there is nothing further amiss.'

He heard the comical stiffness of this exchange.

'Nothing more,' she said gravely. 'My husband says his finger is very comfortable.'

'And yourself?'

'Oh, nothing is ever wrong with me.'

She said this with a jaunty, bright expression. Many women, he told himself, would want him to know that they had suffered and laboured, but were indomitable. They would be inviting admiration. But Silke Kahn meant that she was never ill – just that.

'Do you keep consulting hours?'

'Tehuelche have no watches, and gauchos are usually drunk – at least, when they need me.'

'But you care principally for them, or for those Indians?'

'Whoever has need. And I hope your husband will return, so that I can re-examine his hand.'

'Yes – oh, and we shall pay you! I was meant to say that. That is why I am come. You must tell us how much; without you, we should have been lost.'

She was drifting about the room, gazing at this and that, peering into every angle, the corners of the ceiling, the grey haze of old spiders' webs.

'May I ask,' said Matthieu, 'what are your plans?'

She looked at him quickly; she was a tad defensive.

'It is as Theo said when you saw the aircraft. He will establish a mail service. He will link all the settlements of the coast.'

Matthieu wondered: in that motorised dragonfly?

'He is filled with ideas,' she continued, 'but he's a wonderful mechanic also. And the *Taube* is reliable; the motor is Mercedes which everyone agrees is the best, while the plane is very simple to fly. Theo says that even I could fly it. I should like to.'

And fly out of here, perhaps. Matthieu peered at her. Did she believe in Theo's scheme?

'Might I ask, what is your role to be?'

She looked out of the window, down the estuary to the settlement.

'He intends this to be one of his centres,' she said. 'The ranches can collect their mail, and leave letters for Theo to take on.'

Then, thought Matthieu, Theo was misinformed: farms were fewer and poorer here than anywhere in Patagonia. They sent no letters. He ought to tell Theo this, and then Theo would go away.

'But, what about you?' he asked again.

'Oh,' said Silke airily, 'I shall manage the service while Theo flies our *Taube*, our dove, our *paloma*. There is much to do on the ground. I shall establish agencies at each stop.'

Again she moved almost weightlessly about the room: a *paloma sagrada,* he could not stop himself thinking, and he winced: again she stirred the memory of a graceful Fuegian woman, who had been shot.

He pulled himself together just as Silke turned to him and burst out:

'But I do not understand: what are *you* doing here, Doctor Matthieu? Among these people, in this place?'

He had known that she would demand this. In six years, it had not occurred to anyone else, not one of those drunken, knife-fighting gauchos whom he had sewn together, not one of those Indians whose limbs he'd set or whose children he'd saved from a fever. No one had asked him: what are you doing here? Perhaps they thought it (or him) of no interest.

Silke was scrutinising him, waiting.

'The place,' he began cautiously, 'may be wretched, but the people need care like anyone else.'

'But aren't they savages?' she exclaimed, and immediately blushed. 'Oh, no, they have been very civil to me. But, in the settlement, people say...'

Matthieu interrupted.

'A savage is someone ignorant and inept. The Tehuelche are intimate with their own territory, with skills and crafts that are remarkable. A savage is debauched and has no morals, but you will find few fiercer guardians of a daughter's honour than a Tehuelche father.'

He saw that she was mortified, and he regretted his pompous lecture.

'Please understand,' she breathed, 'that I meet the worst sort, in Montevideo and Buenos Aires and everywhere. I would like to know more.'

Matthieu said more gently:

'I could take you to the encampments. A white woman, taking an interest in them – they'd be charmed.'

'I would so love to!'

'Will your husband...?'

'Oh, Theo has no mind for anything but his *Taube.*'

Matthieu caught a sardonic tinge to this.

'Only,' he said, 'if I am not taking you away from matters more pressing.'

She smiled, 'I think I shall have time. Theo may be returning to Montevideo soon.'

'Your husband is leaving?'

'Possibly.'

'But what about you?'

'I have work here.'

The idea was too bizarre. The aircraft had two seats; Matthieu had concluded that Silke would be flying out with her husband as soon as everything was 'established'. But he might leave her here.

'Good heavens,' murmured Matthieu. 'When will this happen?'

She said lightly, 'We shall see. He proposes a flight tomorrow. He asks, would you like to see the *Taube* fly?'

*

At midday, when he came to the thorn compound, he found that the front had been dragged apart. The Ettrich-Rumpler *Taube* faced out into the open; now Matthieu could see the full expanse of it, and was startled: twelve paces wingtip to wingtip, perhaps more. And yet: the delicacy of those wings hung from their wire supports, of the cloth cover stretched taut by its cellulose dope. A touch from a sharp blade would split it open like the tight skin of a fermenting fig.

The Dove faced outward, debating whether she wished to fly today. But lesser beings, little creatures without wings, made decisions for her; she was like some dowager empress, teetering on spindly legs and wheels, manipulated by her courtiers. She would be informed when and where she was to rise.

Silke stood guard, because a little crowd had gathered to witness the take-off. A few of them had seen Theo's first landing, but landing was a fall, after all; you can do that from a log. To fly, though! None here had ever seen a man clawing his way up into the sunlight. Here to watch came all the population of Bahía Sanlúcar: a few gauchos, the Turk and his woman, a smattering of urchins, two Tehuelche Indians and a brace of sheep men in from the *campo,* laughing, even nervous, not unkind but sceptical.

Matthieu could not see Theo, until he realised that the group was watching a figure moving seventy or eighty yards away. There was something odd about the ground: it was unnaturally smooth. For hundreds of square miles, the earth was peppered with rocks and pebbles and boulders, but here was a smooth stretch, free of detritus.

It had been cleared; the Austrians had paid to have it cleared of rocks. The locals they'd engaged must think it the oddest job ever: tidying the Patagonian pampas. Now, Theo was checking, tossing aside stones.

Silke waited beside the elegant sculpture of the propeller blades.

'Good morning.'

She smiled at Matthieu. How very light her skin seemed, as pale as clouds. He remembered her saying: when the sun shines through the fabric of the Dove, it is invisible in the air. He thought: her skin is like that. Was that a proud smile, or an apology for her husband's obsession?

'You have an audience,' he remarked.

'Theo likes that,' she replied. Her hand went to her white-blonde hair which was back in a loose bun, being worked looser by the breeze.

'Can it be flown in this?' queried Matthieu.

'Oh, we need the wind. We take off into wind. It is air pouring over the wing that lifts us.'

'Ah,' said Matthieu, 'yes.' To a man of science, these concepts would be obvious. 'Like a kite,' he added.

She did not reply at once. Probably it was not like a kite at all.

'As long as the wind is not too strong,' she said at last, 'in which case, Theo would take off backwards.'

Matthieu was unsure, but a little laugh felt appropriate.

Back came Theo, stalking across his stone free ground.

'All clear,' he shouted. 'Some assistance, please, to bring her onto the strip.'

A dozen people crowded around the filmy aircraft, grabbing with their coarse fingers.

'Carefully!' cried Theo. 'Only push where I show you. The fabric is light.'

He bustled round, indicating where it was safe to push. He had two men lift the delicate tail plane with no effort, the whole fuselage tipping forward over the wheels.

'Steady!'

There was laughter. Someone said you could pick her up in one hand, launch her like a dart.

'You'll smash the propeller,' scolded Theo, rushing to push the nose back up before the sculpted blade jagged into the ground.

The Dove rolled slowly out with Theo calling: 'This way! That way!' At the end of the cleared strip everyone let go, to see if she would flutter away before Theo boarded. But he placed wooden wedges against the wheels, to keep her from rolling where she liked. Then came the ladder which he climbed to tweak expertly at the motor.

'Right,' he declared, and everyone backed off.

He took from Silke a leather helmet that fitted tightly over his head and from which his hair sprouted, and leather goggles with small disk lenses which he put around his neck. He ascended the ladder once more, and made as if to stow a large canvas bag. But he did not climb in. From the top of the ladder, he addressed the little crowd, holding up the bag.

'This bag,' he cried, 'will be your link to the world. This bag will contain your letters home, your orders to the merchants of Bahía Blanca and Buenos Aires, your remittances to the banks. Within forty-eight hours, they will be there!'

The gauchos, the farmhands, the two Tehuelche and the traders of Bahía Sanlúcar scrutinised him. Theo (and, at the ladder's foot, Silke) watched for the mood.

'This bag,' beamed Theo, 'will carry your love letters on wings to your paramours.'

The crowd laughed and put up a little cheer.

The Dove waited.

Theo descended again. Now what? wondered Matthieu. The aviator murmured to his wife; Silke moved beside the wheels and picked up two strings attached to the wooden wedges. I should be offering, thought Matthieu, but I haven't a clue.

Then Theo startled everyone except his wife. He reached up, seized the long propeller, and swung all his weight upon it.

The Dove spat, choked, spluttered, and spurted black smoke. The blades chopped, almost halted, swung further, juddered... and spun quickly. The motor clattered and shook, the whole aircraft shook, until Matthieu thought the motor must surely hurl itself out of the Dove's beak and onto the ground. But it settled to a steady growl, and the smoke turned to a blue-grey haze.

Immediately, Theo swarmed up his ladder. In the pilot's seat, he sat with his head high in the air. He slipped on the goggles, gesturing to Silke who tweaked the wedges away from the wheels. The Dove began to roll forward; a thin, apprehensive cheer went up from the watchers. Theo waved imperiously, shouting something that no one heard. Then the engine note changed and the Dove trundled away, lifting its pretty tail.

No talk now; they watched open-mouthed. The Dove ran away along the cleared strip, its wings swaying and its tail waggling, Theo high up like a mahout upon his elephant until they flew, rising, wobbling and climbing on the wind, making a stately turn inland. The watchers saw Theo wave again, and at once the crowd – gaucho and Indian, trader and urchin – all raised their arms, waved eagerly and cheered aloud.

Even Silke waved.

Matthieu found that she was standing beside him. As the aircraft turned above them, the doctor and the pilot's wife laughed. They beamed at each other, and her pale grey-green eyes held his.

The Dove turned again. It passed over their heads, far above, and daylight streamed through the cellulosed wings which gleamed in milky translucence.

Una paloma sagrada. Matthieu, already stiff-necked from looking up, had a moment's vision of a white dove plunging upon some ecstatic apostle. He thought: Theo Kahn's life hangs from thin wires.

There it came again, sailing overhead, looking down on them. Matthieu felt himself observed from above, and he did not like this: he had never expected that his refuge might be prised open from the air. The watchers waved and waved, until it was apparent that the Dove must pass out over the bay. This realisation had a curious effect on the Indians; dismayed, they began jabbering to one another.

Silke looked to Matthieu.

'What is it?' she asked. 'What are they saying?'

The Tehuelche shook their heads, faces dark; they were saying that to fly over the pampas was one thing, for one knew the pampas. But no one knew the water.

Matthieu had begun to smile when he sensed Silke tensing at his side. The note of the Dove had changed: there was indeed something wrong.

The smooth growl was breaking up, cutting, restarting, cutting: the Mercedes that was the best in the world was ailing. The crowd knew it. They saw the nose dip as the Dove turned inland, off that uncertain sea, back over the pampas. It turned tightly, losing height, and the motor continued to splutter, but the Dove was being blown back towards them, out of the north towards the cleared strip of ground, straight back home. The motor died entirely; there was a wonderful silence out of which the glossy thing drifted lightly down, then touched the ground with a faint stir of dust, rolled a little way, and stopped.

The crowd broke forward, running. Silke did not move. Matthieu glanced at her, and saw that she was not looking towards her husband in his aircraft, that she was looking nowhere.

Matthieu asked, 'Has this happened before?'

'Sometimes. Sometimes, yes.'

They stared across the open ground to where Theo had already organised the population of Bahía Sanlúcar to push their mail-plane with its wings waggling apologetically back into its thorn nest.

*

So he must fetch spare parts.

The night before Theo Kahn was to board the monthly sailing of *Luisa Menendez*, heading north, he brought Silke to eat at Matthieu's home. This was the first invitation that Matthieu had issued since he could remember; he had not been a host of dinner parties in Punta Arenas, while in Bahía Sanlúcar, apart from the genial Captain Prothero of the *Luisa Menendez* who sometimes called in just to get off the water, Matthieu had no social calls. But, for Theo and Silke Kahn, he made an effort.

He asked two Tehuelche women to assist, and the Indians prepared a slow roast of young guanaco, more tender and succulent than best lamb.

'Do you want the cheese?' the women asked, and he wondered: would the Austrians appreciate curdled milk taken from the baby guanaco's stomach, a thick rennety paste?

'You keep it,' he told the women.

He went to the store of Rahman the Turk and found dried apple rings; from these, with flour and sugar, a little mutton fat and a swan's egg, he contrived a dessert. He had some *aguardiente*, and a very old bottle of sweet vermouth passed on to him by Captain Prothero ('Not really my thing'), with crystals around the neck.

Matthieu Macanan's house and surgery stood on the bluff where the Río Sanlúcar debouched into the bay. The house resembled a fine doctor's residence much as his surgery resembled a great teaching hospital. There was one residential room only; anything that involved water took place in a lean-to outside. The roof was tin, well nailed-down against the gales, and there was just one refinement compared to the surgery next door: in his living quarters, Matthieu had fitted a ceiling of cream canvas, nailed to rough laths; this ceiling gave some small illusion that his cabin was a house, and a little insulation against the summer heat that throbbed down off the tin overhead. The gaps in the timber of the walls were sealed with mud. He had seen, years ago, the smarter settler houses on the Río Negro where the 'best' rooms were lined with elegant green-and-maroon striped papers sent from faraway Paris, beneath which the insects crept in the mud adobe. But Matthieu Macanan did not aspire to metropolitan style, and was content with boards.

His home was not joyless. There was a small iron stove obtained through Rahman. The furs on the bed were coloured in honey, caramel and crème brulée, cut and sewn into rugs of lovely pattern. Upon the wall there hung a Tehuelche weaving, and two shelves of books. On the lower shelf was a handful of medical texts, a clutch of novels by Victor Hugo, Balzac and Zola, two or three volumes of natural history, and Charles Darwin's *Le Voyage du HMS Beagle,* a set of *Les Tribus de Patagonie,* and a Swedish dictionary which someone had left on *Luisa Menendez*. On the upper shelf was a collection of

French poetry – a true collection, small but giving the marked sense of deliberate purchasing. There was an edition of Lamartine's verse (which Macanan didn't like) and another of Chénier's (which he did). There was Parny's *Chansons de Madagascar,* Boileau and Jacques Delille, Saint-Lambert's *Saisons,* and Gérard de Nerval, Baudelaire and Valéry. Lastly, there was an anthology of old ballads. These had all been purchased over the years through a dealer in Buenos Aires, and delivered by Captain Prothero who, just once, had sneaked a private look inside the pages and grimaced.

The room gave the impression that, with a tad more conviction, there could be charm. And today there was another striped Tehuelche cloth spread over the wooden tabletop.

When the knock came, Matthieu was yet again circling the room wiping everything. He was so absorbed that he had not heard the Indian woman, cooking outside, who had called a warning. The knock startled him. He stared at the door for a long second, until he remembered his manners.

Silke Kahn was wearing a Paisley shawl to keep off the chill: this, in Sanlúcar, was glamorous. Perhaps it was the only finery she possessed, the deep colours in startling contrast to her porcelain skin, grey-green eyes and creamy eyebrows. By the light of two candles and an oil lamp, the fabric's printed swirls of magenta and gold, and the indigo and vermilion stippling, all had an unctuous, savoury quality; Matthieu imagined that he could smell something on the cloth – possibly Mrs Kahn. He felt a carnivorous attraction to the shawl.

She smiled at Matthieu, but there was a fragility in her this evening, unlike the strong woman who had come ashore alone and employed the inhabitants of Bahía Sanlúcar to clear an airstrip. Unlike her quiet firmness in keeping the crowd off the Dove. Either she was nervous, or not quite well. There was a tension between the two, Matthieu thought.

Her husband began chattering before the door was fully open. Theo Kahn's eyes shone. He was leaving tomorrow, he reminded Matthieu; he was anxious to press on with their absurd scheme. Matthieu realised that he wanted rid of Theo Kahn, and that he did not trust the febrile young Austrian – and then told himself that it was tempting fate for a man who expected to be left alone with another's wife to speak of trust.

He welcomed them, seated them, apologised for his home. He suggested, looking round the room, that she might enjoy the braided leatherwork, the bright striped weaving, the buckles beaten from scraps of iron prised from driftwood – all of Tehuelche make. She followed, trying to show interest, but there was something wrong: a lassitude, a despondency. He thought again: isn't she well?

He produced the bottle of vermouth, and the one item of glassware that he owned: a badly scratched whisky rummer in heavy lead glass. He placed the glass in front of Mrs Kahn and offered her a little warm, sweet vermouth; he could not recall any other way of serving vermouth.

But she declined, and asked for water only – and Matthieu again thought: she is not right.

'Mr Kahn?' tried Matthieu, offering the glass and the bottle.

'Thank you,' said Theo, staring at the vermouth. Matthieu wondered: is it that he didn't expect warm vermouth in Bahía Sanlúcar? Or is Kahn thinking wistfully of Vienna, of fashionable cafés on the Ringstrasse, or perhaps of Berlin, of sipping his vermouth *unter den Linden?*

'Vermouth will be very nice,' said Theo politely.

So Theo got a full glass, because Matthieu felt sorry for him. And immediately Kahn began to talk at length about the Rumpler-Ettrich *Taube*, while his wife sat very still and Matthieu bustled about the cramped room.

The roast meat Matthieu served with potatoes and a sauce of onions, both of these cultivated by the Welsh on the Río Chubut to the north, and obtained courtesy of *Luisa Menendez*. There was a fragrant dish of wild celery and nettles, stewed down to a thick paste like spinach.

Silke Kahn picked at her plate, nibbling tiny mouthfuls. Matthieu wished he had not invited them; she was distressed, and he supposed that he must seem like a savage to them, semi-feral.

'It is very simple,' he apologised.

'No, believe me,' Silke sounded sincere, 'the lamb is wonderfully tender.'

'Not lamb, Mrs Kahn: young guanaco.'

She stopped eating. Matthieu thought: she's going to be sick.

'Did you kill it yourself?' said Theo.

'I'm no huntsman,' protested Matthieu. 'The Indians provide me with meat, sometimes horse, sometimes rhea which they like better, though it's not to my taste. Guanaco is the best. It is part payment for my services.'

Silke nibbled at the meat.

'How do you manage?' Theo was eating enthusiastically between gulps of vermouth. 'I mean, this meat is very fine, but how can you stay here so long on your own?'

'I'm not on my own.'

'Come, you know what I mean. You're still a young man, but you have no wife, no... comforts!'

I can hardly believe such impertinence, thought Matthieu.

'And there is no one here your intellectual equal,' his visitor charged on. 'What books do I see there? French verse! With whom do you read and discuss French verse? You even set your home apart from the rest of the little settlement. To whom do you speak? And can you do without the delights of civilisation?' Theo looked pointedly at the vermouth bottle. 'May I...?'

He refilled his own glass.

'But I enjoy Tehuelche civilisation.' Matthieu glanced at Mrs Kahn. She was frowning at the table, distracted or puzzled.

'I almost think you are serious!' Theo's laugh rang too high, too bright with vermouth.

'I am quite serious,' said Matthieu, thinking that European company had its drawbacks.

'Well! But what brought you here – 200 miles from anyone beside half a dozen hardcase gauchos and Rahman the Turk?'

'Again, you forget the Indians,' Matthieu replied, increasingly irritated.

'Oh, but you had no need to come so extremely far from *Kultur* if you wished to study some Indians.'

'I'm not here to study them.'

'Or to be nice to them, or whatever. You could have worked from a mission station – aren't there lots? I see missionaries everywhere; some are Austrians. They'd have had you, and there would be all the Indians you could wish, and better wine.'

Theo Kahn reached for the vermouth bottle. But his wife passed her hand across her brow.

'Silke?' Her husband spoke too loudly, and she winced. Theo saw this, and said, 'Silke, do you have your headache?'

Matthieu saw that her face was flushed. Her eyes had narrowed; her forehead glistened, taut and uncomfortable.

'What is wrong?' he enquired keeping his voice low, for he saw how she recoiled at Theo's loudness.

'Silke gets the most dreadful headaches.' Theo spoke for her. 'It takes over, and she can hardly speak.'

'I am poor company,' she whispered.

'My dear Mrs Kahn,' breathed Matthieu, 'do you wish to lie down?'

'I am afraid...,' she began, but did not say of what she was afraid: lying down in a stranger's home, perhaps.

Matthieu saw her glimpsing the fur bed through eyes half-closed.

'Come, please.' He was the doctor, after all; he took her elbow and steered her to the bed. She subsided, helpless.

'Theo,' she murmured, 'please... my laces...'

Her husband clumsily unlaced and freed her feet, in their grey woollen stockings; a faint hot tang passed across the room. Released, Mrs Kahn rolled away from the light.

'This happens,' said Theo, sitting on the bed. 'The pain is horrible for her. She speaks of flashing lights and an awful tightness. This is why she has not eaten your excellent meat.'

He seemed embarrassed.

'Perhaps I can help,' said Matthieu. 'Please, keep her warm.'

He indicated a cover which Theo hauled across his wife.

'One moment,' said the doctor. He took a spare oil lamp and lit it, then stepped outside and went round to his surgery.

The wind had eased for the first time in days, and he could hear the South Atlantic surf on the sandbar of the bay. Overhead, stars blazed from north to south, and out to sea. The full moon was high, its light bold and thrilling. As he returned, carrying a small bottle of thick frosted glass, Matthieu felt strange exhilaration: he had a patient. Not a gaucho with a stab wound; not a native with pneumonia – but a lady patient. He was ashamed of making such distinctions, but nonetheless...

Inside, Silke Kahn lay face away from the light, with a fur rug and her Paisley shawl over her. Theo sat by her, holding his glass of vermouth (refilled) and peering at Silke as though she constituted a great puzzle.

Theo looked round as Matthieu re-entered. He saw the frosted glass bottle.

'You have something for her?'

'This is supplied as a cough remedy,' said Matthieu, 'but it has been shown to have considerable powers of pain relief also. It has a bitter taste, so I shall mix it with a little sugar.'

He went to a dark corner of the room, opened a box, brought items to the table and began to measure out small quantities.

'Silke?' said Theo softly, 'Silke, dearest? Doctor Matthieu has medicine for you. How extraordinary, in this remote place, to find the one person to help us.'

Theo picked up the little bottle, peering at the label and the trade name: *Heroin*, from the Bayer Farbenfabriken.

'A German medicine,' he reassured her, 'made in Elberfeld.'

'I don't know this,' she murmured, sounding anxious.

'Doctor Macanan says this is effective...'

'No,' she whispered.

Matthieu did not insist. He re-stopped the glass bottle, saying that he had common aspirin next door also; he would fetch that. But Theo Kahn was following him, so that Matthieu stopped just outside, looking up at the stars as Theo emerged. There was something to be said, obviously.

'Doctor...'

Theo pulled the door shut. Yes, something to be said. Matthieu waited, smelling the warm vermouth on the Austrian's breath.

'You know, I am leaving tomorrow. Silke is not travelling with me.'

Matthieu protested: 'Can that be wise? To leave her, if she is unwell?'

'For Silke these headaches are not out of the ordinary.'

'But these are not gentle surroundings. Your wife can hardly take care of herself.'

'No, Doctor, and so I ask: will you take care of her?'

'I?'

'Who else? Would you have me entrust her to Rahman the Turk?'

'He is a good fellow. His wife is...'

'Doctor! The Turk barely speaks decent Spanish. You have no need for concern; Silke will be no trouble for you. In an hour or two she will be on her feet, laughing. I only ask that you keep an eye out, offer advice, that sort of thing.'

Matthieu stared at the moonlit sea horizon.

'Doctor?' The Austrian's tone was curious. Wheedling.

'Herr Kahn,' said Matthieu, 'I still do not know why you leave your wife here. I do not understand it at all.'

'But did I not explain? She has her work, for our mail service. She is to write to all the farmers...'

Matthieu's stare stopped him. Kahn changed tack.

'Also, you know something?' His voice altered: it became oleaginous. 'You know, a husband does not always want his wife at his side. Not in the city. What do you say, Doctor? You and I, we're not old...'

What was Kahn hinting at: a world of Viennese mistresses in gaming clubs? A circle of artists in Paris and Rome with their 'models'? Did he believe that Matthieu had frequented society balls in Punta Arenas? Society for Dr Macanan had been shepherds creeping up the wooden stair with dripping chancres on their penises.

'I can't imagine,' said Matthieu coldly, 'what you might be implying.'

Which was quite untrue.

Kahn stood beside Matthieu, both of them gazing ahead as though the sea would speak the awkward bits for them.

'My wife Silke is the dearest possible... and so competent, and devoted also. But in special ways that I think a gentleman will understand, she is not... Well, taste is such a personal matter. I find in myself a certain – what to call it – disinclination. Those very pale eyes, you know.'

But Matthieu did not know, and would not hear any more. He went to his clinic to fetch ordinary painkillers.

And came back to find Theo Kahn gone.

For a moment, Matthieu supposed Kahn must have stepped behind the house to urinate. But as minutes passed, Matthieu grew puzzled, and then angry. Mrs Kahn lay on his bed, smothered in caramel furs, motionless. Matthieu waited. Twice, he opened the door to look out. He walked round his tiny house and clinic, its fenced corral and sheds, but he found no one. He stood some minutes on the river bluff, peering in the direction of the moonlit settlement a few hundred yards away, seeing nothing but one or two lamps glimmering. He heard only the surf that hissed on the sand bar.

What could he do: go after Kahn and drag him back? To what purpose, if the wife was too incapacitated to move? Should he insist that the husband carry her away to the mercy of Rahman the Turk, or load her onto *Luisa Menendez* like a bale of wool, and ship her off to lodgings in Buenos Aires, to lie helpless on a bed while Kahn went whoring? Was that what Matthieu should insist on?

Perplexed and cross, he remained in the moonlight looking over the river. He saw a black shape cross the gleaming water: an owl launching from its sand hole in the opposite bluff. The owl seemed far more decisive than he felt.

At last, he went back indoors. Silke Kahn had not moved, and from her slow breathing, Matthieu did not imagine that she would be stirring very soon. In the light of the oil lamp, he could in fact hardly see her; only a slight tousle of white-gold hair showed like pale surf on the beach.

There was no other bed. Matthieu sat at his table, pushing the abandoned meal aside, the apple pudding ignored. Weary, he put his elbows on the table and placed fingertips in the bony inner corners of his eyes. The notion of bed teased and tormented him. He folded his arms on the table and rested his forehead, but was comfortable for no more than half a minute. At last, he stood, took a rug across his arm, and turned the lamp over the table as low as possible. He walked once more round to his clinic, to lie on the unpadded boards of the examination couch, hearing the wind return to lift the iron roof that shifted and creaked with a faint scratch of grit.

*

'Theo has gone,' said Mrs Kahn in the morning.

She was sitting on the edge of the bed – his bed – and speaking with a quiet, clear conviction. Matthieu wished to exclaim: *Yes, the boat called, and your fine husband is fled from Bahía Sanlúcar to the stews of Buenos Aires and Montevideo.* But she knew this.

'Shall I take you home?' he asked.

'Home?' That meant: the lean-to storeroom of Rahman the Turk. 'Oh, thank you, yes.'

'Do you have anything there to eat? You must eat something.'

'Thank you, but no.'

'I must insist,' said Matthieu. 'You took almost nothing last night.'

'I am very well, believe me.'

'At least, let me make coffee. For both of us.'

She studied him – then nodded.

'For both of us, Doctor.'

'Please do not call me doctor.'

'Then, what?' She peered at him. 'Am I to call you Monsieur Macanan? I hardly like that. Your first name – was it Matteus?'

He blushed with dismay: he hadn't meant any of this. He did not know what he had meant.

'It is Matthieu.'

'In that case,' she said, watching him closely, 'I shall be pleased to call you Matthieu.'

'Yes...' he breathed.

'Matthieu,' she repeated, tasting it.

He began to brew the coffee. She watched him a moment, then turned her attention to the two shelves of books, tugging down one volume of poems after another and studying them in surprise.

'My goodness,' she murmured. She was engrossed in Lamartine.

'They are at your disposal,' he said. He had never loaned his books.

He put out bread made by Aisha, wife of Rahman – rough and stale, but it could be dipped in coffee, or salted. They took breakfast together. She was as lively now as she had been subdued the night before. Matthieu noticed that, in Silke, pallor indicated better health, whereas rising colour was the mark of her headache.

She spoke of her childhood (in Carlsfelden by Linz, the Burgermeister's daughter), her school (the inevitable convent), her longing for training as a musician, perhaps a violinist. But her father had vetoed this, saying that the daughter of a Burgermeister did not perform in public like a chimpanzee. He had allowed her to take basic instruction in first aid so as to be decorative at the local hospital. So – said Silke gaily – she had eloped. She'd begun a systematic flirtation with the Technical Assistant to the Clerk of Works in Carlsfelden, bewitching him. When her father was in Salzburg on business, she'd twisted her paramour's arm so hard that he'd carried her off to Linz, then to the Argentine. They'd been living, she said, on Theo's technical wits.

Matthieu gazed at her: the pale grey-green irises, the almost white eyebrows, the hair like cobwebs tied back by an orderly spider.

'An interesting marriage,' he said.

'Interesting?' She suspected irony. Her eyes were now wide open, whereas in the evening they'd seemed pinched. They were, he thought, remarkably large, clear and bright, inviting him straight in.

'Unusual,' offered Matthieu gently.

'It was unusual,' she agreed. Her voice was a little distant – and she had spoken in the past. 'Theo has never been unkind to me. He is very proud, you know. And very ambitious for his mail service.'

She considered that ambition and that mail service. She said:

'I've told you my terrible history. Now you must tell me yours.'

'I don't have one.'

'You have a story.' She was not going to let go.

'Well – my father was a pharmacist.'

'And how many children did your mother have?'

'Myself only,' replied Matthieu. 'She was sickly.'

'But you studied.'

'At Montpelier.'

'Then your father was more proud of you than mine of me.'

Matthieu gave a deflecting smile. 'I should like to give you something.'

It was on a shelf above the bed: a brooch of silver. The Tehuelche

Indians, he said, obtained silver dollars from traders, and could work the metal marvellously. This brooch was in the shape of a star, the points incised with feathering. Silke touched the tips with the pad of her little finger.

'It's sharp.'

She continued to finger it, as though working out what the gift meant; Matthieu wondered if he should have done this. She made a decision and pinned the brooch to her breast – but let her shawl fall over it, partly.

He walked with her along the bluff towards the settlement. A pall of thin cloud stretched over them like pale grey felt. The wind pricked them: a warning of rain. The dozen or so wooden buildings stood in a line, facing across the bay and the sand spit that was the only protection from the entire weight of the South Atlantic. They paused a moment and regarded the sea.

'If you sailed,' Matthieu said, 'directly east at this latitude, you would not touch the extreme tip of South Africa, not even Australia, and would scarcely clip the uttermost point of New Zealand, before completing the earth's circle and smacking into the Chilean Andes at our backs.'

She gave a little breath of a laugh, and took his arm.

Behind the settlement, they could see (though neither mentioned) the pen of thorns in which the Dove waited for Theo Kahn. They came to the first buildings: the grand, locked shed of Home & Imperial Wool – built for an influx of sheep and an outpouring of fleeces, neither of which had yet occurred – and the small house of Home & Imperial's agent, who came rarely and went soon but kept a half-caste 'housekeeper'. Then there was the home built for Scottish missionaries who had stayed two years until the wife died of pneumonia and the husband fled; the house was now used as a bothy for shepherds or gauchos come in for supplies. There was the shack of Jimenez the horse dealer, with his stables and corral behind; there was the police post, established by the Argentines in that same expectation of the wool trade, but now manned only a few days a month; and in the middle of these, the *boliche,* the general-store-cum-bar of Rahman and Aisha, also waiting to make their fortune.

To which Matthieu escorted Silke Kahn, wrapped in her paisley print shawl and a short fur cape, which he had insisted upon against the wind.

They passed the open front door; inside, Rahman was hammering furiously at something, while Aisha shouted at her daughter. They turned the end of the clapboard building, whose timbers were scoured out by sun and gritty winds like an old man's hands with the flesh shrunk away. Here was the door of the storeroom Silke occupied — the heart of her husband's airmail empire.

There was no light. She laid the cape on a small table, then she opened the twisted shutter, so that salty brightness washed in. Matthieu looked round. There was a candle standing in congealed wax on the table; there were two stools, two tea chests by the window and, on the earthen floor in the corner, a leather portmanteau. In the dimness at the back, he saw a bunk bed, crude and massive, with horsehair mattresses. The room was cold; it smelled of mildew.

Slowly, Silke Kahn unwound the paisley wrap from her shoulders, as though she wished to be prevented.

Matthieu said: 'You cannot possibly stay here.'

'It suffices,' she returned dully.

'It does not. You do not even have a fire.'

'But there was nowhere else. Where else is there? I would have rented somewhere better...'

There was an edge in her voice. She had done what her husband had commanded: she had prepared the way for Theo and the Dove.

'There is nowhere else,' she murmured again, looking out of the window at the Atlantic, the sea light on her pale eyebrows.

So Matthieu heard himself say:

'You shall stay with me. No, it is certain: I can't leave you here. You shall have the other room of my house. There is a fireplace, at least. And Rahman has beds to sell, with leather straps.'

She objected: 'But that is your surgery.'

'No matter. Mostly I go out to my patients. Or they can sit at my dining table well enough. I shall make it over to you.'

'Oh... Only until something better can be arranged.'

'Something better, of course.'

'When Theo returns.' She was looking at him quizzically.

He could hardly believe what he had just done. For an instant, he thought of the journey he had made to reach this place, to attain this refuge, how he had nearly died seeking seclusion.

'We may be obliged to build,' Silke said. 'Perhaps near to you.'

'Near to me?' he replied, startled. She heard this.

'Oh, but our home should be close to the Dove, of course.'

'I expect so,' urged Matthieu. 'In the meantime we shall inspect the aircraft each day. We can find a boy to watch it. I must speak to Rahman, and get the room prepared for you.'

So it happened, before he was scarcely aware of it: Matthieu Macanan, who had lived alone for a decade, took in a lady lodger. As he hurried home, he saw with anxiety and resentment that his privacy had been jemmied open. He was doing exactly what Theo Kahn had intended.

But above these grumbling notes rang a different sound: Matthieu's heart was singing.

Five

HOUSEHOLDS

They circled, they minced around each other.

The facilities of the house were basic.

Matthieu found this mortifying. When she first arrived, Silke Kahn was delighted with everything, but Matthieu was palpably anxious to get it right. So she humoured him, and smiled to herself at his fastidiousness.

On the table in his erstwhile surgery, she found a little cluster of pretty stones: pink and green, some almost maroon but shot with black, and some sparkling quartz.

Matthieu reddened.

'I thought, there was nothing appealing in here. These came from the riverbank.'

'You fetched them for me?'

'Yes,' he blurted out, 'a penguin does the same, a Magellanic penguin, when proposing a dwelling to a lady penguin...'

He stopped, covered in blushes. She smiled, having no idea what he was speaking about.

Of a morning, they tacitly agreed that he had first use of the lean-to wash room. Afterwards, he would go to the front of the building and knock on the door.

'I am done.'

He would pace slowly upstream; when he was suitably distant, the young woman would emerge from the front door with her towel over her arm, and slip round to the rear of the house where the wash-room stood. He took care not to look behind him at this moment, but his other senses always detected her emerging. He would walk perhaps half a mile along the stony bluff, and he established the habit of reaching a certain large piece of creamy quartz by the path, a rock shaped, he thought, like a crouching hare. Here, he would turn back; the quartz hare measured Silke Kahn's time in the wash house.

Of the other 'facilities', not a word was said. Whenever he or she walked briskly out to that small cabin perched over a laboriously dug pit forty yards from the back door, the other would always be fixedly considering the sea.

Mid-morning, Matthieu went out. Silke, left alone, wrote letters to farmers and to traders, to tell them of the imminent airmail service. She had with her a supply of good writing paper and creamy envelopes, such as the merchant classes of Buenos Aires and Montevideo use to correspond with cousins in Mar del Plata and Bahía Blanca. What – wondered Matthieu – would a sheep rancher on a Patagonian *estancia* make of such a document? What would Rahman the Turk? These letters began to stack up on the bookshelf in Matthieu's room, sealed and ready for despatch. The letters were all the same, the formal address always the same: *Muy señor mío*. Only the envelopes were unmarked. Silke said:

'If I meet a gaucho going out to any of the *estancia*s, I can address one of these and hand it over in an instant.'

Matthieu did not like to tell her that the nearest *estancia*s were far inland, by the lakes at the foot of the cordillera; that, although the authorities had parcelled out the territory, and although some blocks on the map were sold, there was as yet no one who had made a profit out of the hinterland of Bahía Sanlúcar. The crop here was thistles and *calafate* berries; the harvest was pebbles of obsidian and porphyry. Farmers had come and gone; one or two had brought sheep. But the sheep usually died and so did the ambitions.

He watched the little stack of letters build up, for writing gave some purpose to Silke's day. He promised that, whenever he heard of a rider passing through Bahía Sanlúcar, he would ensure that a letter went that way. There were few riders, though from time to time Matthieu would ostentatiously take a letter from the pile in kindly pretence (and discreetly destroy it). When the stack threatened to topple, Silke stopped writing, and began to read her way through the volumes of French verse instead, beginning with Saint-Lambert's *Saisons*. There was no word from her husband who, Matthieu believed, was too busy whoring.

One morning, Matthieu had a suggestion for her.

She had washed some clothes, lugging a wooden tub down a steep path to the river. She must hang them out somewhere; he saw her with a loop of cord in her hand, studying his own clothes line that stretched from the building to a corner of the corral. Two of his thick cotton blouses swung gently. Although there was plenty of space on the cord, she seemed reluctant to use it. He was about to call to her – *Please, make free!* – when he considered the intimate garments that might be involved. She would not want those hung out like flags.

Then he thought: she has hardly once left the vicinity of this house.

'Mrs Kahn?'

She looked round, the loop of cord dangling by her flank.

'I think,' she said, 'that after some days of my addressing you as Matthieu, you might now call me Silke.'

He hesitated – then continued:

'I'm going to the Indian camp today. Would you join me? I'll be visiting the old *cacique*, Coromín, and it might be of interest, if you don't think it all too rustic. Do you ride? I'm no horseman, but that's how we get about here, for we don't have the wings of doves. Mrs Kahn...'

'Silke.'

'You can't be confined to the company of no one but myself, and some dusty old poets.'

She considered this.

'My husband will be back soon.'

'I'm sure. But there'll be no steamer for another week, you know.'

'Another week?'

'Pretty much. *Luisa Menendez* stops on her way to Punta Arenas, and on her return, but any number of delays may occur. Captain Prothero tells me the currents in the Strait are among the world's fiercest.'

'Ah. Then at least another seven days.'

She was studying him so directly.

'Let's go to your Indians,' she said.

He chose for her, from his mules and ponies, a mare they called a *rosada* for the creamy pink in her colouring, while his own mule was cinnamon. He had only one leather saddle, but there was an Indian thing also, a frame of wood over which skins could be laid, and this she could ride side-saddle. He told Lipi his boy to prepare the animals, and he fussed about giving orders which were blithely ignored. Matthieu was a nuisance to Lipi.

'Shan't you be cold?' he asked Silke, looking at her light woollen jacket. The day was sunny, but the breeze never stopped. 'I'll give you a fur.'

She accepted the light fur cape that he gave her. He looked at the mule and at the driftwood serving as a mounting block; he wondered how she would get up, and saw that she was thinking the same thing.

'If you'll allow me, Mrs Kahn.'

'I will allow you,' she said, 'only if you agree to call me Silke.'

He gave a slight bow.

He placed one foot of his own on the mounting block, then took her by the waist and lifted her. The movement was not so very elegant. He felt the lower margin of her ribcage under her jacket, and thought his thumbs must have bruised her. But she smiled down, pulled the cape around her and took the rein, waiting.

For a moment he did nothing but gaze back up at her; she allowed herself to be admired. He saw how the colourings flowed into one another: the *rosada* of the pony, the cape's honeyed fur turning at its tips to gold, and the young woman's hair so blonde as to be almost white, tied back to pour down her neck. There was, in her look, in her pale delicacy, in her light frame, little to remind him of a young Fuegian woman whose image was scorched into his memory – except for a particular unperturbed dignity; a disdain for embarrassment; a peaceable and amused tolerance of everything. Yes, he had encountered this manner before.

The memory startled him. He shook it off to concentrate on the present.

Matthieu mounted stiffly his cinnamon-coloured mule, with a

renewed sense that he was more awkward in the saddle than anyone in Patagonia. He could still feel Silke's ribs on his thumbs. The boy Lipi took up the lead rein, and pulled Matthieu's mule after his own. Silke did smile a little, when she saw the doctor led along the riverbank like a child on a pony.

They rode slowly: being led on a string, Matthieu of necessity rode slowly. They went along the banks of the Río Sanlúcar travelling westward, inland; if they had continued 200 miles further, they'd have been climbing the Andes; in 250, they'd have reached the Chilean border, high in the cordillera. But they rode just a dozen miles, and gradually the summer landscape softened. On the plain, heading away from the salt, there were the beginnings of the tawny, tussocky grass that supported the Indians' horses and the herds of nervous guanaco, the pumas that preyed upon the guanaco and the humans that preyed upon them all. The river below them was clear now, the level down in the dry months; below the bluff along which they rode, there was a margin of grass that was green and fresh.

To north and south were phosphorus plains and basalt flats. They saw, far off, a shallow salt lake that was almost dry, encircled by a quarter-mile band of glistening, sticky salt crystals. But the river cutting and its marshy water margins showed flowers: cowslips and tiny orchids, yellow, white, pink and purple among the haze of flowering grasses. As they rode, a rolling fuss of water birds rose before them and settled behind: snipe and swans, ducks and geese. Little swallows skittered in gusts, showing white chests and dark blue wings, settling in the *calafate* bushes with their electrical chattering, nibbling at the indigo berries.

'Such colours, I'd no idea,' she called in delight. 'This is quite lovely.'

He smiled and felt happy; she had that quality. As he relaxed, the mules and pony sensed the change, and picked up their feet. They jogged along in bright sunshine, following the river across a shallow grassy basin where the lightest of breezes dropped to nothing, to stillness. The birdsong intensified; there were larks even.

She said, 'I've not felt so pleased since I came to Patagonia.'

Her hair swung at the back of her neck as the animals ambled across the pasture; they must be hauled on the bit, or they would stop and gorge.

He pointed ahead: thin plumes of smoke, vertical in the still air. Another ten minutes, and they came among horses, forty or fifty, filling themselves with new grass and wild strawberry plants.

Then the tents, tawny or white. There were a dozen or more, complex structures of skins draped over ridge poles, tall in the centre where a person might stand upright, and broad like the carapace of an enormous woodlouse, except that they carried fur to the outside, to break the force of driving rain. Around the tents were stacks of firewood, and between them the ragamuffins scampered and the women busied. A handful of old dogs slept in dust hollows, snapped at flies and chewed at their own hindquarters. But there were no men.

Matthieu, Silke Kahn and Lipi halted the pony and mules at the edge of the settlement.

'Makan!' shouted the children in greeting, 'Makan, they are hunting!' skipping about them, staring at the gleaming white woman that Matthieu had brought.

'Oh, hunting?' answered Matthieu with regret. He turned to Silke. 'I'm afraid I've chosen our day poorly. Most of the men are out chasing guanaco and rheas.'

'Then let's speak with women and children,' replied Silke so cheerfully that he felt stupid. And before he could reply, she had jumped down and was wandering through the tents with dogs prancing and urchins hanging on either hand, hauling her along to see the armadillo they had tied to a stake and were tormenting. She was almost skipping; the children seemed to catch her pleasure, and frolicked about her. An older girl joined them, with tresses of beaded hair to which Silke pointed delightedly when the girl swung them about. Silke waved to Matthieu, calling:

'I'll be back!'

He watched her go, glimpsing at the far end of the tents the captive armadillo. He disliked seeing creatures tied to stakes for others' pleasure; he'd seen it before. He had also seen before the horse tied to a post behind the tent, a pinto with a battered Spanish saddle.

'Sor Juana?' he called.

But when the woman appeared, she did not give him her usual beam.

'Oh, Makan,' she said, sounding embarrassed. The woman stayed in the tent doorway, fingers playing with the edge of the hide flap.

'Juana,' nodded Matthieu, not without formality, 'I came to see if Coromín's knee was healing.'

Still the woman did not step aside.

'Coromín isn't hunting, surely?' enquired Matthieu, 'with that leg? He's not riding?'

An older, gruffer voice called, with a hint of resignation:

'Makan, I am here.'

So Juana let him enter, and there, seated on rolled furs and with a shaft of dusty sunlight thrust down between them like a sword of truce, were two men. One of these was not an Indian.

'Ah,' nodded Matthieu, 'Señor Margall. I'd no idea that you'd business with Coromín.'

The other regarded him coldly. He was a man with a tight-clipped beard and watery eyes.

'I've a right to business here, have I not?'

'Quite so. And I wonder what that business might be?'

'Señor Doctor, with respect, it is none of yours. I was paying my compliments to the *cacique* here.'

'I am sure.'

'And now I am leaving.'

With that, Margall – a tall, bony figure who had to stoop even in the centre of the tent – took his leave.

'What was Margall wanting?' asked Matthieu, hardly waiting till the other was out of earshot. The *cacique* sighed.

'Makan, sit with me. My knee is hurting today...'

'What was Margall doing here?'

'It's so sore...'

Often the Indians had said to Matthieu: *Play straight with us, we don't like dissembling.* This dissembling in Coromín made Matthieu angry.

'I know Margall's business,' he said, answering his own question. 'A land agent's business is to sell your land from under you. But usually he doesn't bother to ask the Tehuelche. So why did he come when there's a hunt?'

'Makan,' said the old voice, 'I hide nothing from you.'

'Not from me, but perhaps someone sent Margall word that the men would be absent...'

'Sit! Must I say it again? You are in my home.'

Matthieu blushed: he was misbehaving. He peered at Coromín, who reclined with one knee lifted over a wooden saddle and gazed back at Matthieu with an unnatural fixity. In the shadows, the woman Juana sat holding on her lap a terrier that she petted in a distracted, ungentle way while she stared at Matthieu.

'Did Margall offer you money?' said Matthieu.

'Oh!'

The *cacique* looked aside, and Matthieu knew that he was right.

'He's offered you money to move the tents, hasn't he? It must be that. This is the only decent ground near Sanlúcar. I hear there's an American woman, very rich, a Señora Hendry Morgan...'

'I know nothing of Morgan.'

'No, you don't need to. You just need to take Margall's cash and move the camp. Then there'll be no dispute when the government sells...'

'Makan, you understand a great deal, but not everything.'

The eyes, narrow slits in the *cacique*'s tired face, studied Matthieu.

Coromín said: 'Are you perhaps angry with me?'

'I've no cause to be.'

'But are you?'

Matthieu Macanan looked at the tent floor, pursing his lips.

'You should know,' said the *cacique*, 'that I have sent letters to a lawyer in Buenos Aires. He will present our land claim to the government.'

'Then you will need,' observed Matthieu, 'every *centavo* that Margall puts in your pocket.'

'It does not go in my pocket,' said the *cacique*.

And Matthieu saw weariness, defiance and dignity tussling together in the old man. He was about to apologise, when there was a stir behind him. She pushed in, thrilled with everything.

'Matthieu? Matthieu, they have quite the prettiest...' She saw the old *cacique*. She did not hesitate, nor fall about apologising; she knelt on the mats, and the shaft of sunlight entered her grey-green eyes and her white gold hair, which shone from within. She held out her hand to the *cacique*.

'*Guten Tag*,' she beamed. 'I am Silke Kahn. I am from Austria.'

Coromín blinked at her in astonishment, struggling to sit upright.

'Juana? Juana!'

'Yes, what now...'

'Furs, look. Bring those...'

'But they're not so...'

'At once!'

'Never mind me,' protested Silke.

'Juana, I tell you!'

'I have better ones,' objected Coromín's wife, 'if you'd let me...'

It's a long time, thought Matthieu, amused, since any Tehuelche got into such a fuss over me. From the moment the *cacique* had set eyes on Silke's gleaming hair he had been galvanised, twitching like a frog's leg – though a twitch was all the ruined knee could manage.

'And you are with Makan?' he beamed at her. 'Oh, Makan, it is unfair. I could have found you a dozen lovely Tehuelche girls with hair as black as pitch, but this is sunlight.'

'Please,' Matthieu blushed. 'Mrs Kahn is visiting...'

Silke laughed.

'I am here,' she interrupted, 'because I choose to be.'

'Well, I don't understand,' said Coromín, 'but I'm pleased. Young lady, our Makan works hard for us. He cures all our ills. See how well he's made my knee.'

Before the *cacique* could begin leaping about for the entertainment of Silke, a child scampered into the tent.

'The horses! The horses!'

When the *cacique* rose, it was Silke who got to him first, offering her arm. Out they went, Coromín beaming with pleasure.

There were thirty horses – forty, perhaps, in the dust and confusion – streaming into the camp. Over almost every wooden saddle there hung the carcass of a rhea or guanaco, the legs stiffly jutting. Over each carcass was slung the leather-thonged *bolas* that had brought the quarry down. The horses were exhausted from a hard chase; they steamed and stank, and hung their heads or shook them. But the riders were roaring their triumph, mocking one who had tangled himself in his own *bolas*, applauding another who had taken two animals with one cast and was boasting his head off, while those riders who had run out of things to say just shouted generally.

Out came the women, out came the young girls, the ragamuffins and the crones, yelling applause, yelling questions. The hunting dogs trotted among the tents, sore pawed and proud, while the old, sleepy hounds opened one eye, then closed it.

Fires! bawled the young men. *Get the fires blazing!*

'Miss Silke,' purred *cacique* Coromín, clutching at her elbow with his bony claws, 'what a good day it has been for our boys. Stay with us for the feast, no? There will be dancing.'

Matthieu began to whisper that they should be leaving, that the Indians would get drunk, that it was a bad idea. But Silke was full of pleasure and questions.

'Matthieu, shall we stay? To see dancing? Oh, we must!'

He realised that he was jealous!

'We can stay, if you wish it. We must ride home at night, but the moon is full.'

She hardly heard him. She went to the ponies to wonder at the lovely little dead guanacos, playing with their soft ears while praising with her ringing laughter all the young men who had slaughtered them.

Matthieu wanted to run after and associate himself with her.

'A fine young lady, Makan.'

Coromín, propped on his crutch, studied Matthieu.

'Yes,' Matthieu replied, brusque. 'She will not be here long. She has a husband and they are wanting to set up a business at Bahía Sanlúcar, but nothing may come of it.'

They watched Silke move gaily among the horsemen, several of whom remained in the saddle preening.

'That's a shame,' remarked the *cacique*.

'Why so?'

'Because I could invest Margall's money, on my people's behalf.'

The fires had been revived, stacked with wood. The afternoon lethargy of the camp had vanished; everyone chattered and fetched, gutted, skinned and sliced. Matthieu noticed two men emerge from a tent carrying a small wooden cask at which they tapped and tugged excitedly: *aguardiente*, from the store of Rahman the Turk. Matthieu felt a dread: he should have obeyed his conviction; he should have acted; he should have taken Silke away sooner.

Coromín said, 'I will take in all their knives and guns before they start on that cask.'

He lurched away on his crutch, shouting to the men with the cask, shouting to everyone, demanding attention. Matthieu saw the glances, the resentment – until, with shrugs, the men began delivering pistols, an antique blunderbuss and several muskets, with a nasty cascade of knives, all to Sor Juana who carried them into the dark of the *cacique*'s tent.

'You see,' said Coromín, 'how sensible we are.'

'Let us walk by the river,' said Matthieu to Silke.

They went with a cloud of small children.

'The riverbank is so hard and stony at the sea.' Silke gazed at the rich, soft ground either side of the Sanlúcar. 'But look here, those pretty strawberry plants!'

'In winter, the water is cold as death,' said Matthieu. 'The Indians hunt rheas by driving them into the river. Their legs grow so stiff with cold that, when they reach shore, they cannot run.'

She shrugged: 'Everyone has to eat.'

'In the winter here, many starve.'

The children were pointing into the clear water, shouting *Fish! Fish!* and hurling stones. Stubby perch flitted in the shallows.

'What a way to catch them!' laughed Silke.

'They don't eat them,' he replied. 'They'd think that very disgusting.'

'You know everything,' she murmured, 'and I nothing.'

Matthieu was sorry.

They walked on, under plumes and spray from the children pummelling the water with rocks.

She said: 'When we arrived, there was someone else in the *cacique*'s tent. I saw him ride away. There was a bad feeling.'

'His name is Margall.'

'Why did Señor Margall make everyone uneasy?'

'I wish he did. I wish the Indians entirely mistrusted him. Margall is a land agent. The Indians are being squeezed off; they have nowhere to go. Coromín knows it. He's watching the last days of his tribe. They number half what they were when I first came.'

She looked back at the camp, at the bustle and shouting and smoke of roasting, and he could see admiration in her eyes.

'But why?' she protested. 'How are they starving? It doesn't seem so. The young men and girls are vigorous.'

'They get diseases I can't prevent, pneumonias and fluxes. People like Margall give them drink, and they fight. They die stupidly.'

'Oh.' She stooped to pick an agate from the water margin. 'But look...'

She was gazing at a pair of enormous carmine dragonflies hovering by a clump of rushes.

'And look at those!' She had spotted berries both crimson and ivory-white. 'What are those? Can't they be eaten?'

She seemed to have grasped the hopelessness, and was trying to fend it off with the delights of nature.

He said: 'They're tea-berries and yes, they can, but those look shrivelled, so they've been left.'

Glancing down, he noticed how the ground under her feet was mossy, and how it shone with wet where she walked. Silke looked again towards the camp, and the excited preparations.

'Can one believe that it is ending for them? I cannot!'

Her face was wide open. Strands of her silken hair lifted hopefully. Even her dismay had a freshness. Matthieu wanted to speak – but when she turned to him, he saw something he did not understand: the look of hope was directed at him. It made him uncomfortable.

Dusk was coming on. There were shouts from the encampment.

'They're ready.'

They were roasting on the spit. The children had been sent to gather wild spinach for stewing with swan's eggs and rhea fat.

'Makan, Makan!' they called, but it was Silke they led by the hand, leaving Matthieu to follow obediently. Coromín waited on a roll of rugs by his fire, patting at a place for Silke while shouting instructions at two youths turning the spit. The young men began hacking at the roast – but again they were berated by Coromín: what were they thinking of? A fine lady visitor could not be presented with lumps of dripping meat. So there was a great scrambling for wooden bowls, wiped out with rags. A man gave orders to his little girl who scurried into a tent, returning with something which she held out to Silke: an apple, rather shrivelled and mottled.

'Oh!' cried Silke, and the girl was struck shy and fled to her mother. 'Matthieu, look, it's an apple. Where on earth…?'

'The old Spanish settlement on the Chubut,' he replied. 'The place is deserted, but the orchards are still there, completely untended of course.'

He felt piqued; he had managed to offer her only dried apple rings.

'The savour is intense,' she murmured.

Now there was shouting: the young men had begun to drink. They were tipping *aguardiente* from the cask into wooden cups, spilling it and arguing. Matthieu saw Coromín frown and bite his lip.

'Who will dance?' Coromín cried out suddenly. 'Bring the music. Bring it at once!'

But the Indians nearby glowered: *Who are you to hurry us, old man?* Matthieu felt pangs of pity.

There was a drum, improvised from a bowl with a skin stretched over it. There was a flute of bone, and a little horsehair bow placed against the lips of a thin-faced man, who plucked out of it a curious buzz. The women sat on capes facing Coromín across the fire; the crones began to sing nasally, the younger wives attempting to follow. Four men could be glimpsed in the shadows by Coromín's tent, dressing themselves, jabbing rhea plumes into each other's headbands.

To Matthieu's relief, Silke seemed to be watching these, and not the boys and their cask.

'Come on, come on!' Coromín was urging. Again, the glances: they disliked being hurried; they had all night to drink and dance. But the *cacique* was fretting, patting at Silke's arm, wanting to get the entertainment started.

The circle of women opened. Through the gap came men with fur capes held up around their faces, showing only eyes and the rhea plumes waving above their black hair. They processed round the fire, shuffling or stamping as the drumming and thin fluting continued; with twanging from the horsehair bow, the tempo increased. The four dancing men threw aside their capes, revealing straps of small bells slung from one shoulder to the opposite hip – *jing, jing!* They hopped and bobbed, dipping their plumed heads left and right as though their necks were broken. They were already awash with *aguardiente*.

Matthieu glanced at Silke; her dish of nibbled meat and spinach put aside, she was observing intently. Behind her, Lipi sneered at the savages. The first dancing men moved out of the circle; others came, with more feathers, more bells.

The moon was rising, the sky clear and the air chill. Matthieu felt it in his clothing, felt his back cold, even while his front towards the fire was toasting. He saw Silke's pale skin gleam, and he saw Coromín murmur to a youth who ducked into the *cacique*'s tent to re-emerge with yet another fur cape which he draped around Silke, who smiled her thanks. The drum pounded on and on. Matthieu thought: she must be weary of this, surely. Unvarying, tuneless.

But now it varied. In the gloom beyond the fire, someone laughed, mocking, sharp above the drum and the old women's drone. A laugh loud with alcohol. There was a terse answer. Matthieu saw faces turn and peer out into the darkness; men moved to intervene. There was a shock in the ring; figures lurched forward, staggering because someone had blundered into their backs. Others looked round to protest. Coromín lifted his chin, straining to see, but there were flames and a crowd between him and the argument. The old women continued chanting doggedly, but the younger wives' faces were anxious.

There were still three men dancing, lurching, stamping and bobbing their plumed heads around the fire circle while the straps of bells chinged and jingled on their chests. These men showed no interest in the dispute, until there came an enraged shout: this electrified one dancer who ran from the circle. There were cries and shrieks: a man had fallen, another was upon him, others clawed at both. The dogs bayed furiously – and only now did the old women stop their song.

Silke looked to Matthieu. He grabbed at Lipi who was grinning and shuffling his feet as though impatient to see blood flow.

'Bring the mules,' Matthieu snapped. 'Bring them behind the *cacique*'s tent.'

The boy was reluctant, his eyes heavy and rolling; perhaps someone had given him *aguardiente* also.

'Get on with it!' cried Matthieu. Silke rose to her feet and Sor Juana took her by the hand, tugging her towards the tent even as Coromín teetered past the fire towards the trouble, and Lipi trotted in the direction of the hobbled mules.

Matthieu caught the glitter of the moonlit river streaming through the lush meadow, flowing to the distant, peaceable settlement at Sanlúcar and the sea. Then he noticed that the shouts had changed from the coarse screech of a fight to a beseeching. They called his name:

'Makan! Makan!'

There was a knot of figures between the tents, and a dark bulk which they lifted like a roll of carpet and carried to the light of the fire, shouting for help, for water, for rugs, for justice. They lowered their burden: a young man with one side of his neck slashed open, and blood spouting onto the dirt.

'Makan! Makan!' they shrieked again.

The young man gazed with astonishment at the faces gathered over him, saw Matthieu Macanan, and opened his mouth to speak. But his throat filled with blood which bubbled and sprayed the onlookers. Everyone cried out, turned aside and wiped at their faces. When they looked again, the youth was dead.

*

The moon was above them, the river a highway of pewter.

'Do you know his name?' she asked quietly. She brought her mount alongside his, behind Lipi.

Matthieu knew: the dead boy was Coromín's nephew.

'Alonso,' said Matthieu. 'His name was Alonso.'

He was frowning into the moonlight. He said:

'I must go back in the morning.'

'Go back? Why? The poor boy was dead.'

'There'll be others. There'll be more trouble tonight.'

A few moments of silence, riding alongside the metal river.

'Do you go there every day?'

'I go whenever they need me – but there's often little that I can do.'

'You seem to care for the Indians,' observed Silke, 'more than for your own sort at the settlement.'

'My sort? Gauchos and feather traders? The Turks?'

On they went, beside the river that bubbled over pebbles. In this stillness, without the wind knocking their ears, they could hear their own breathing.

They were nearing the settlement; the buildings appeared in the moonlight like boulders on the bluff. Even the thorn-hedged corral – in which the Dove slept – even this looked natural. Beyond, the sea lay in an oily stillness, as though playing dead.

The next moment, her pony stumbled. It went down on its front knees. Silke, side-saddle, was thrown past the pony's shoulder, staggered clear and tottered two steps before sprawling. The pony was already gathering itself up, even as Lipi stopped the other animals and Matthieu jumped down.

'My God, are you hurt? Are you hurt at all?

'Not in the least.'

Silke was back on her feet, brushing the palms of her hands on her skirt, smiling a cheerfully shocked smile.

'Really,' she protested, 'I'm not hurt at all, though the poor pony's knees...'

'But your hands – I think they're cut. Why in God's name did we ride home in the dark!'

'It is not dark,' she replied, quite calm. 'There is a moon, and we delayed because I wished it.'

She peered at her stinging palms that had taken the brunt.

'I do think, though...'

'Oh, heavens, they're cut.'

He seized her hands and peered down at them, turning them this way and that to catch the moonlight: there were dark streaks across the palms, beginning to run. He flicked the dust away with his forefinger, as though he would spit on her hands to clean them.

She said, 'Do you have a handkerchief?'

'Of course!' he blurted without thinking – and began searching for something he had not carried in a decade.

'Señor...' said Lipi, holding out some rag. Matthieu took it, flapped it out vigorously, stared at it a moment but was none the wiser, and bound it around Silke's left hand.

'I think,' she said, 'that I should walk this last bit. We are so near.'

They were by the quartz hare, half a mile from home.

So Lipi led the animals away towards Matthieu's house, and would light the fire against their arrival. Silke took Matthieu's arm. They went in silence on the path along the bluff, and the deeper the silence, the more Matthieu felt her clinging to his arm, and the more he wanted her to cling there. He felt the pity of situations and loneliness, and all the reasons for a heart to be generous, and all the circumstance that got in the way. He saw the ocean lying nearby, and sensed the woman trusting in his arm, and he wanted to speak but he did not know her. He felt Silke's hold on his right arm tightening, and he wanted to weep.

Matthieu began:

'I was once present – a witness – at a murder, on Tierra del Fuego. I saw a group of natives, Fuegian Indians, murdered by Europeans. I... could do nothing to stop it. There was nothing I could do, absolutely nothing. There was a priest there, a big, powerful man, and he could do nothing either.'

His voice shook with the fear that lies beneath all anger. He forced it steady.

'Taking the Indians' land is a sort of murder. It leaves them weak as kittens, and you see what happens.'

'But it was certainly no fault...'

'It's the fault of anyone who does not stop it.'

'Why,' Silke wondered, 'do you take it so much upon yourself?'

She stopped, and turned to him. Her free hand went up behind his head, pulling his face to hers, and she kissed him.

For an instant he was too astonished to react. Then he gave slightly towards her. Their mouths moved across each other, so that he sensed the very faint invisible down on her upper lip. Confused, he bent over her, his forehead pressed to hers, her delicate hair in front of his eyes. Through it, he was aware of the gleaming water in the pit of the bay behind her.

They stood like this half a minute.

'We shall grow cold,' she whispered. 'I think the breeze is rising.'

They moved on with her again grasping his arm, and his mind racing. In spite of the intoxicating moment, Matthieu's imagination rushed elsewhere. He thought of her husband, in Montevideo or Buenos Aires or wherever Theo was and whatever he was doing. In Matthieu's mind, a fear was gathering, but he could not tell yet what this fear was. He did not think it was jealousy, but fear of something as yet unclear.

When they reached the house, they could see the mules safely corralled. In the half-light, the silhouette of Lipi shuffled away towards the shack his parents inhabited on the near side of the settlement.

Matthieu pushed open his door; the fire was alight, its flames illuminating the corners of the room.

'Sit,' he commanded, steering her to a bench. 'I must dress your hand.'

She did not sit on the bench, but on the edge of the bed heaped with furs. He lit the oil lamp, placed his implements and dressings nearby, then sat beside her. So, again, he tended to an Austrian hand, dabbing and padding; the wound was only slight, and he had little excuse for his slow turning of the hand back and forth in the lamplight, or for his caress of her fingers. But he needed none, for Silke sat quietly, gazing at what he was doing.

After a long minute of this, he stopped and rested her hand within his. They did not look at each other's faces, but stared at their hands. They said nothing, but the room was not silent: on the far side of the table, the fire rustled. Outside, the wind had of course returned, with the sound of sand tossed onto the tin roof that shifted overhead, the sound of his swallowing, and the breath of both of them. He felt his chest tighten, and all the muscles of his abdomen tense, while in his mouth the saliva welled up. And yet, the more he willed himself to be still – the tip of his little finger stirring against the side of hers – the more he felt something building in him which he would not be able to contain. His face grew taut, with a curious prickling sensation. As he turned his look, very slowly, towards Silke, he saw that she was watching him and that in her eyes there was anticipation. He was about to speak, but she pre-empted him with a swift move of her hand to his cheek, to pull him round to her. And they sank together onto the thick waves of fur, pulling each other close. She slipped one long leg, trailing acres of warm skirt, over his thigh, right up to his waist, while Matthieu's hand clasps at her hip.

Even as this happened, however, even as the warm shape came eagerly towards him, Matthieu felt his own resistance and reluctance. Almost every strand of him wanted to draw closer, to shed restraint, to plunge into this – but there was something else: a distaste, a scruple. It was that ill-defined but rapidly growing fear. Even as his hand buried itself in the fine cobwebs of her hair, he knew that he was not breathing quite as fast as she, that he was not quite as fervent as she. He stopped kissing her; he drew his face back, he looked at her clear grey-green eyes. She said nothing, but her hands went to his waist, tugging at his clothing. He detected a hint of panic in her – as though she knew that if this moment did not drive on to its conclusion, it might never return. And so she was working at him, exciting him, eager and busy – even as he was becoming still.

It was no good: the first moment had passed, and the fury of the blood in Matthieu's head, the seemingly unstoppable momentum, had passed also. Silke stopped; she looked at him in dismay. Matthieu felt himself subsiding back onto the bed – as it were, relaxing, except that he was anything but relaxed. He stared up at the canvas ceiling – but it was not this that he saw; rather, it was a memory.

'What is it?' she whispered.

What could he say? That he saw the image of a tall woman, strong boned, clear eyed, a figure so handsome as to be noble, a figure who, divested of her clothing with the assistance of a religious sister, he saw to be covered in the disgusting pustules and rashes of sexual disease...

He could not speak. He took a deep breath; he sighed it out. He clasped her hand, but felt his strength gone. When Silke, biting her lip, looked down the length of him and ran her hand over the cotton across his stomach, he knew that desire was still there – but that a very particular horror was mastering it.

'Is it,' she said, 'that I am married? That I have a husband?'

Matthieu could not, in courtesy, lie there without responding; he nodded, though he did not speak. Yes, that was it: she had a husband

– and her husband was now among the disease-ridden whores of the cities where he had undoubtedly often been before; he was dipping into a vat of infection; he must have infected his wife. That was it.

'I suppose,' murmured Silke, 'that you are of a higher character.'

Oh, no! he wanted to wail. He wanted to grasp her by the shoulders, tell her firmly and clearly that she was quite wrong in so many ways: that he wanted her, dreadfully so; that he was still young and had been without love for more than a decade; that he was lonely; that his body cried out. But he was terrified of what she surely carried within her. The ghastly clinical precision of a medical text gripped him: the lubricant fluids in the female genitalia; the bacterial load in syphilis; the permeability of mucous membranes...

Silke Kahn rested her extraordinarily fair head beside his shoulder.

He sensed her face close to his, felt her thigh that lay across him tighten and squeeze both on him and on her own sex, until a little tremor ran through her. He felt the tightness of his own desire so intense that he almost stopped breathing, but the fear was not dissipated. Every sort of venereal scourge crowded back into his mind: whimpering shepherds and their ulcers; their poor wives speckled with rashes; a slavering syphilitic in Punta Arenas with his brain rotted.

At last, he felt Silke's grip on him, the grip of her whole body, loosening in a failure that she completely misconstrued.

'You think very badly of me,' she whispered. Her tone was not self-pity but resignation, as though she had known this would happen.

'No,' he said in misery, 'not at all.'

'But I think so,' she persisted, 'because I am a married woman, and I am wanting something terrible.'

Matthieu, suffocating, swung his feet down and sat on the edge of the bed. The lamp was burning low; he could reach out and turn up the wick, but he did not. The fire needed fuel, and he stood and dealt with that. Glancing back, he saw Silke lying on her side on his bed. The hand that had been caressing him was now under her cheek, and she watched him without reproach, only bodily hunger and disappointment. He felt a rush of tenderness for her, and sat running his fingers through her cobweb hair.

'Stay with me,' he breathed.

*

Just before dawn, he heard the vipers under his floor; Matthieu had not heard them for some time. There came the familiar slitherings and soft hisses of their conversation. He thought: they are discussing the change in my household. For Silke Kahn was still there sleeping; she and he lay under two furs, with no sound but the usual wind nudging the house, and the snakes below.

Then the servant boy knocked on the door, beating diffidently with the side of his fist.

'Señor Doctor,' Lipi called, 'Señor, there are Indians.'

There were three, waiting by the surgery. The boy would not let them in because that was the room, surely, where the white-haired señora would be sleeping. So Lipi was puzzled when Matthieu came from his own door, nodded to the Indians, opened the surgery and took everyone inside – and the señora was not there.

In the other room, Silke Kahn heard through the timbers loud accounts of the sequel to the previous evening's disaster. She rose, and straightened her clothes and hair.

She came out of the building, and saw in the distance Lipi trotting away on a mule. She opened the surgery door; two Indians turned to look at her. But a third man, seated by the table, did not look, because his left eye was hanging loose from the side of his gashed face, which Matthieu was supporting with a clean boiled cloth. The man winced and gasped, trembling with shock. He had, nonetheless, an overwhelming urge to see who had come in the door.

'Sit still,' snapped Matthieu.

Silke saw the ragged shambles of the face; she put a hand to the doorframe to steady herself. Then she saw that Matthieu needed six hands, that the Indians were chattering indignantly but were no help. She stepped forward, took the cloth and supported the man's cheek, taking care not to crush the eyeball.

Matthieu, without discussion, relinquished the task to her, reaching for implements and salves, sutures and strapping. They worked in murmurs.

'I must return to the encampment,' he said. 'Matters got out of hand, and there are people who cannot be moved.'

'Then we shall go as soon as we have fixed this person's face.'

Matthieu attempted a stern look, but she forestalled him:

'You will recall, perhaps, that I received nurse training at Carlsfelden.'

Matthieu saw that the Tehuelche were nodding urgently. The Indians departed first, hurrying home to their crisis while Matthieu re-gathered his bags. But as he opened the door to call for Lipi, he stopped, gazing out at his mules in horror.

'What is it? My dear, what is wrong?'

'Lipi,' he said. 'He's not here. He wanted to spend the day gathering crabs; he will have left by now. Damn the boy, today of all days I need him!'

He stared at the corralled mules as though at a nest of cockatrices.

'Can you not go without him?' she asked. 'Is it for leading the mule?'

Matthieu murmured in despair, 'Of all days. I cannot on my own...'

Silke became brusque.

'Then allow me. We can't fail our friends today.'

He glanced at her, uncomprehending.

'It is,' she announced, 'just a matter of holding the lead rope of the mule. I can do that as well as a small boy.'

He peered in disbelief.

'You?'

'Of course, me. I shall lead your mule today. We shall all be quite safe, and we shall reach the camp directly and be of use to them.'

He did not answer, but continued to stare.

'I am quite as strong as Lipi,' said Silke, somewhat tartly. 'What is more, I have on two occasions flown the *Taube,* which I daresay requires quite as much coaxing as a mule. Or are you ashamed to be seen?'

He shook his head.

'Then come,' she was firm, 'with no delay.'

Moments later she handed Matthieu into the saddle from the mounting log, the doctor mute and helpless, as though he was the patient stripped of dignity. Silke handed up his bags; he looped these over the mule and sat waiting for her, watching as she tied the lead rope securely between two animals.

'Now we are ready.' She clambered from the driftwood log to perch side-saddle, leading him away from the house onto the riverside track.

What would become of his reputation among the gauchos, were he to be observed led on a string by a woman along the Río Sanlúcar? Even Matthieu Macanan might have been dismayed at the thought – but then, this was not his sort of pride; perhaps of all men in Patagonia, he cared least for those sorts of dignity. He had quite other concerns, and at the encampment the Tehuelche were too frantic with their own troubles to notice.

They began work in the tents, crouched over men who had slashed wildly at each other with machetes, men who did not scream because, twelve hours later, they were still too drunk to feel much pain. Silke's presence calmed Matthieu. To begin with she merely held, passed, dabbed and pressed as *per* his instruction. But there was too much to do; half the encampment males had cut each other up. Matthieu, about to embark on stitching a wound that ran the length of a forearm, was called back to another man who was thrashing about and had cast off all the careful bandaging of ten minutes before. As he dithered, he found the curved suture needle and the boiled thread taken from his hands.

'I've stitched the ripped fabric of a Dove,' said Silke. 'so I can manage this.'

Matthieu went to Coromín's tent.

'I thought that you took away all weapons before the boys got drunk.'

'They took them back again,' said Coromín. 'They crawled under the edge of my tent. Or maybe they just found new things, nice and sharp; I don't know. I am an elder, not a king, Makan. I have influence, not power.'

He watched Matthieu easing a pad off the hip of an elderly man who had been stabbed not very severely, and who moaned for rhetorical effect.

'Not just the young,' murmured Coromín. 'These things never used to happen.'

He watched Matthieu a minute longer.

'Makan,' he said, 'I have something I wish to ask you.'

'Anything,' replied Matthieu.

'Yes, I think so,' said the *cacique*. 'You are the best of friends. I have told Juana so; I said, Don Makan will never fail us.'

'What is it?'

'Not for me, Makan, but all the...'

'What is it?'

'Will you go to Buenos Aires for us? We need you to go to Buenos Aires to speak with a lawyer. To present our claim, no one better than you.'

Matthieu was kneeling by the old man, apparently examining the wound in his side. But the casualty now peered at the doctor, puzzled, for Matthieu was not looking at the wound, nor at his face, nor the bloody clout, nor anything.

'Makan? Will you go, please? We have money to send you on *Luisa Menendez.*'

'I'm sorry – no.'

'Do you say...?'

'I cannot go.'

'It will cost you nothing. We will pay.'

'It's not the money.'

'Listen,' said the *cacique* with more urgency. 'There are men here I could send – there are still some in one piece. But *cristianos* won't listen to an Indian. They are like Margall: they talk fast and they have no regard for what we say. But a respected doctor...'

'I am not respected.'

'You are one of them! Better than them, an important qualified man, a special man. They will listen to you.'

'I am sorry, but no.'

'I don't understand: why will you not? You have seen Margall here, you know what is happening. Look at you working here, while Miss Silke is also...'

'I cannot go to Buenos Aires,' said Matthieu. 'Do not ask me again.'

With that, he got up and left the tent, the injured man gazing after him in disbelief, and Coromín also.

*

He did not tell Silke of the *cacique*'s request, or of his refusal, but of course she noticed that something had affected him. Matthieu hurried to leave, gathering up his equipment and steering her out between the tents. Coromín stood at the entrance to his home, gazing in silence as they departed, and Matthieu saw Silke puzzled by this, sensing his embarrassment and anger. He could tell she knew there was something wrong – but Matthieu did not explain.

That evening, he lay staring at the fabric ceiling in the flicker of the fire. As the light of the flames lit the unevenly stretched fabric, throwing agile, elusive shadows, he thought of the tiny creatures that lived up there, unnoticed and undisturbed. No one bothered them. If a bug was to creep out clinging to the underside of the cloth, and drop into the lamplight on the table, it would soon be in trouble. But if it kept to its own dim world, it could be as busy as it liked.

Matthieu Macanan would stay out of the light; he would not go to Buenos Aires. He recalled the Tierra del Fuego waterfront, and the red-faced murderer hinting at rumour in Buenos Aires, stories which would soon resurface if he was to start making awkward claims on behalf of savages and their rights to the wilderness. Buenos Aires would soon remember those unwholesome tales about Matthieu Macanan. He would not go, he would not discuss it with Coromín, and he would tell Silke nothing.

She was beside him, asleep. A strand of her light hair was tickling his cheek, near his left eye; he knew that it was just one strand, triggering sensation through the even smaller hairs that stood out from his own skin. He did not move, but lay considering every feeling she caused in him. There was the sound of her breathing, a soft tide in her nostrils. There was the movement of her chest that produced an infinitesimal tugging of the rug over his forearm. There was her warmth felt all down his right side, but there was also a pocket of air by his feet which was not so warm, caused by the cover lifted between them. There was the slight sense of tipping inwards, caused by her weight in his bed, even this bed with its unyielding horsehair mattress on hard wooden boards; this dip, he found, required a discreet tensing in a few muscles of his flank and thighs, to keep him steady. He was not, in her presence, fully at ease.

Without any doubt, he wanted her there. Her presence was far more than physical. He thought of her at the Indian camp, kneeling by a man whose hacked shoulder she was suturing, making the Indian smile by her cheerfulness, even as she stabbed with her needle. Matthieu recalled the man's eyes captivated by the airborne wafts of shining hair. He thought of her riding home, pointing out the mineral colours on the ground, the jet and chalcedony that he, Matthieu, had years since stopped noticing. Of her drawing him out until he became almost a raconteur, bragging of trapping wild cats in tangles of *calafate* and staring into their black eyes. Of how she had squirmed at his stories of eating puma hearts raw, and of roasting skunks and armadillos: 'You'll try them if you stay another month,' he'd declared, just to tease. Of how they had discussed the hardcases and peculiars, such as the community of self-exiled Americans who still flew the flag of the Confederacy over their north Patagonian farms. Of how they'd shared the lore of horse colours and horse racing, and his laughable fear of everything to do with horses, fears compounded by the horse-hurt men that were brought to him. Matthieu had not talked so much in months, or laughed so, and it was wonderful provided she did not insist he talk about himself, did not prise him open…

'What are you thinking about?' she said, in the dark. 'I can feel your muscles; they are holding you still, when really you want to move.'

It was true; he was becoming cramped, but had not wanted to wake her, because in bed it was better that she was asleep.

She slid an arm across his chest, and hugged him. She placed her lips against his ear, and closed them gently on the lobe, tugging.

'Tomorrow,' he said, 'should we not inspect your Dove? We've not been for two days. What if it has been damaged?'

'I shall repair it,' she breathed.

There was a short silence.

He said: '*Luisa Menendez* will call towards the end of this week. She'll be sailing south again.'

Her fingers were sneaking through the front of his heavy shirt, toying with the chest hair. He tried again:

'Your husband may be returning.'

Still nothing. Her fingertips roamed over his chest. He heard a slight change in the rate of her breathing. A hint faster – the tiniest hint. Then she stopped exploring his chest, and was doing something with her own clothing. She pulled his hand across, guiding it in through the front of her own blouse, to rest on her naked breast and the nipple swollen tight. There was no helping it: he stroked, he cupped the breast, he teased the nipple and the broad areola.

She moved again; her whole form tensed and trembled as she slid her hand down his front. When she arrived at his crotch, he was hard and ready for her, and she began tugging at the clothing, pulling it up to get at him.

But he stopped her. He took his hand off her breast, and he stopped her, pressing her palm down against his hard member, but not letting her move. She tried to stir, even under his imprisoning hand, but he would not let her.

They lay still like that. Matthieu stared into the dark, marvelling at the torture endured by them both. He heard the faintest whimper, one plaintive little note from her, and her breath became uneven. Then she extracted her hand and turned over, away from him. Her back curled and she drew her legs up. He became aware of a slight rhythmic movement in her that grew stronger, as though to begin with she was trying to conceal it but gave that up. Her breathing took on a slight rasp as though her nostrils were flaring. Then, with one soft expulsion of breath, and with a ripple that spread through the fur mantle, she lay still.

Beneath the house, he heard the snakes whisper.

*

Every morning, they worked together in his clinic. There was no lessening of need, but Matthieu noted that certain Indians were cool towards him; they must somehow have learned of his refusal to petition Buenos Aires. He noticed that his patients – men and women, gaucho and Indian, trader and child – all adored Silke. However sick or hurt, they beamed at her gratefully, and sometimes reached out to her hair, so different from their own, touching and purring with pleasure. She smiled, apparent tranquillity incarnate.

Matthieu observed and admired.

It was best if they went out. They often rode to the Tehuelche camp. Matthieu thought that Silke's eyes were, so to speak, wider than those of ordinary people. She watched the Indians breaking and training horses, and she would relate to Matthieu how they crafted saddle and gear from nothing but hides and scrub wood. She sat with the women by the tents and watched how they sewed capes of fur, into which the awkward shape of the skins was cunningly fitted like a jigsaw. She would try her hand at this, and mocked her own clumsiness, while the women patted her fondly. She would convey to Matthieu all she had seen, so that his own enjoyment revived also.

Each succeeding day, Silke Kahn appeared to him more angelic – or, more like a dove; she had fluttered into his life in the most improbable way. But she was ever more tense, possessed by an ache for his affection. She could not touch him without a piercing tenderness, and could not look into his eyes without torment.

He could not help staring at her. He loved to watch her move, for she went about so lightly that she left no footprint. This was literally true; the ground was so hard and stony that nobody left much mark, but Matthieu would solemnly examine the way she had just taken, looking for footprints and seeing none, and making her laugh. For a short while, things would be lighter between them.

They checked daily that the Dove was unharmed, and sometimes noticed signs of a visitor. One afternoon they found the wooden ladder placed against the fuselage: someone had wanted to look inside. But when Silke lifted the canvas cover of the cockpit, nothing had been disturbed. She smiled down on Matthieu, her pale skin suiting the colours of the Patagonian sky. From up there she could see over the thorn fence. Her look – when she gazed out across the plains – was ecstatic at the freshness, the air itself bright with South Atlantic salt.

One afternoon, Silke took the cockpit cover right off, and said to Matthieu:

'Would you like to sit inside?'

He followed her instruction, climbing slowly into the front cockpit, fearful that he might put his coarse foot right through the delicate fabric. Silke climbed into the second space, and stood on the narrow floorboard to reach over his shoulder and tell him what was what: the controls of a Dove were few. He tried the pedals for the feet, from which wires ran to the tail. He grasped the control stick, its iron ring covered in tightly-sewn leather; from the shaft of the stick, more wires passed through small blocks, then up the short mast and out to the wings to warp them (the Dove had no flaps, no ailerons, only this twisting). He tapped the compass, and the tube of pink fluid that would tell the speed. He fingered the brass taps and valves by which the Mercedes sipped its fuel. There was nothing more. Matthieu ran his hands over these controls, trying to imagine flying but finding his imagination incapable. Flying meant nothing to him; it was something most people never thought about. Matthieu tried recalling Icarus; the 99 horsepower Mercedes didn't fit that story. He noticed that the Dove had begun to accumulate a lot of dust; it was filling with Patagonia.

So they sat high up, the French doctor and his Austrian lover in an earthbound Dove, looking out at the plains. It was ridiculous, though no one was watching.

But each evening the awkwardness returned. They would walk along the river bluff to the bay. They purchased foodstuffs – dried beans, flour, sugar, tinned meat and fruits – from Rahman or Aisha his hook-nosed wife, or their tubby daughter who was getting no schooling here. For the news, they would take an *aguardiente* with the gauchos from distant farms who came in to Rahman's store for provisions. Silke would drink too; she was neither proud nor retiring. And with Rahman there would always be a quick exchange: *Any sign of Luisa Menendez? Of Señor Theo?* No, none.

And each night he sensed the unbearable tension in her. He felt her fear of intruding, of becoming unwelcome, even as her body crept closer to him. Sometimes, jokey cuddling would work, chattering about the cold outside to take their minds off the heat indoors. With luck, she would fall asleep. He kept very still, or, if she turned on her side, would fit himself to her back.

One quiet night, she heard the snakes rustling, and she sat up in alarm. He lit a candle, to show that there was nothing in the room, and to assure her that it was entirely natural to have a nest of lancehead vipers beneath one's floorboards. By the candlelight, she gazed at him as though uncertain whether he was not quite mad. At last he blew the flame out, and they lay not talking but not sleeping either, listening to their liaison being discussed by the serpents below the floor.

For some more nights they lay like this, and it was almost bearable. But one evening, after they had been gazing at each other over the table, after small talk, after they had distracted themselves with pages from *Germinal*, after they had prepared for sleep in silence, they slipped under the fur mantles and he immediately felt her edging nearer. He could do nothing about it; a moment later her hand, hopeful, was creeping across. It wasn't secretive; her trembling could be sensed in every corner of the bed. There was nothing sly about it; she could hardly take him by surprise and, as for going gently, the process was costing her terribly. She buried her face into his neck, eyes tight shut. She touched his abdomen, his belly. Her hand inched downwards.

It was too much for Matthieu. He rolled towards her, his own hand reaching across to her flank. Immediately, she gave a cry of hope and became more urgent, pulling at his clothing. Her other hand took hold of his, and pushed it between her thighs. Without a word they agreed what was to happen: the rhythmic rising and falling, the pressing of his thumb against a deeper recess. This lasted very little time; it needed very little time, because they could not contain themselves.

After which they stroked each other's hair in silence, partially relieved, largely dismayed. Together they had entered a blind alley.

*

The next day, she was distracted. She hardly seemed to notice even the Indians, who glanced at Matthieu as though they held him responsible for this behaviour.

When they walked again to inspect the Dove, her mood was flat and distant. They paced once round the fragile, lifeless thing and pronounced it all intact, then went without further comment to Rahman's store, and made trivial purchases to give themselves something to do. There, Matthieu heard Silke ask Rahman yet again if there was any word of the *Luisa Menendez* – somewhat absurdly, because until the Dove began its regular flights, almost the only way word of anything could come was by the *Luisa Menendez*.

It was not her illogic that upset him: it was that she appeared so keen to be gone.

That night she ate nothing, but complained of her headache, not wanting to be touched. She lay on his bed turned away from the light, not speaking. He sat by the fire, pretending to read a book of poems but seeing only her, and listening to the rain on the roof. He realised that he was addicted to her, and could not do without her; that now she alone made this place tolerable – this place that he had tolerated for years without her. He thought this unfair; he wanted her to depend on him also. He glanced at the neglected stack of letters regarding Theo's airmail service, now gathering a film of dust on top of his shelf of French poetry.

Then she startled him, getting to her feet, blundering to the door. He saw her face puffy, red and tear-streaked as she pulled the door open and fell out into the night. He heard her retching emptily.

After two moments, with her eyes reduced to piggy squints, Silke reappeared and made her way slowly back to the bed.

'Silke,' he said, 'this is much the worst I have seen you. I can't watch and offer nothing. Won't you try the medicine I offered before?'

'What is that?' she whispered. 'I don't recall.'

He went to the door.

'I shall fetch it.'

He was back a moment later with the small frosted glass bottle.

'This is made in Germany,' he said, 'by the Bayer company; it can be trusted. It is reported to be very effective against such particular pain. You can take it as a draft, or I can prepare an injection…'

He waited; Silke made no response. He stood looking down at her, and saw on her face a wince that spread from the temples to every part of her skull. He saw the puckering eyes, and the tears springing from them, and he could weep at the injustice of pain.

'Yes,' she breathed at last, 'thank you, yes.'

So he moved promptly, and had the *Heroin* syringe ready. He turned her arm towards the lamp, seeking a vein while praying that his needle was sharp. There came the slight pop through her skin, but he flinched more than she did. Then they both waited.

Some minutes later, she breathed:

'My dear, that does seem wonderfully good.'

For long moments, they were silent. She lay gazing up at the ceiling; he realised that just having her eyes open and tolerating lamplight was progress. He sat with his poems, from time to time sneaking a glance at her. She dozed lightly, but deep sleep did not come. He noticed that the horrid redness of pain had faded a little. He saw her stretch her limbs out, wriggling her toes and ankles, up and down, wriggling her neck also, stretching it this way and that. She did not seem quite so uncomfortable now, but looked exhausted.

She was looking at him.

'What are you reading?' she murmured.

'Some old French songs.'

'Read me an old song.'

Unthinking, he read the first verse he saw:

> *Beneath the blossom of an apple tree*
> *In the month of May,*
> *A while ago, my sweetheart soaked me*
> *With love's spray...*

Matthieu stopped reading; he did not look at her, but turned the pages of the book. Silke reached for his hand, and whispered:

'We are the most bewildered people on earth, you and I.'

She glanced down the bed; there was a blanket of coarse brown wool folded at the foot.

'Dearest, the rug – could you...'

The fire was low; he hurried to cover her.

'Don't sit up.' He feared some rush in her head re-igniting the pain.

'Stay with me here,' she said. So he sat on the edge of the bed, meaning to stroke and soothe her to sleep.

'Silke,' he breathed, 'Silke...'

Her eyes were clearer now, and it was as though he could see her thoughts ordering themselves, marshalling to take hold on her situation.

'I was not always like this,' she murmured.

He looked down at her, touching her hair with one finger, waiting.

'Only,' she said, 'since my marriage.'

He hardly understood. Still he waited.

'I expected,' she continued under her breath, 'some feeling. One does expect a little: that is normal. One thinks of warmth, of closeness. But I do not blame Theo.'

She closed her eyes against the residual pain.

'For what?' prompted Matthieu.

She could not answer; he saw her brows wrinkle and her lip curl slightly, and a pallor pass through her skin. He thought: she is going to be sick. But the instant passed.

'Our marriage was my doing. I wanted to escape from Carlsfelden.'

She was still clinging to his left hand, squeezing it against her belly, low down. Between her closed eyelids, Matthieu saw a tiny gleam forming: a tear. It was not, he saw, a tear of pain, but something else. Silke turned slowly on her side. When she spoke again it was so quietly – into the rug – that he was uncertain that he had caught what she said.

'He has never touched me.'

'Touched?' Matthieu had seen them arm in arm.

'Privately – as one touches a wife,' she said into the rug, pressing his hand. 'I was never to Theo's taste in that way, not at all.'

The silence rang with questions.

'So…' tried Matthieu.

'So it is not such a wonder that I get this ache, is it?'

Matthieu began, slowly: 'When your husband goes to Buenos Aires…'

'Boys,' she whispered into the bed: 'Only boys for Theo.'

It was all she would say. The next instant, Matthieu realised that she was asleep.

He gazed down at her, and looked at the wisps of her delicate hair swirling across the rugs and pillow, at her flushed cheek and still slightly puckered brow close beside him. A tide of tenderness surged over him, and self-reproach at his obtuse fears.

As he looked down at her, not moving for some long while, he became aware of a curious ache in the muscles of his own face – not unpleasant, but growing – and it puzzled him for a moment, until he realised that he was smiling so delightedly that his unpractised cheek muscles were beginning to grumble in an amused sort of way. For an instant he could not quite understand what had happened, until his mind caught up with the sensation of pure joy that was running freely through him. He felt no fear. Doubt and revulsion fell away so rapidly that he could scarcely recall what had ever come between them. He could not take his eyes off Silke, filled with desire which he allowed to swill through him unchecked: for two centavos he'd undress her right now – except that nothing of the sort: he would not touch her, she must recover, she must sleep, she must be better, he would see to that. But then, then certainly! It must be deferred, it was so much the sweeter for being deferred – but no more headaches.

He eased his hand free, and stepped as quietly across the room as he could to restore a little life to the fire. Once it was crackling genially, he turned back to regard her, and found that everything about his looking at her had changed. He studied the form of her curled under his rugs not with the fear he had experienced before, but with adoring familiarity.

He sat beside her again (on the bench, so as not to trouble her by shifting the bed) considering her skin that continued to slowly change colour, passing through a faint blotchiness as she reverted to her normal pallor. Towards Theo, Matthieu felt little, except perhaps gratitude. An unconsummated marriage? No marriage at all, even the Pope would agree!

Self-seclusion, retreat, denial: how beside the point; Silke Kahn was his life. Of course, he would now behave with the utmost generosity to anyone who called upon him. It was so easy, so clear; he would, for example, ride as soon as it was light to the Tehuelche encampment, where he would apologise to Coromín, make his peace with them all, offer his services to travel immediately to Buenos Aires and make strenuous representations about their land, and scorn anyone who tried to stop him.

He contrived to work his way to the inside of the bed by the wall, laying down carefully and pulling some of the rug over himself without disturbing Silke. There he remained on his back, gazing up at the ceiling dappled with the flicker of the fire, turning to let his look burrow into her haze of hair, drinking up the scent of her, and in happy, charitable weariness dreaming of everything that could now happen. Matthieu finally drifted away into a doze – until his boy Lipi hammered on the door, calling something about a ship.

Eight
DAFNE

There was a small tramp steamer in trouble close offshore. A dry gale was blowing; her engine, struggling to cope, was labouring and losing. One of her twin boilers – strangely oversized for such a little vessel – had burst. The tramp had been steaming at extraordinary speed as though she was pursued, and the boiler had split so suddenly and so violently that two crewmen had been trapped in a far corner of the engine room, and had been flayed alive by superheated vapour.

The second boiler was undamaged; by isolating the burst, it was just possible to maintain steerage way. But, although No.2 boiler was intact, the piping was not. Airlocks kept the pipes juddering fit to tear their joints apart, while fractures and twisted valves hissed away the precious head of steam. Very little pressure was reaching the triple-expansion cylinders; only the feeblest thrust was available, and few knots. The little ship just kept her head to the north-easterly gale, but made no progress. The dark shoreline was creeping closer. The crew glanced at each other apprehensively.

Only the moon – full and bright – gave Captain Hase any help. On the cramped bridge, the master and his first officer peered at the charts and at the look of the land barely a mile away. The Patagonian coast was so unvaried that any inlet was readily visible; they were staring, in desperate hope, at what might or might not be Bahía Sanlúcar.

'Do we try for it?' wondered First Officer Schultz.

'Certainly,' replied Captain Hase above the wind. 'The engine's shaking itself to pieces. We don't have the power to ride this out.

If we don't turn into the bay, we'll be grounded on the outer shore.'

'If we are wrong about the bay, and there are rocks...'

'No choice,' insisted the master, 'and I am not wrong.'

'Sir, once we turn across the wind toward the bay, there'll be no getting back out, not in this. We cannot be sure...'

In the teeth of the gale, Captain Hase allowed himself a half-second to feel irritated by his First Officer. Schultz was very able, and knew it. Schultz was a nephew of the commander of the *Scharnhorst;* his uncle, guessed Hase, was now rocking in a watery grave off the Falklands; still, one watched one's step with Schultz who was also the military liaison officer aboard *Dafne*, reporting directly to the *Kaiserliche Marine*. Hase had the feeling that Schultz was compiling a dossier on his captain's failings.

'I am not wrong, Schultz. I have sailed this coast a great deal, and that is Sanlúcar. It's nothing much of a bay, but it is shelter.'

'Very good, Sir.'

So they turned *Dafne* towards the shore and, with the gale heaving at her, she made a wheezing rush for the safety of Bahía Sanlúcar. She very nearly made it.

*

At first light, there came that banging on Matthieu Macanan's door, and Lipi calling:

'Señor, Señor Doctor, a ship!'

Surfacing, Matthieu was appalled; *Luisa Menendez* was here, and with her Theo Kahn and all the complications possible. By his side, Silke gave no sign of waking. Matthieu momentarily thought of rousing her, of turfing her out of his room and into the surgery minus any semblance of dignity, like a student caught with a prostitute in his room. He thought of the warmth of her head, the heat trapped within that angel's hair, and he flinched at the thought of shabby concealment.

But Lipi knocked again.

'Señor, a ship!'

If it was Captain Prothero and *Luisa,* why did the boy not say so?

Lipi knew very well what that quaint old tub looked like. Could this, possibly, be something else?

Matthieu eased himself out from behind Silke without waking her, and went to the door. The boy looked unusually excited.

'Not *Luisa Menendez*, Señor – another. They have a problem on the sand.'

Soon afterwards, Matthieu stood on the bluff in the chill early morning light, together with most of the population of the tiny settlement, staring down at the tramp steamer grounded on the sandbar that almost (unless you know the way in) blocked the bay. She did not look damaged; there was smoke coming from her stack, but there was also steam issuing rather oddly from under a hatch cover on deck, as though it had got lost and had wandered inside the boat looking for an exit. There were men on the foredeck, peering over the bow at the water and the cold grey sand. They looked safe enough, but their ship was thoroughly stuck.

Captain Hase returned the stares of the settlement population, and tried not to betray his feelings. He knew the Patagonian coast well, and he hated it. Not all of it: he liked the far north by the Río Negro, where there were giant butterflies that would drift out to sea and take refuge on ships, and where at night the wave crests prickled with phosphorus. He liked the far south, enjoying the antics of penguins and the sublimely hostile landfalls of Tierra del Fuego, where mountains draped their skirts of evergreen beech into the Beagle Channel. There, you could watch for the naked primitives who burned fires on patches of clay on the floors of their canoes, even as they bobbed between icebergs. Gunther Hase appreciated the far south, and the distant north.

But in the middle coast of Patagonia there was next to nothing, only comfortless harbours like this with no facilities, no help. Just now, however, Captain Hase must be thankful for this haven.

From *Dafne's* bridge, Hase considered the prospect around his ship.

On reaching the coast, the Río Sanlúcar ended with a long, low gravel spit that turned north up the coast for perhaps a mile. Behind this protective spit and parallel to the sea, the estuary ran northward also, before at last accepting that it must venture out into the Atlantic swell. At this point on the coast, the warm Brazil current, coming down from the Equator, met the frigid mass of the Antarctic stream from the south. Into the ensuing turmoil emerged the Río Sanlúcar, a piddling flow which took one look at the ocean and dropped its load of silt.

At the north end of the harbour spit was the mouth of the river, quarter of a mile wide. There was a sand bar, cut through by a deep channel maintained by the river swirling round the corner and out into the ocean. The channel was deep enough for a small ship such as *Dafne,* but – like the entrance to some tiny fishing harbour – it was little more than seventy yards across. And *Dafne* had not found it. *Dafne* was sitting on the sand bar. Indeed, *Dafne* had gouged herself hard into the sand, driven on by the gale.

On the north side of the river mouth the bluff was low; Captain Hase saw a row of cowed wooden buildings, with a few small boats drawn up on the beach below. From this bluff, *Dafne's* embarrassment was being studied by a little group of windswept figures.

'Schultz,' Hase called tetchily, 'where's your glasses? Who are they?'

The First Officer peered through black binoculars.

'Just people, Sir,' he observed. It was the sort of snide answer that made Hase detest him.

'Ah yes, people – thank you. What people?'

'A couple of cowboys,' said Schultz unperturbed, 'a woman or two, some Indians I think, and a handful of brats.'

'No soldiers? Nobody looking official?'

'No, Sir.'

'Then we must go and introduce ourselves,' said Hase. 'Plain coats, mind – no uniforms, or remove any badges at least.'

As he was rowed the short distance to the northern beach, the captain was thinking hard. He was anxious to keep curiosity at bay; he would rather give bland explanations up there on the bluff than have anyone prying on board *Dafne.* Who could tell what Argentine authorities might be here, what telegraph lines might run south to Gallegos or north to Comodoro Rivadavia, or what vessels might come calling. Hase was frankly dismayed at his position. As a commander in a belligerent navy, he could stay in this neutral harbour only twenty-four hours. Fortunately there was little belligerent about *Dafne*; she was again flying a Chilean flag and as they had fled north from the disaster at the Falklands, Hase had ordered the name at the bows and stern to be obliterated; a crewman had been dangled over the rail in heavy seas to slop black paint over the lettering. They might convince these locals that she was what she seemed: nothing more than a coastal trader. If, however, the Argentine navy came prying, they would not keep their secret for long.

But there was no point in attempting to re-float *Dafne* at high tide if they had no power; she'll simply be driven onto the rocks. Hase needed to make repairs, and there'd be nothing here in the way of resources. His chief engineer was very good, hand-picked for the exploit, but several of the crew were hurt – quite apart from the two who had been steamed alive, and who needed urgent burial. Bucholz the mate was a steady man, but no mechanic. There were eight others left, apart from himself and Schultz, the sole military professional. So Hase was quite sure it would take him more than twenty-four hours to sort the ship; he could not see it being done in less than three days. And then – where was he to go?

For in that special compartment in the hold was a precious cargo for which the Kaiser waited. There was no prospect of *Dafne* sprinting anywhere now. What could Hase do? Try limping home by some out-of-the-way route, sneaking through the chill mists off Iceland perhaps, hoping to avoid the British Grand Fleet? Or perhaps off-load and bury the gold on some island off Africa, to be picked up by U-boats? Every notion that came to him seemed more preposterous than its predecessor.

Moreover, he was haunted by nagging doubts about his crew; their morale had been severely dented by the rout of the Imperial navy off the Falklands, by the boiler explosion, and by the sight of their comrades dying with their skin in tatters. Unusually even for a Chilean vessel, the men were all of German extraction, so they were loyal – were they not? But to whom, exactly? Some he liked and trusted: Vollmert had been exceptionally strong and hardworking, but he'd been one of the casualties of the boiler burst; Matz was straightforward, an innocent; Bagan was amusing. Hase was aware, however, that one or two – that man Sahler, for instance, with his lank hair and endlessly searching eyes – were cronies of Schultz. Sometimes he'd see Schultz and Sahler standing close to each other, not obviously conversing nor yet whispering, but with something passing between them.

Thus, as Captain Hase climbed the gully that led from the beach to the settlement, he was preoccupied. Only when he, Schultz, and the two sailors who had rowed them stood on the bluff facing the cluster of locals, did Hase pull himself out of his gloom and make an attempt to communicate.

Although of German stock, Hase was Chilean born; Spanish was his first language, before German. He was a straightforward man of honest manners, happy to treat with simple folk. Faced, however, with Rahman and his wife Aisha, with their giggling teenage daughter and her wiry hair, with a cluster of snotty urchins, and with two hung-over Tehuelche Indians who had bought a flask off Rahman last night and slept out in the open afterwards, Captain Hase found conversation hard going. He wished he had gone along with the two seamen whom he had instructed to take a walk around the settlement to see what was what.

Until a new figure appeared; the group parted to let him through, and the situation changed.

The newcomer was a man of perhaps forty years, Hase guessed. He wore plain but good clothes which had seen plenty of wear but which had been meticulously mended. The man had elegant features with a southern, slightly olive colouring and with a somewhat elongated nose, and this desolate little place must have something to recommend it, for the newcomer looked uncommonly happy. Hase decided that he'd never seen a man so transparently cheerful, so likely to burst into laughter. The eyes were intelligent and searching; Hase thought: If anyone is going to see through us, it will be this man. But he thought also: Here is someone I can speak with.

In fact, the other spoke first.

'Good morning,' he said in Spanish. 'My name is Macanan, Matthieu Macanan.' He held out his hand. 'Is your ship damaged?'

Hase was surprised by what he was sure was a French accent, and taken aback by the cultivated courtesy.

'Nothing that a day or two of repairs won't put right; then we'll refloat and be on our way.' The captain spoke with forced conviction.

'That's splendid!' said the Frenchman.

But Hase recalled something more sombre.

'Two of my crew were fatally injured in an engine-room accident. We must have a burial. Perhaps you'd be so good as to help us locate a suitable spot? Out of your way, of course.'

'Patagonia is at your disposal,' the Frenchman remarked, glancing over the vast pampas. 'Are the rest of your crew safe?'

'Some injuries,' replied Hase. 'Mr Schultz and I do what we can. We hope to find a doctor at Rivadavia.'

'I can assist you!' said Dr Macanan, and explained himself. He seemed so pleased to help.

Hase stared: a doctor, here? He'd pay in gold for that.

A new quandary presented itself to the captain: should he risk asking Macanan on board ship, or insist on bringing the injured ashore? The doctor was a godsend, but he was also surely a Frenchman – an enemy of Germany. While Hase dithered, the two other sailors, Bagan and Sahler, came running back. They were so excited that for a moment the captain could not understand what on earth they were talking about.

'Oh, you'll like this,' laughed the Frenchman.

So everyone went to look.

Captain Hase had never actually seen an aeroplane before – not in the flesh. He had read reports but, a seaman to his marrow, hardly thought such things credible. Or at least, he thought them rather improper. When he entered the thorn windbreak and stared at the Dove, Hase was inclined to dismiss it as a joke, a fantasy, a plaything. First Officer Schultz, however, had a keener military instinct.

'What a bizarre object, Schultz,' said the captain, by which he meant: ridiculous. On getting no reply, he looked at his First Officer, whom he often suspected of ignoring him deliberately. Schultz was staring at the Dove with a fixity that Hase found unnerving.

'Schultz?'

'Forgive me, Sir,' said Schultz at last, 'yes indeed, very extraordinary.'

'Well,' observed his captain, 'it seems to have impressed you, at any rate. Doctor, are you the aviator?'

Matthieu laughed.

'I am shy of sitting on a horse, Captain; the thought of going up in that thing makes me faint. It is, I believe, a Rumpler-Ettrich *Taube* with a 99 horsepower Mercedes engine – but don't expect further enlightenment from me.'

He told them of Theo Kahn, expected any day, and about the airmail service. There was a lack of guile that decided Gunther Hase: he invited Dr Macanan on board ship.

'But forgive me,' said Matthieu, peering at the crudely obscured lettering. 'What is your vessel called?'

'The *Chloe*,' replied Hase off the top of his head; he had quite forgotten to choose a replacement. 'We changed owner just before sailing, and have not got round to repainting her name.'

Hase disliked lying to this doctor, to whom he warmed. He glanced at Schultz, hoping that his First Officer had registered the new name; Schultz gave a barely perceptible nod. Not long afterwards, Matthieu having collected a bag of essentials, they rowed back to '*Chloe*'. There, Matthieu dressed burns, strapped two broken ribs and debrided a raggedly gashed thigh. Hase watched with gratitude.

'Captain, may I have a word?'

Schultz drew him out of earshot.

'Sir, that aircraft – I have been considering: if the pilot does indeed return in the next day or two...'

'Come now, Schultz. Don't start building schemes upon that flimflam, that basket of string and linen.'

Schultz smiled patiently.

'Flying is taken very seriously by our commanders, Captain. We have, I believe, more than two hundred aircraft serving the Army in France, while our dirigible airships...'

Gunther Hase guffawed like a catarrhal donkey. But Schultz persisted:

'We have bombed Paris from the air, Sir.'

'Schultz, what possible interest is that to me here? Are we to be lifted off the sandbank by balloons?'

'I ask you to hear me out, Captain.'

Schultz gave Hase a steely look to remind the captain of his First Officer's unusual status. Hase grimaced.

'Say your piece.'

'Thank you, Sir. I observe that the *Taube* is designed to carry two. I propose that, at the first opportunity, one of us flies to Comodoro Rivadavia to make contact with our people in Buenos Aires.'

'You're not getting me in that thing!'

'I myself could undertake this mission, Sir,' said Schultz. 'If, as seems likely, *Dafne* is no longer...'

'*Chloe.*'

'Yes, Sir. If the ship is no longer able to fulfil the original plan, we must adapt. I can make the new arrangements. We may rendezvous with a submarine in the Caribbean if we can get that far, or off Brazil, although the U-boat would be operating at the limits of its range.'

Gunther Hase gagged on this bitter pill: the *Dafne* scheme reduced to limping up the coast looking for a submarine, while Schultz won plaudits in a Dove.

'And you can set all this up from Rivadavia?'

'No question, Captain. I have only to send a coded message, and Buenos Aires will do the rest.'

So, thought Gunther Hase: the *Kaiserliche Marine* had half-suspected all along that *Dafne* wouldn't make it.

'I have to get to Rivadavia,' urged Schultz, 'and the aircraft is the way to do it.'

'Why would the pilot agree to take you?'

'He is an Austrian, Sir. His duty is clear, and I shall lend him a sword.'

'What for?'

'Flying, Sir,' said Schultz. 'As a temporary officer, he will wish to wear a sword. It will focus his mind upon his duty.'

Thus, the plan was made. The moment he gave his assent, Captain Hase detected in First Officer Schultz a renewed self-importance, and – Hase also sensed – a curiously dangerous idea of license.

'Aeroplane or no aeroplane,' the captain grumbled, 'we still have to re-float *Dafne.*'

'*Chloe,* Sir,' said Schultz.

A sailor appeared in the companionway, grinning down at them.

'Beg pardon, Sir,' he blurted out, 'but there's a woman on shore. She invites the officers to dine.'

*

'My husband,' said Silke, 'is an engineer. He has adapted the *Taube* for long-distance flight.'

Matthieu Macanan listened quietly, supposing that it was obvious he was not her husband. He felt the two visitors at his table glance at him, and believed they must sense the adoration he felt for Silke. He returned the German captain's look, and saw that the man was smiling at him in a gently knowing way.

'We look forward to seeing that,' said Gunther Hase courteously.

'You say the problem is slight?' Schultz enquired, leaning across the table keenly.

'Ridiculously slight,' replied Silke, 'merely a seal on a valve, ten minutes' work for Theo when he returns, though it takes weeks to fetch it.'

Schultz was regarding her across the empty dishes, nodding and grinning, seemingly fascinated by her white gold hair.

'You have, for a lady, uncommon technical knowledge,' said Hase in honest surprise.

'In Patagonia,' replied Silke, 'one cannot be always ladylike.'

Matthieu placed more dried dung on the fire and returned to the table with the bottle of *aguardiente*, remarking:

'Frau Kahn is also a skillful nurse. There is little that I can teach her.'

'But who are your patients, Doctor?' asked Hase. 'You surely don't practice to a handful of children and cowboys?'

'Oh, the Indians!' declared Silke. 'They keep us busy.'

'Indians? We saw one or two...'

'There are dozens,' said Silke. 'A whole tribe.'

'And where are they?'

Matthieu did not want the Germans to know this: he could not quite say why. For all that he adored the bright ring of Silke's voice, he wished just now that she would keep quiet.

'They camp in this region sometimes,' he said.

Schultz said, 'Maybe we shall visit them.'

'They are not nearby.'

'Just an hour upriver, and so interesting,' said Silke.

'It's a difficult ride,' Matthieu insisted.

He did not like the way Schultz was staring at Silke – but he could hardly be surprised, for tonight her beauty had a ceramic glint. The officer could not take his eyes off her.

'There are no other farmers here, Doctor?' asked Captain Hase.

'As you will see,' replied Matthieu, 'this is poor country.'

'Then how do these Indians of yours live?'

'They are not mine; there's none prouder on God's earth than the Tehuelche. They trade in feathers and salt. Above all, they hunt.'

'What is the quarry?'

'Pumas, condors, guanaco – like a small woolly camel. The fur and meat are both excellent; you have just been eating it.'

'Excellent,' agreed Schultz. 'So, they have firearms?'

Again, he leaned slightly forward, as though interrogating an informant.

'They prefer,' Matthieu evaded the precise question, 'to use the *bolas,* three stones wrapped in leather and attached to a long rope. It entangles the animal's legs, and the hunter can then dismount and cut its throat.'

Schultz fixed Matthieu with that hard stare.

'They have many horses, these people?'

'They are horse-crazy!' Silke laughed. 'Dozens and dozens, every man with his *tropilla,* and every *tropilla* with a *madrina,* a lead mare, so they do not stray. An Indian would not walk into his tent if he could ride to bed.'

'So,' smiled Schultz, 'many horses.'

'And beautifully trained,' she enthused, 'a joy to see. They have no notion of hurting the animals, or of training by fear.'

Schultz – thought Matthieu – rather believed in training through fear.

'That is so Austrian of you, Frau Kahn,' said Schultz, 'so Viennese, and charmingly sentimental.'

Matthieu noted the captain eyeing his First Officer with distaste.

'But the Indians are much oppressed,' exclaimed Silke.

'By whom?' asked Hase. 'We've seen no soldiers, no police.'

'No, but by moneymen and politicians who sell the hunting lands from under the horses' hooves.'

'You know so much about these people.'

'Oh, I don't! Dr Macanan tells me everything.' She treated Matthieu to a beaming smile. 'He is here to redress this.'

'Frau Kahn considers you a saint, Doctor,' said the captain.

'I rather think,' Matthieu parried, 'that the Tehuelche regard Frau Kahn as an angel.'

She laughed and blushed, her skin like roses, and that hair waving...

'And I think,' said Hase, 'that we have a ship to sort out, and that we have imposed on your time. So many more agreeable things to do than amuse the likes of us.' He looked about the room. 'You have interesting books.'

'French verses,' Schultz remarked. 'Where do you buy those, Doctor? Not traded with your wild Indians, I expect.'

'I send to Buenos Aires.'

'Heavens, what a little oasis you have made for yourself, and so incongruous. How you must yearn for civilization.'

Matthieu said nothing.

'Come, Schultz,' growled Hase.

The Germans rose; in the process, Silke Kahn found herself facing First Officer Schultz. In the cramped room, they were close. Schultz was a tall man; Silke looked directly into his eyes, which unblinkingly returned the look.

'Good evening, both,' Captain Hase bowed.

When the Germans had gone, Silke wanted to know:

'Why do you not want them near the Indians? Matthieu, you did everything to discourage them. The Tehuelche are not your preserve.'

Matthieu, tidying the room, sensed a belligerence.

'There are too many outsiders,' he replied, 'interfering.'

'They weren't interfering. They were simply interested.'

'In Patagonia, you will find, that is impossible. No one is just interested.'

He knew this was amiss. He looked round; she had reddened.

'What is wrong?'

'You patronise me.'

'Oh, now...'

'Yes, I think you do. But I came here by myself. I am not helpless or stupid.'

'Far from it.'

'I give you every credit for teaching me how things go here, but also I have found out for myself...'

So she continued a stream of tart remarks. That's what she would call them, thought Matthieu even as he flinched: remarks and observations. As she tore into him, he saw how the flush suffused her face. He saw her brow lined with stress, and a tightness in her cheeks, under the eyes. He heard her voice pinched and weaker, as though speaking was becoming painful.

At last, she stopped, and sat on the edge of the bed.

'Go gently, sweetest,' he ventured. 'I think...your headache?'

She had closed her eyes. She was poised, assessing the approaching pain like a foot soldier in an outnumbered army watching the enemy come on. He waited. At last, she felt for his hand.

'Forgive me,' she said, keeping her voice terribly smooth, as though the vibrations of speech might shatter her defences. 'Forgive my ranting at you. Really, I must learn to relax, mustn't I? You see, it's not so easy, I have bad habits and I'm paying for that now. Please, that German medicine, the *Heroin* – could you give me that again?'

*

She remained in his room; it was not how he had envisaged this night, but Matthieu was content to lie beside her. They slept peacefully, with promise lingering between them like a scent. In the morning, however, she said she still felt unsteady. She did not think that she could assist Matthieu today: would he mind? She would remain here in the house and rest, and then later perhaps she would do a few light chores.

A message came: Matthieu was called to a gaucho fallen from his horse some hours south. The man's leg was badly broken, the jagged bone jutting through the skin; he could not be moved, and was lying under an improvised shelter. Would Dr Macanan please oblige, and hurry? The weather was bad...

Matthieu was inclined to oblige the whole world. He thought of his planned visit to the Tehuelche, of his apology to Coromín, and of the trip to Buenos Aires – but all that could wait a day. He took Silke's hands and kissed her on the forehead. They stood close, face by face, arms at their sides with fingers interlocked, breathing into each other's ears. Their cheeks touched, barely so: they could feel the fine contact of hair.

'À bientôt.'

He squeezed her hand and set off with his medical bags, on his mule with Lipi leading.

For a while, Silke lay down on the fur covers in the darkened room. But the morning sleet had ended, and she realised that she was bored. She rose gingerly, and decided that if she was careful, she could move about and be a little active. She opened the shutters and began to clean and tidy, nothing too vigorous. It amused her to act the housewife – Dr Macanan's wife. She thought of Matthieu: how had he taken her account, two nights back, of Theo's neglect? She did not yet know exactly; she had fallen asleep.

Thinking about this, she stopped in front of the bookshelves by the head of the bed. She stood contemplating the Darwin and the Zola, and the volume of birds with coloured plates. For once she ignored the poetry. She thought of tugging out the Swedish dictionary and looking up something obscene: *testicle* perhaps – always supposing that Swedish dictionaries admit the testicle. Or *desire,* or other words that she wished to see on the page. But her eye fell on the medical books. She pulled at the dark blue buckram of the pharmacopoeia.

She studied the flyleaf: the black ink, the handwriting neat and positive, a tad smaller than she'd had expected:

Matthieu Daniel Macanan
Université de Montpelier.

She tried to imagine Matthieu as a student. Did he sail through his course winning prizes? Maybe he was out of his depth, but she thought not. Was he pushy and ambitious? Possibly not; perhaps he was cowed and exhausted, overawed by professors and richer, more arrogant classmates. She could not readily link that hazy university past to the man with whom she found herself living. She thought of him with the Tehuelche: gently firm, reassuringly confident. The Indians esteemed him; to Silke also, Matthieu was a doctor of magic, her most ferocious migraine banished by his medicine.

She replaced the pharmacopoeia and took down a volume of anatomy, with tinted plates. She turned the pages: the grim grey layering of ribs and pectoral muscle; the skull opened to reveal a brain but no soul; the unfeeling heart, dangling in mid-air with its great vessels severed. There were the bones of fingers with no sensation, and the nerves of a hand that could not caress. Next, startling and shocking, gaping at her from the page, there stared, as it overwhelmingly seemed, her own pudenda, touched up in colour. Spread apart, as though to stress its emptiness, was a vagina. There was a dry urethra, and the labia stretched in a grimace. There was a small protuberance also, a clitoris, that reached out like an anemone.

She turned the page, and blushed. There was the male organ, drawn erect.

She stared at it. She put out a finger.

Behind her, the door opened. She snapped the book shut.

'Matthieu?'

It was not Matthieu. In the doorway stood a tall, athletic figure in a peaked cap and a blue-black jacket that, although it had no visible insignia, nevertheless looked like uniform. He was a man who had surely attended the sort of school where small boys wear military uniform.

'Good morning,' said First Officer Schultz, entering without permission to her dismay. 'What are you reading?'

He stepped around the table to take up the book from the table. It re-opened.

'The male re-productive system,' Schultz observed. 'Good heavens.' He peered at the annotated penis. 'This was never meant for ladies.'

Silke thought: I should tell him to leave, he has no business here.

Then she thought: I have none either.

'I was looking for Dr Macanan,' said Schultz. 'Is he...?'

She thought: you'd not have walked in like that unless you knew.

'Out on his rounds?' Schultz seated himself at the table, and studied her. 'Mmm? Out and about?'

'He's visiting a patient.'

'And will he be gone long?'

'I can't say. Probably overnight. I expect two nights.'

'Oh, unfortunate. Our repairs have gone well, you see, but we cannot yet move the ship, even with the high tide; our power is much reduced. I hoped to ask Dr Macanan's help.'

'You want him to push?'

Schultz gave a cold smile.

'Is Dr Macanan very strong, would you say?'

He was jeering. Silke said nothing, and Schultz laughed:

'No, don't worry; I've a notion of horses. You mentioned Indians living nearby with numbers of horses.'

Silke sat mute on the edge of the bed: like a child, she thought, interviewed by its parent.

'You see,' continued Schultz, 'we have cables and ropes, plenty of those. The mouth of the estuary is remarkably narrow; from the stern of the ship to the beach is barely sixty metres. Teams on the opposite shore might pull almost directly astern of the ship. Given the right tide, with our engine doing its best, it can be done – with horses. We will pay your friends with coal. We have abundant coal, but we are short-handed; if they will assist us in jettisoning coal, we can lighten the vessel and they can keep the coal. We can be away on the morning tide. What do you think, Frau Kahn?'

'I wouldn't know.'

'But you're such a practical woman. You've seen the horses?'

'Go to the camp yourself, and ask.'

'So I shall. And the doctor will not be back till tomorrow evening at the earliest. We'll miss him. A shame.'

His gaze upon her was uncomfortably direct, while his eyes had an unpleasant shine.

'Well, thank you for the advice. Here you are with your husband far away, and you're in command of the doctor's home. I daresay Dr Macanan could scarcely manage without you – Frau Kahn.'

She could not meet his eye, though she noticed that his skin looked oily and stale.

'For a lady of strong character, the company of Dr Macanan must be very stimulating.' His eyes explored and dissected her, opening her out like the pudenda in the book. 'Tell me more about your doctor. What do you know of him?'

'I?'

'Yes, you.'

'Your tone is offensive, Herr Schultz.'

He ignored her.

'You are intimate with Dr Macanan. What is his family?'

'It is no concern of…'

'But do you know?'

'He is a good man who desires to help people,' she said, bewildered by the other's shifts and feints.

'But why help Indians? There are plenty more deserving.'

'Dr Macanan makes no such distinction.'

She had become shrill.

'And you agree, Frau Kahn?'

'I assist Dr Macanan where I can. He will do anything for them.'

She stood, and began moving things about in a parody of tidying. She placed cutlery in a wooden box, then took it out because it had a film of mutton grease. She lifted tins and jars from one side of the shelf to the other. Schultz stretched out his long legs, and leaned back to survey her.

'If you have a *grande amour* for Indians, Frau Kahn, why did you come here in that aircraft – that Dove?'

'I don't understand you.'

'Well, the Indians will not benefit. They will be harmed.'

'Why?'

'Oh, come: it is obvious. The moment the land speculators arrive, the farmers, the miners – and the post – your Indians are lost. You are their angel of death.'

Now her translucent skin flamed in anger.

'What nonsense!'

He laughed at her.

'Oh, yes. And it is nonsense also that your Dr Macanan will do anything for his Indians. Twenty-four hours, and already I have learned things. Dr Macanan will not agree to help them by going to Buenos Aires. They asked him to take letters to the High Court about their land, but Dr Macanan cannot be bothered. The Indians are most upset.'

'I don't believe you.'

'I daresay,' he answered, 'but it fits the picture, doesn't it? His being out here, back of beyond. He surely has something to hide. Punta Arenas is remote enough for any man, my God, but he moved here!'

'You know nothing about him.'

'But I'm curious. What is he hiding?'

'Dr Macanan is a private person.'

'In his position, one would be. When is your husband expected?'

'Soon.'

'Is he aware that you live here with the doctor?'

'I have the room next door.'

She cursed herself for lying, for showing irritation. Silke stepped to the door. If there had been a garden, she might have insisted that they go out, take the air, walk about in full view. But there was no garden, and nobody. She stared out, praying for two mules returning, one leading the other.

Schultz was eyeing the bed. 'Those furs look warm.'

Silke didn't move.

'Are they warm, Frau Kahn?'

He was close behind her, breathing down her neck so that the hairs prickled. She caught alcohol on his breath – not foul, sour, stale drink but new, sharp and strong.

'Are you his mistress, Frau Kahn?'

She made to step outside – but his hands closed on her hips, firm and controlling, his fingers pressing hard and bruising the pelvic girdle. She froze, fearing to incite him, trying not to gag at the reek of spirits, so incongruous with that smart, stern jacket.

'It is provoking,' Schultz said, 'to think of an Austrian lady set up in sin with a Frenchman. I spent last night not liking it.'

Neither moved. If she could remain silent and still, he must at last release her and leave.

'Very provoking,' he murmured.

He breathed in her ear; softly, he blew through pursed lips, directly into her ear. She flinched, she pulled her head aside, the tiniest movement but she clearly recoiled from him. So he gripped her harder at the waist, and she gave a tiny sound, a mouse squeak. Excited, he pulled at her: one, two awkward steps back, he dragged her while she was off balance, and his grip was so firm that she could not twist to face him but moved backwards into the shadow, if only to keep from falling.

So she could not stop him: he had her alongside the table before she could think. With a powerful jerk, Schultz turned her, put one hand to the back of her neck and pushed her down – it was not violent, just a slow movement, but powerful – down over the table. She saved her face from slamming onto the planking by thrusting her arms out wildly, but she was spread-eagled. He heaved at the hem of her clothing and tore away the undergarments, kicked her feet apart and exposed himself, and as she attempted to twist aside, perhaps hoping to spit or bite or kick, she felt his hard flesh shoving at her...

Except that the vile thing did not happen.

There was an explosion of noise, of shouting, several voices shouting. There was a sideways wrench, and someone collapsing to the floor such that the entire house trembled. She lurched away, barking her shin on the bench, throwing herself in the direction of the window where she too stumbled and fell to the boards, and looked back across the room.

There were three Indian men. One had his arm in a sling and a bandage across his chest: she knew his face, she had helped Matthieu with him. The others were staring down at a dark heap on the floor that groaned and attempted to rise, until the nearest Indian swung his foot back and gave an enormous, vicious kick that would have broken the leg of a horse, but which had the effect of turning the victim around on the smooth wood. Schultz lay still, with the Indians peering down. When Schultz groaned, a part of Silke thought to cry out, *No, don't hurt him...* but it was a small part.

The Indians stood in the centre of the room, uncertain of what should be done when one caught *cristianos* in the act of rape. They stared at Silke, sprawled by the wall, waiting to see whether she could walk or talk. They did not mean to be rude.

Silke sat up against the wall, trembling. She looked again at the collapsed thing that was Schultz, fearing that he might swarm towards her on all fours – so she made herself stand. She felt faint, and stretched out a hand to the corner of the table. When she was upright, the Tehuelche appeared to recognise her.

'Señora, who is this person?' enquired the tallest, still on guard over Schultz. 'Is he from the ship?'

Silke nodded.

'We should kill him.'

She put her hand over her mouth not in prudery but to stop herself vomiting.

'He must be killed,' they all agreed.

Still their manner towards her was strange. They offered no concern, no assistance; but she saw that they were acutely embarrassed, and that their outrage was intense. At her word, they would have stabbed Schultz to death, there on the floor, slashed his throat, stamped on his windpipe. In horror, Silke sat on the bench by the table, pale and weak.

Without another word, the men seized Schultz by the arms and hauled him to the door, dumping him into the fierce sun outside. The bundle of him looked less threatening but also less predictable, capable perhaps of pulling a revolver on them. But the Indians had experience of the drunkenly murderous. One of them crouched again and searched him, extracting an automatic pistol from inside the jacket. The Indian waved this in the air, shouting angrily, waving it again until Silke was afraid the gun would go off and she'd be killed after all.

Now the Tehuelche hauled Schultz across the yard, propped him up against the fence and, finding a length of rope, lashed him to a post. They stood back, discussing Schultz like a sheep for the slaughter, while the man with the broken arm jerked this up and down in its sling as though Schultz should die for having interrupted his treatment.

'Dr Makan is not here,' Silke called out, propping herself in the doorway. They turned – and her legs gave way. She collapsed on the threshold.

*

Her head was split wide apart by pain. The slightest movement brought on a knotted grimace and, if she could have seen herself, she'd have been horrified by the lurid flush of her face. She found some relief in pressing her skull hard into the horsehair mattress, such that the scalp was tugged a little this way, a little that. It seemed to help – until someone began chopping at the other side of her brain with a blunt axe. She felt nausea rising, swelling and washing about like filthy water in a dock. She felt cold, she shivered horribly, and the shivering shook her skull and rattled the sore grey matter. She groped for a rug to pull over her, then realised with vague surprise that she was lying on Matthieu's bed. She could not recall making her way there. She only remembered the assault, and standing in the doorway, and feeling very unwell. Someone must have lifted her.

This gave her a small thread of hope: there was the glass bottle of Matthieu's *Heroin* somewhere in this room, which dealt with her pains as nothing else could. She attempted to sit up – and it was as though, from the sea of nausea, a wave of cement bulged up; she was knocked flat again, retching. She lay with her mouth slightly open, concentrating on the cold air of her indrawn breaths as a tiny relief from her agony. At last, very slowly, she managed to roll to the edge of the bed and let her feet down to the floor. She sat facing the door, which was closed. The window shutters were fastened also. She was profoundly grateful for this; the thought of daylight was so dreadful as to almost lay her out again.

She peered through the dark towards the chest under the window; the bottle of *Heroin* was in there, she was sure. She planned the next manoeuvre meticulously, because she suspected she had the strength for one attempt only. She half-crouched, with her hands grasping the wooden bench and then the table as she inched her way round. She sat a moment facing the shuttered window, her brain thrashing in her skull like a cat in a sack. Then she launched herself towards the chest, scrabbling at the clasp with her fingers.

The chest was locked. Crushed, she slumped to the floor with her cheek on the cold box.

She heard voices arguing: inwardly, she begged them to stop. She began to pay attention to the sense of having been almost violated but not quite; the discomfort that remained was more indignant than invaded. She felt damp, and realised that she had wet herself, which seemed unimportant. But those voices outside were speaking about her. It was not over.

So she dragged herself back to the open door; by taking deep breaths, she was able to control the nausea. The sunlight smacked her in the face. She glimpsed figures standing, but the man tied to the fence had gone. The glare was too much; she leaned, closing her eyes.

The voices fell silent; she sensed faces turning upon her. Footsteps came rapidly.

'Silke!' cried Matthieu. 'My God...!'

She let herself be supported into the house and lain down again.

'Keep still,' he was urging. 'Keep still.'

'What is happening to that man?'

'He doesn't matter.'

'Tell me,' she tried to insist.

But the nausea grasped her by the throat; she rolled onto her side and retched – but nothing came. She felt a hand on her forehead, stroking at her in absurd eagerness.

'Matthieu,' she whispered, 'do you... do you have that... that bottle...'

'At once, of course!'

He jumped up; the mere force of this, transmitted through the horsehair of the mattress, was enough to jar and jangle her sore head. He did not go to the chest under the window, only to the lower bookshelf, at the end of which was the bottle of white powdered *Heroin*.

'I left it here, don't you recall? You could have taken some in water...'

She heard the soft fricative of the ground glass stopper, and a spirit sterilising lamp being lit. He took her arm, and pushed the cream cotton sleeve up to her shoulder. With her eyes shut, she traced what he did by sensation: the slight tug of the fabric in her armpit, the cool of his fingertips as he searched for a vein, the pop of the needle through her skin, and at last the curious warm lovely ache that spread up into her shoulder before fading.

Her pain began to ease. She lay with a rug over her, curled against his flank. In place of the hammering inside her skull, there came a convoy of sensations and emotions arriving in turn: self-disgust, then euphoria; a luscious warmth like an infusion of sweet dark chocolate, then a second wave of pain followed by the relaxation of all her muscles; shock and then comfort, childish terror replaced by utter confidence, bodily revulsion with physical surrender – all were there.

She drifted in and out of sleep.

Later, she found that Matthieu was stroking her hand.

'Now you must tell me,' she said carefully. 'What of the German?'

'I've no wish to speak of him.'

'But I have.'

'The Indians have him at the camp.'

'What are they going to do?'

Matthieu did not at once reply.

'Tell me.'

'They say, he must be executed.'

'They wish to kill him?' she whispered.

'They demand,' answered Matthieu miserably, 'they say that I...'

She opened her eyes.

'They expect you to do this?'

'They say that you are my responsibility.'

She sat up slowly.

'Shall you?'

He lifted his hands in protest. Peering into his eyes, she felt far more sorry for Matthieu than for herself. She took hold of him.

'Nothing happened. The Indians came.'

'But if they had not!'

'But they did.'

Their gaze was interrupted by knocking.

'Don Makan? Don Makan!'

Three Indians stood at the door; one was *cacique* Coromín. Both Silke and Matthieu looked at the Tehuelche in weary apprehension – until Matthieu stepped out, and walked away from the house speaking with them.

In the shade within, Silke moved herself tentatively to the bench by the table. She could see, through the half-open door, Matthieu confronted by the three Tehuelche. Only the occasional word reached her, but she hardly needed to be told the argument. I am not an executioner, Matthieu would be protesting. Don't you value her honour? – the Indians would insist.

Poor Matthieu, she thought again: poor Matthieu, striving to do right, ensnared by ever more complexities, and now probably wishing he could hide away again, somewhere yet more remote, some lost Andean valley. The men continued their argument, standing out in a hard white light with the interminable wind swirling little twists of dust about their feet. She saw the Tehuelche adamant, sure of their justice. She saw Matthieu glance her way, saw the anxiety, the sweat of the dilemma on his face, an habitual belief that it was all his own fault, the desire for her approval. She wanted to run out to him calling: *It's nothing to me. Don't do any such thing for my honour!*

Then, the discussion stopped in its tracks; the four outside all turned to look at something – and a moment later there came into view on the river bluff another group of men: four or five, in a trim group with one leading the way. Captain Hase marched briskly at the head of four seamen dressed in dark blue woollen jerseys. Each sailor had a carbine slung over one shoulder; Silke saw with relief that, as yet, the carbines stayed slung.

It was getting worse, it would get far worse yet, she was afraid. She rested her face in her hands a minute, hearing the voices raised outside. She supposed the German captain was demanding his first officer back; she hardly supposed the Indians were agreeing. Lifting her look wearily, she was surprised to realise how military Hase now looked, and his men; they were in uniform, they'd given up pretence. She could see the confrontation, the gesturing, the hands on hip, the defiance all round – and saw Matthieu in the middle, struggling to keep the peace, to calm the Germans, to placate the Tehuelche, to compromise. And it was about her. All this masculine rage was about her.

Silke opened the door wide and stood surveying the squabbling men.

Again, the voices fell away. There came from Hase a sort of punched-out gasp: '*Mein Gott…*'

The sailors tensed as Coromín moved – but he was only walking to his pony, hauling himself stiffly into the wooden saddle.

'We wait for you, Makan,' he called. 'We expect you this evening.' Coromín urged his pony a few paces towards the house. 'Miss Silke, we offer our respects. This shall end as it should.'

He raised a hand towards her, and Silke felt all the weight and weariness of Coromín's pride. With a puzzled glance at Matthieu, and a last shot of contempt at the seamen, the Indians departed. A moment later, Hase too saluted crisply in Silke's direction and was about to approach her when Matthieu put a hand to his arm, speaking quietly. Hase stopped, considered an instant, then ordered his men about, and the five of them marched away along the bluff towards their grounded ship.

Left in the white sunlight stood Matthieu, responsible for everything no doubt, and with Silke Khan watching from his door.

'THE CHARACTER OF THE COAST'

from

SKETCHES OF THE PATAGONIAN SEABOARD

by

Huw Asbury Prothero

The sea and its rainbow ways are the first delight of a mariner's soul, but for the master of a steam packet calling at ports up and down a coast, there is more: the unfolding drama of life. From aboard *Luisa Menendez* I observed every shift in the character of the Patagonian littoral. I visited at harbours large and small; I gathered news, saw the sheep stations, wool depots, meat refrigeration plants all raised up in brash optimism, or subsiding into rust and decay if they failed, as so many have.

For that is a harsh, unforgiving seaboard. From Bahía Blanca to the Strait of Magellan, a voyage of near a thousand nautical miles, there is but a handful of passable anchorages. Sailing within sight of shore, you observe each day an unvarying low bluff, stony and bare, enlivened by nothing more than knots of grey scrub in the streaming dust, or sheep huddling on the skyline, or a shepherd's hut. Landings are tucked away up estuaries, with neither mole nor lighthouse.

Ashore, you see in the pioneer faces only doggedness or drink. A fresh enterprise is established: on your first call delivering supplies and new equipment, they greet you with brave talk, crisp printed handbills advertising services or calling for hands, new offices with a smart frontage (and a shanty behind). But on your return a month later, already there will be scowls, wind damage to buildings and machinery, bad water, disease among sheep and men, and everyone going about with grit-reddened eyes.

In government offices where I had business, maps on the walls recorded the purchase of Patagonian land. The grid of numbered holdings, scantily marked in 1900, filled steadily with names, and was progressively coloured with a pale green wash. In the south, the newcomers were Spanish, German and Scotch, and Welsh of course.

The land purchases advanced upriver, spreading north and south so that Patagonia on the map seemed subject to a creeping green stain. Yet today the grand sheep concerns are anxious. Grazing in Patagonia was never lush; there is twice the nutrition in the grass of little Wales than in all that vast Argentine expanse, where the huge flocks devour everything. Even a modest farm may support 10,000 sheep; there are some, such as the great hacienda at San Gregorio, with 100,000 animals. With each year, the pasture is thinner, the returns less, and the mighty barons of mutton must extend their territory.

Miss Dinah Morris – latterly the keeper of a lodging house at Río Gallegos – at one time rented rooms to shepherds, men who reside in corrugated shacks on far stations, deprived of the power of speech after months without human contact. Here, save for their horses and dogs and several thousand muttons, they live entirely alone. The snow drifts may be four feet deep; the kettles freeze solid overnight. Miss Morris once accommodated three men so desperate for conversation that they had set off for Río Gallegos in the teeth of a four-day blizzard; they arrived at her door having survived by curling up inside disembowelled ponies.

Of the Tehuelche Indians I saw less, since they were never a maritime or fishing race and largely kept away from the coast, preferring the stony seas of the open plain, and their swift ponies, and the hunt. They stayed by the fresh rivers, for salt water was of no use to them; they could not drink it, nor could their animals. A man could not set up his tent of hides, or hold a dance or slaughter a foal for a funeral – not on the waves! So the Tehuelche briefly appeared at the trading stores of coastal settlements, but soon departed. Dr Macanan described them as the gentlest of people. They had no martial skills that ever I heard. In the hunt, in pursuit of young guanaco with its meat like tenderest lamb and its fur as soft as beaver, they were inexorable, but in Indian camps there were very few fights – at least, not until we introduced them to alcoholic beverages.

The gentleness of the tribes showed in their adoration of children. Parents loved their offspring with indulgent kindness, allowing the young great license, seldom chiding or rebuking. This affection vitiated their obsequies, as my friend Dr Macanan described to me at Bahía Sanlúcar. The Tehuelche, he observed, were poorly equipped in those rites and ceremonies by which we channel and control grief. In particular, the death of a child would lay them low, for they had no notion of a benign Creator to whose unknowable purpose the death might be ascribed. Nor could they accept ill-fortune as an explanation; it did not adequately account for the calamity of a child's demise. In such a case, the parents might well slaughter a whole herd of horses and burn all the family possessions in an outpouring of despair. Anything that reminded them of the lost child – any item the infant may have favoured or handled in the family tent – all would be destroyed, all trace expunged, as the parents strove to free themselves from sorrow.

Dr Macanan enjoyed cordial relations with the Tehuelche. Locating his practice at Bahía Sanlúcar, he went often among them, offering assistance in exchange for payment in kind or a modest cash fee. Dr Macanan kept a little surgery where many a bruised and broken native would be repaired. They held him in high esteem – as, on one occasion, I myself witnessed.

I had determined to seek Dr Macanan's advice; several paying passengers on *Luisa Menendez* had, on consecutive voyages, succumbed to intestinal cramps and fevers, and I was concerned that this trouble, if unchecked, would soon result in all human traffic avoiding us entirely. I had taken on a passenger, an American engineer, at Río Gallegos, and he had hardly settled into his cabin and taken a first cup of coffee than he vomited. So I determined to consult the physician of Sanlúcar

With *Luisa Menendez* riding at anchor, and with a bottle of vermouth in my coat pocket as a gift, I walked along the bluff from the main settlement towards Dr Macanan's residence. I soon saw that others had preceded me: there were ponies tied up outside the clinic. Their colourful trappings and wooden saddlery I knew to be Tehuelche. The door was open, and from within I heard groans, urgent whispers, and one calming voice.

I was presented with an horrific spectacle: an Indian lay upon the examination couch, held down by two of his fellows, for agony was making him squirm. Dr Macanan was examining the man's right arm. The limb was snapped above the wrist; a horse had kicked it violently, and the lower portion jutted at right angles, splintered bone bursting through the skin. It was a gruesome wound, but Dr Macanan maintained his calm; his visitors fell to silently admiring the skills of a professional.

Dr Macanan treated all patients with equal compassion. Be they naked savage, lord of some grand *estancia*, roaring boy or pursuing policeman, he did his best for all. He made no distinction, and earned the trust and respect of each, taking payment from those who could, deferring it for those who could not.

His wants were utterly modest, his home as humble as it was neat and presentable. He was, however, a man of common sense and practical ability. I once asked if I could supply him with a barometer, an item of utility in those storm-tormented environs. I offered to purchase one for him at the chandlers in Bahía Blanca. But he declined, indicating to me an arrangement upon a shelf: nothing more than an empty sauce bottle inverted in a marmalade jar, and part-filled with water whose rise and fall gave a barometric reading. This served as well as any brass aneroid.

I questioned him as to the satisfaction he obtained from arduous work in self-imposed isolation – for at Bahía Sanlúcar he had (at first) recourse neither to the play of female fancy nor to energising intellectual discourse, but had to make do with Indians and rough traders. I recalled that, in Punta Arenas, his skill had been widely valued, yet I now found him very far 'out of the limelight'. Surely a man of his ability could make a great name for himself in Buenos Aires; what need this penitential posting? But Dr Macanan merely observed that he was doing what he had been placed upon this Earth to do.

It is a considerable question: whether Patagonia has benefited from European settlement. Energy and ideals abound, but so do drunken desperadoes. We can by no means be proud of the record. But as long as there are such as Dr Macanan to be met with, the great Balance Book may perhaps remain 'in the black'. The world will see what generosity means, and will marvel at what men can do.

Seven

AN ANGEL OF DEATH

Late afternoon, a group of horsemen approached Bahía Sanlúcar along the coastal track from the south. They moved with a professional steadiness; they knew where they were going, and knew that hurry was bad for the horses. They skirted the *salinas* – broad salt pans that littered the plain with their sterile, crackled whiteness – and the ponds of brine which, in some incomprehensible manner, the wildlife found drinkable. They rode their animals down steep ravines and up, their *tropilla* of pack ponies and spare mounts following without demur. They observed distant groups of guanaco but, although the men were well armed, they did not break into pursuit; they had their itinerary and their instructions, and were not the sort to put these aside on a whim.

Several weeks before, they had started out from Punta Arenas, along the narrow foreshore where the wooded slopes crowded down toward the Strait of Magellan, where the red deer nosed through beech and magnolia, and where on the tree bark grew edible fungi that the men picked off in passing. Then they crossed the marshy lands by the Argentine frontier at Bahía Posesíon, just before the Strait opened to the pounding Atlantic. North they went, onto the grass plains of Patagonia, glimpsing the snows of the Andes to the west, riding among thickets of *calafate* heavy with new berries, and freshwater lakes loud with geese.

Next, they had followed the telegraph wires that traversed the wide expanses of grazing towards Río Gallegos. Here was a town of sorts, and a massive refrigeration plant shaking and hissing, freezing up mutton to be freighted to Liverpool and Baltimore. Here were vast corrugated sheds packed with 400-pound bales of wool waiting for a ship, and trains of wagons that brought the bales from the *estancia*s, with wheels twice the height of a mule and hauled by teams of twenty. Here were bars, here were women.

But the group of horsemen had not stopped; they had continued across the shelterless plains, leaving behind even the poor shade that the scrub could provide. Much of central Patagonia was as treeless as the sea, but the grass was still relatively abundant here; sheep in their thousands grazed thousands of acres, though the dust filled their fleeces until the sheep were camouflaged grey-brown. Now the party had divided, ranging over as broad a swathe of country as possible. The travellers had sought shelter at the sprawling *estancia* houses whose timber cladding was bleached and weather-scoured till the grain stood out like old washboards. They'd exchanged news with Argentine, English or German managers, eating in bunkhouses with the shepherds and shearing hands. They were on their best behaviour; such men would normally carry, in a colourful woollen sash at the waist, long knives with silver handles – but these they kept tucked in the saddle gear. They would take a drink with their hosts, but always paid their share. Although the group leader was happy to refill his glass, and although his face might become flushed, this was kept firmly under control. At the end of each evening, the private notebooks came out, the quantities and qualities of everything recorded. For that was their mission.

Together again, moving on, the party skirted the Indian encampments on the plains. From a low hill crest, they had the spectacle of several hundred guanaco and rhea together, pursued, enclosed and slaughtered by a ring of Tehuelche horsemen. The newcomers took telescopes from leather sleeves on their saddles, and a careful note was made of the Indian numbers, and of the interesting scarcity of firearms. An astute observer might note a narrowing in the survey leader's eye, a flare of distaste for anything to do with natives – but that was hardly uncommon.

Then, as they continued north, the grasses gave way to rubble and scoria, and to harsher light, but the four gauchos and their European captain rode on with the same single-mindedness. Lightly equipped, they had no more than essentials, but what they carried was well-chosen and in good order. They gathered just enough meat as they moved: a rhea one day, a puma the next, brought down with smart shooting, minimal expense of ammunition and minimal pursuit. Galloping meant danger: of the hoof going down a rat burrow, or the opening of a ravine whose trees might not rise above the level of the plain, and gave no warning. These men took few such risks; they did not rush about, they did not waste time. They might, however, see a group of armadillos sunning themselves on rocks; on the leader's nod, one man would dismount, walk quietly and make a kill before the prey knew a thing. The armadillo would be cooked by hot stones placed in the stomach cavity.

Day after day, they worked their way north, separating to visit every *estancia*, discreetly recording the arrangements and management of the sheep in each area, noting the quality of the land and asking after vacant or underused tracts for this was early 1915, and not all of Patagonia had yet been bought up or leased; there was still territory uninhabited by anyone who mattered. By the time they had crossed the Río Santa Cruz at fifty degrees, even these toughened men were saddle sore, but were too professional to mention it. On they came, always north, their leader everywhere making notes in the black books stored in watertight wraps for delivery to his employer.

And so they approached the Río Sanlúcar.

Now the scenery was increasingly inhospitable. But here and there, inland, were pockets of surprisingly rich grassland, small fractions of the vastness of Patagonia but substantial enough to spark interest in an investor.

That was the point. When their tour was complete, the team would inform their employer on several matters: what was the nature of the land still available? How could this best be turned into money? Where the land was occupied, was it worth a bid?

*

By late afternoon, as they neared the bay, the wind dropped as it often did at this time. The sky had lost its morning sheen and now had a milky flatness. When even the breeze was lifeless, when the stones in any direction offered no enticement, when the Andes cordillera was not in view, when it was neither hot nor cold, when the wildlife was all elsewhere and the ground beneath you was the colour of nothing much – then it was easy to fall prey to lassitude.

Even these single-minded riders were glad to reach the Río Sanlúcar. The bluffs over the river caught the early evening sun and gleamed warm and golden, with tiny grains of quartz spangling everywhere. The sheltered river, with its pockets of green in the meanders, its flowering bushes, delicate grasses, and blooms in sky blue, yellow and scarlet – the only simple, bright colours in fifty miles – these were a relief after long days out on the stony flats. But what the men saw first was the natural hunting trap, a bend in the river into which one might drive a flock of rheas on the bluff, so that the flightless birds, cornered, launched themselves over the edge with their useless wings outspread, to stagger about half-stunned at the bottom while a man easily killed them. That was what the newcomers noted: the utility of a place.

At the Río Sanlúcar, the track turned inland a mile to where the river was easily forded, and over they went. Then, back toward the sea, riding downstream. Soon they could see the settlement overlooking the bay, and the spit of land that sheltered the estuary from the Atlantic – and, to their considerable surprise, they could see dithering there a small ship, with the surf swirling about its stern, and men on deck.

They were so astonished by this sight that they rode straight past the first house they came to, and hurried on. They saw next the corral behind the settlement, the high thorn fence that surrounded the Dove.

'And what in God's name is that?' one demanded, peering at the pen.

'All in good time,' said their leader. 'We'll find this Turk and set up for the night. Then the questions.'

Half a mile back, however, a person who had been busy in his outhouses as the newcomers trotted past now stared after them. Matthieu Macanan had got no more than a glimpse of the riders, and four of them meant nothing to him at all. But one face gave him such a jolt that he felt faint and had to take a grip on himself. His heart raced; he stepped back into the shadows. There his pride and his courage rallied and he did not collapse but he felt a tightness in his chest, and outrage. He wanted to shout after the horsemen: *Turn around! Get gone!* With a stiff walk, he returned to his house, entered and sat in silence.

Silke – who had been resting on a bench looking over the bay – came in and saw him.

'Matthieu,' she began, 'I have been considering... What is it? Matthieu, what is wrong?'

He did not even look at her. He was sitting bolt upright, as though afraid he might lose his balance.

'Matthieu, speak to me, please.'

He lifted his hands from the table, and murmured:

'That's too much.'

She sat and took his hand.

'What is too much, dearest?'

Matthieu did not reply, but his glance lifted towards the open door.

'Is it those men who came by? Do you know them? Tell me, please: what are they here for?'

'I don't know why they are here,' he breathed.

She sat, putting her hand on his, alarmed by his expression – or rather, the absence of any expression, for shock had punched Matthieu's face to a blank.

'But do you know them?'

'Four of them not at all.'

'But one? Who is he?'

'He is an estate factor,' said Matthieu. 'I met him once on Tierra del Fuego. His name is Lovell.'

*

At the premises of Rahman the Turk, a deal was struck, a camp established, the horses fed. Supplies were needed for a trip upriver, planned to follow after one day's rest break. Immediate stores were replenished: Rahman's simple daughter, her greasy locks thrashing about her face, ran back and forth taking the newcomers' orders, trotting in to her father who dug into his stock, set out provisions, and drew up an account. Two accounts, in fact: one was for goods charged to the expedition's budget; the second was paid out of the men's pockets, and consisted of nothing but tobacco and brandy. Most men in these regions required a stiff drink of an evening, but the newcomers, though they drank deep, never lost control. It was methodical, and measured. They sat by their fire only after the camp was ordered and organised. Once set about their bottle, they stayed seated and calm, and they took turns; each evening one of the four took no brandy, and remained fully alert. This was most professional. Mr Lovell fully appreciated the comforting glow of spirits himself, and considered it useful in prising confidences from others. In bars and bunkhouses across Patagonia, he had shared brandy and bonhomie with dozens of unwitting informants.

With his gauchos seeing to the *tropilla,* and the dinner cooking in Rahman's kitchen, Lovell walked to the waterfront to stare at the ship. He wanted to know everything: what she carried, where she was bound, what she was doing here. 'Repairs', Rahman had said; something to do with a split boiler. Lovell decided that, given the chance, he would use his favoured instrument of interrogation – the brandy bottle – upon the ship's captain or officers. Germans, apparently, or Chilean-Germans.

Half an hour later, the Turk and his daughter came to the fireside with a pot of stew and some coarse, semi-leavened bread that was impenetrable by saw or drill unless soaked in the stew for some minutes. The gauchos were seated on wooden provision boxes. For a minute or so, they ate in greedy silence. Then Lovell took a last piece of bread, wiped his tin plate and set it on the ground, stretching his legs towards the fire to warm the soles of his boots, and saying quietly:

'The ship, Rahman – tell me more.'

Rahman glanced towards the bay (from here, they could not quite see the water below the bluff) and he frowned.

'No good,' he mumbled.

'Ship's no good? Repairs, you say.'

'Other trouble,' Rahman grumbled again. The Turk hadn't taken to the Germans or Chileans or whatever they were. He'd expected to get trade out of them, as he would from any passer-by, but they seemed to have ample provisions, and the captain kept his crew on a tight leash.

'Come on, spill it,' urged Lovell, offering Rahman his own brandy, which the trader declined with a gesture.

'When they came,' said Rahman, 'two were dead.'

He described how two steam-blasted corpses had been buried behind a knoll half a mile along the shore.

'And?' prompted Lovell, hearing in Rahman's tone that there was more.

Lovell was blending his tin mug of brandy with another of coffee, clacking their edges. Watching him, Rahman decided that Lovell's party was a strong card, professionals who would pay well. But professionalism, he thought, was only a veneer; anyone was subject to passion if the trigger was right. Cautiously, watching for reactions, Rahman told the newcomers about Schultz, about Silke Kahn, and about the Indians.

When he also mentioned the doctor with whom Mrs Kahn lived, Lovell frowned.

'Devil of a place for a doctor. What's his name?'

When Rahman told him, Lovell sat back in astonishment quite equal to that when he first spotted *Dafne* on the sandbank.

'He's here, is he?'

His companions were not interested in doctors; they wanted to know about the arrest of Schultz. Their collective blood boiled: a white man, an officer, captive and menaced by savages? Lovell looked from one to another, gauging the mood.

'So,' someone said, 'what might we do about that?'

'We might not be letting it pass,' said Lovell into his fortified coffee. 'Where exactly have they got him?'

'I don't know,' shrugged Rahman. 'But the boy Lipi will know. He's there every day.'

'What about the German crew?' asked one of the gauchos. 'Why don't they fetch him? He's their officer. With us, and them, and good rifles...'

But the trader was shaking his head.

'Why not?' pursued the gaucho.

'Something about the ship,' mumbled Rahman. 'I don't know... They don't let nobody on board.'

'Is that so?'

Under Lovell's stare, Rahman felt uncomfortable. In Lovell's stocky frame, his chubby thighs thrust out towards the fire, his thin, scratchy voice, his narrow eyes and the restless movements of his hands that twizzled a length of leather thong about his fingers – in all this was something unsettling. And Lovell's face: ruddy from drink, or the fire, or some other heat – it made Rahman uneasy.

'Well,' mused Lovell, 'even if they let no one on board, they must come ashore themselves. Unnatural for seamen not to came ashore.'

'Two at a time,' said Rahman. 'He lets two off at a time. There's two on shore just now; their boat's on the beach. I see them walking to the point.'

'Oh? Taking the air, are they? That's sure to give a man a thirst. Nothing like taking the air to put a man in mind of a dram, I'd say.'

He glanced along the foreshore towards the barren point, where the two sailors might even now be strolling. There were two flecks visible in the dusk – were they just guanacos? No, here they came. Lovell could take his time.

'We shall be hospitable,' he breathed into his mug; within an hour, Mr Lovell knew a good deal about the little ship *Chloe* – or *Dafne*, as some unguardedly called her – and her cargo. And Rahman nodded to himself: given the right trigger, men would do anything.

*

Mid-morning the next day, Matthieu Macanan returned to the Tehuelche encampment upriver.

He rode, as ever, on his mule that was the colour of something burned in the bottom of a pan, led on a rope behind Lipi. Matthieu had often wondered if he should be ashamed of his abject riding; in his early days at Sanlúcar he'd seen some smirks (though, so far, no one had joked about Silke taking the lead rein). But Matthieu cared little for what people thought; he only cared that the mule did not throw him or kick him. Something about the very smell of a mule or horse made him tense. Lipi at first did not like to lead Matthieu around the district on a rope; now, however, these two were a feature of the landscape, always moving slowly.

Today there was something odd in Lipi's manner. The boy seemed shifty, as though he knew something but wasn't saying.

They followed the familiar trail along the riverbank. There was one great advantage to being towed: one could think about other things. But today no amount of brooding or fretting helped Matthieu. How was he to prevent the murder of Schultz, that he himself was meant to commit? And how was he to appease and mollify Silke for everything that he, Matthieu, either did or did not do? How could she maintain that fearful calm, after what had happened, and Schultz still near? And what new horror brought Lovell? Would that evil, calculating drunk have any more regard for Tehuelche life than he had had for Fuegian? Matthieu thought of Lovell at Porvenir, mocking him. And he winced, remembering his own failure.

So now Matthieu felt that he must rush to grapple with these troubles immediately, before more appeared. He almost wanted to jerk the lead-rope from Lipi's hand and to thrash the mule into a fast jog – but he must plod along the riverbank at this grimly sedate speed, sore and stiff, imagining all the worst things. He glimpsed below the bluff the bright yellow berries weighing down the *calafate* bushes over the water, and beneath them the gravel that was rich with red cornelian and pretty green chrysoprase, with jasper, sardonyx and obsidian littered about as though someone had been breaking bottles – and he thought sadly how little the pretty stones and berries now helped.

As they neared the Indian encampment, Matthieu noticed that Lipi had become agitated, twisting about in the saddle, looking in all directions as though packs of pumas were near. He noticed other unusual things: a cluster of horses, loose and un-hobbled, with their tack hanging loose but no one minding; a crowd of women outside the perimeter, seemingly without occupation or purpose, craning to peer between two tents back into the camp; no children playing by the river, no children visible at all.

As Matthieu drew close, the women saw him and two came running, waving their arms in confused gestures that might have meant *Stop! Turn back! Flee!* or equally, *Quick, for pity's sake, come this way!* Lipi stopped; Matthieu stopped.

'Don Makan!' screeched the nearest woman. 'They have the children! They have them, they say they will kill...'

So Matthieu knew that it was getting worse.

The story was garbled, was changing, was interrupted by shrieks one moment, then by everyone telling everyone else to be quiet because something was happening, had happened, was about to... *But be quiet!* On the far side of the camp, one tent in particular was the centre of attention. The women glared at it while, nearby, a tight knot of Indian men glowered ferociously. In front of the tent, two men holding rifles faced them: a European, and a gaucho in a cape with a long knife in the sash at his waist. Behind the tent, Macanan glimpsed five horses saddled in Chilean leather, another gaucho holding them, and three more unsaddled. He could not see five men, only three. He did not understand. He did not understand how so few men could keep at bay a crowd of thirty or more furious Indians.

But the whispered distress of the women began to make sense: there were children in the tent, six or seven; there were also men with guns inside. The men with rifles would shoot the children – unless the German officer was handed over.

Oh dear God: Lovell would do it. Lovell would not hesitate. Matthieu realised that Lovell was the grotesque solution to his own dilemma: he, Matthieu Macanan, would no longer have to shoot Schultz who would be either freed or butchered.

But when he thought of the children, Matthieu wanted to rush shouting through the tents to take Lovell by the throat – though Lovell would doubtless club him down. The children! The Indians could not bear the loss of seven children. How had this happened? How had *cristianos* duped seven children into a tent? What smiling wickedness? Somehow it had been done, powered by Lovell's contempt for all things native.

A familiar figure appeared at the tent entrance. Matthieu hurried across the tussocks and the bare dirt, crying:

'Lovell! Lovell, let them go!'

At which the stocky, red-faced man beamed at him.

'Doctor! Good Lord, so it is you, after all these years.'

That raspy little voice, just the same. Matthieu stumbled to a halt. Behind him, the crowd of Indian men shuffled forward. They carried cudgels, they carried long machetes; two carried antique muskets that might have been left behind by Magellan.

'Get back!' Lovell snapped. When the men continued to creep closer, he did not heft his rifle at them, but raised his voice instead, calling:

'Merryweather!'

'Here.'

A face appeared at the entrance: a big man glancing out at his boss while barely taking his eyes from the interior where, Matthieu supposed, half a dozen terrified children shank from him. The man had a rifle in his left hand and a pistol in his right.

'Shoot one,' commanded Lovell.

Merryweather turned inside the tent and fired the pistol once, purely for effect. There came small, terrified cries. Sixty yards away, the women screamed. The knot of Indian men swayed. Again, Lovell called:

'Merryweather...'

But he did not have to say more. The men at the front of the group put out their arms and held their friends: *Stay back! Stay back!*

Lovell smiled genially.

'That's right, just you keep your distance. Wouldn't want any injuries, would we, Doctor? You'll oblige me by not coming too close either. Don't crowd me, if you don't mind.'

'What in God's name are you doing?' Matthieu demanded.

Lovell raised his eyebrows in mock surprise.

'What are we doing? Saving you from a spot of bother is what we're doing. Removing an obligation on you to murder a European gentleman... Here he comes, look.'

Through the crowd, two Indians were pushing a figure in a dark blue jacket that was filthy and torn. Schultz' face was filthy and torn likewise, his hands bound fast behind his back. The Indians gave him a shove; he lurched forward, falling at Lovell's feet.

'Pick yourself up, man,' said Lovell, adding to one of his gauchos, 'Help him.'

The gaucho knelt and untied Schultz, who rose and glared at all the world, even while trying to understand the strange assembly, and these liberators at whose identity he could only guess.

'Good morning to you, Herr Schultz. If you'd like to pass round the back of this tent, you'll find horses saddled. Are you fit to ride? Mount up straight away, please.'

Schultz, rubbing at his wrists, strode through the tents to the horses.

'Good man,' nodded Lovell. 'Merryweather – you ready?'

'Ready.'

'Bring them out.'

Seven small children stumbled from the tent, prodded forward by three men. The children were tied in a string with their hands at their backs, were hauled out into the light by that very large European who held the rope's end and a rifle in one hand, and the big, cold revolver in the other. He flicked the cord to make them move like a batch of little slaves heading for the slave market, utterly terrified, tear-streaked and big eyed.

'Oh, let them go!' cried Matthieu as the children searched for their fathers in the crowd, and whimpered pleas for help.

'In present circumstances, Doctor, that would not be a smart move. Lead on, Merryweather.'

The slaver hauled at the children on their cord. One or two tried to refuse; he jerked their wrists. There were distant sobs and shrieks from the women, while the men cried out in anger, but were restrained by their friends. The children tottered away behind Merryweather.

'Right, let's be off,' said Lovell. 'I want a word with Herr Schultz. Tell your savages to keep their distance, Doctor – a good distance. If they behave themselves, they'll have their bairnies safe and sound. You tell them.'

Lovell moved after Merryweather and the children, with one eye always on the crowd who came after, step for step. Behind the tents, the horses waited, the nine horses. Lovell decided that seven children was one too many; the last on the string was unleashed, and pelted back to its parents. The others, bound in pairs, were bundled onto the three unsaddled horses. A dozen Indians ran for their own mounts.

'No!' cried Matthieu. 'For God's sake don't pursue, don't go near!' They ignored him.

'What are you saying to us?' Coromín snapped bitterly. 'You tell these men to forget their own children? To let them be carried away by your *cristianos*?'

Matthieu stared miserably after the horsemen towing the children: like himself towed by Lipi. The Tehuelche riders now shadowed them at seventy yards distance.

'If you had killed that sailor man as we requested, this trouble would not have come.'

'I didn't ask you to seize him.' Matthieu now saw the Indian women rushing in among the tents.

'No, you said nothing,' retorted Coromín. 'Nothing of use at all.'

He stamped away, shouting at his women who in turn began furious recriminations of the men: it was obviously their fault, they had allowed the raiders near the children, they were contemptibly duped. Coromín called back over his shoulder:

'You look after Miss Silke, Don Makan. See if you can do that.'

*

Matthieu tried to imagine what Lovell intended. He could not expect merely to return First Officer Schultz to the ship, release the children, inform the Tehuelche that the matter was closed, and ride away. Even if no child was harmed, the rage in the encampment was incandescent. Somewhere out on the trail, Lovell would be murdered very soon.

So: what would he do? Lovell was hardly the sort to flee. Was he thinking to sail away with Captain Hase? Why would he want to? The man had come here for some purpose; Matthieu could not imagine Lovell shelving his mission for a boat trip. But Matthieu could hardly forget how Lovell despised natives. Possibly he regarded them with too great a contempt to accommodate them in his planning at all.

Matthieu heard the outraged discussion amongst the Indians:

what they would do, whose throat to cut first… He was not included in the debate, was not asked for an opinion. The Indians closed ranks against him, turning their shoulders, shunning him. He stood in the centre of the village but outside the circle, feeling nothing but cold. The wind was rising. He must go home, to whatever further catastrophe was gathering there also.

He called to Lipi for his mule, and trailed back along the river. He expected to be overtaken by twenty or more Tehuelche horsemen riding to the slaughter, but he was alone with Lipi all the way.

They reached Bahía Sanlúcar after nightfall; lights moved here and there in the settlement, but that was usual. The *cristianos* had their camp behind the Turk's store; he could not see any activity there.

Lipi corralled the mules and scarpered into the gloom. Even Lipi's company might have been desirable for one more moment, for one last word of respect. Matthieu could not imagine what welcome he would get from Silke; she could not know what had happened – and yet, this strange night, she might do.

He went to the front door and almost knocked, though it was his own house. He felt need to give notice of his arrival. He stood a moment more – then put his hand to the latch and went straight in.

Silke was sitting on the bench by the table. In her hand she had a hair brush, and her long, silvery-cobweb hair was down about her shoulders. She was not brushing. The hair glistened in the light of the oil lamp but its sheen was hard, more snakes than angels. The brush lay in her lap, clasped like a cudgel.

'Oh…!' Startled, her eyes dilated in the lamplight. 'Have you heard?' she breathed. 'They have the children in the pen.'

'The pen?'

'The *Taube* pen! They have the children, six children inside the thorn corral, with the *Taube*. They are prisoners. The men threaten to burn them!'

However Matthieu tried to grasp this situation, it always slithered ahead of him and got worse. He began to shake his head…

'Yes, I have seen everything!' she insisted. 'I was at the Turk's when they arrived. They pushed the children into the corral, and there are thugs standing guard on them. The little ones have no coats, no food or water.'

'The men will come,' Matthieu said, 'Coromín and his people.'

'Oh, they are already here,' she cried, throwing the hairbrush onto the table.

'How can they be here?' He was mystified. 'They did not pass me... Can they have ridden straight across the salt lake? Perhaps they can do that. I was plodding along the river.'

He paused, struck by the absurd gentility of his own amble on a string held by Lipi.

'Well,' she rushed on, 'they are here. They have made a camp among the Spanish ruins, and they are in a rage for murder. I think they will kill every *cristiano* in Bahía Sanlúcar, every gaucho and Turk, you and me also.'

'And the ship's crew? They have guns, and their officer is rescued; they will surely side with Lovell.'

'Who is this Lovell?' demanded Silke, and Matthieu felt some tiny gratification that he had information she did not.

'He is leader of the thugs, who must have delivered that man back to his ship.'

'Then you haven't heard?'

He groaned: now what?

'The mutiny!' she shouted at him.

He gazed at her in perfect stupefaction.

'Oh, Lord!' Silke turned on the spot as though trying to pull a runaway horse in tight circles. She spoke with laboured control:

'The German sailors have turned against their captain. Actually I do not know if they are Germans or Chileans; they seem to be both. Your Mr Lovell and the man Schultz have turned the crew and they have seized poor Kapitän Hase who is I think a decent one. Lovell says the ship is stuffed with gold...'

'Gold!' blurted Matthieu, laughing.

'So they believe, and Lovell pretends he will take it to Río Gallegos for safety or some nonsense but of course they will steal everything.'

'And Schultz? Run off with gold also? He doesn't seem the type.'

'What type is that?' she demanded, and he could hardly say: the sort who rape but are too disciplined to steal.

'I do not know what that man is about,' she said, 'but I daresay they will all kill each other. That is what will happen. They will use the poor Indians, and then they will fall out and kill one another, I am sure.'

'What is Lovell demanding?'

'Oh!' she threw up her hands rhetorically, 'nothing much! The Indians are to be their slaves. They are to unload coal from the ship, to help her float. Then they are to bring all their horses to the north beach with ropes and pull her off. Perhaps they are to swim underwater and dig with their hands. But they cannot have their children back until this is done, and if they do not agree, then your Mr Lovell will burn the children alive among the thorns – along with *die Taube, naturlich*.'

Matthieu whispered:

'Lovell is mad -- or there is a great deal of gold.'

'No doubt both,' said Silke airily. 'Lovell is mad and his fellows too – but this is what they are saying must happen tomorrow at dawn. The Indians must unload the ship, and then pull it off. Or the children are burned.'

Matthieu went to the window and opened one shutter, peering through the gloom towards the settlement.

'What can we do?' he whispered.

'I do not suppose that you can do anything,' she replied. 'Maybe you could have done earlier.'

He wondered: Am I to blame? He generally believed that he was. He looked back into Silke's eyes, and saw that she did not really hold him responsible for these grotesque events. But if he did not do something…

'I shall speak with Lovell tonight,' Matthieu said.

He could not imagine why Lovell might listen. Silke looked at him with (he thought) some approval. He wondered: could I have forestalled this? I did not bring Lovell; I did not invite that ship; I did not pack it with gold; I did not urge Schultz to… to… His panicky logic drained into the gravel. He saw that misfortune had been stalking him across Patagonia, and had found him at last.

He should have known by now that flushed expression of hers. Silke sat slowly on the bench, her eyes stunned by her own frailty.

'Matthieu, dearest, have you got… can you, quickly, before this starts…'

He was at her side with the *Heroin,* relieved to have the means of lifting her pain; perhaps her anger could be curtailed likewise.

He thought: now we depend on one another.

*

She slept for an hour. When she woke, somewhat calmer, she insisted on coming with him. He considered the possibility of violence. Against himself? That seemed unlikely; he was no great threat to anyone. Against her? The Indians would not permit that. Against the Tehuelche? Possible, but Lovell needed their labour; harming them would not float the ship. Against the children? That was appallingly possible, though nothing was threatened until the morning. But Lovell was here, and where Lovell was, violence was.

She was coming – and if anyone could calm the Indians, it might be Silke. If anyone could civilise Lovell, it might be her. Before they departed, Matthieu dug in the chest under the window. Kneeling, he made sure that he had his back to Silke. He took from the box a revolver, and tucked it out of sight.

They went in darkness along the river bluff, guided by weak moonlight on the water. The wind coming off the sea was making both of them shiver. She did not hold his arm though she was close, her skirts brushing back and forth against his long coat. To begin with they were silent, listening to the river trickling over its stony bed, hearing the wind and the distant surf, and their own gravelly footfall. There was nothing unusual to be seen as yet, but that was because the cluster of buildings lay between them and the *Taube* pen.

'The Indians are at the Spanish ruins?'

She nodded. He peered in that direction, but could make out nothing. He dreaded the reproaches of the Tehuelche almost more than he dreaded the savagery of Lovell.

They neared the first buildings. To their right, the ship's black bulk crouched on the sand bar. Matthieu listened, and imagined that he caught the waves breaking against the far side of the hull. There were no lights – or was that a glimmer through a skylight? He glimpsed an unfamiliar shape on the foreshore which he decided was a beached rowing boat. Someone had come ashore.

'Where are the Germans?' whispered Silke.

It was one more thing that he wasn't sure of.

'I believe Lovell and his people camped behind Rahman's,' he said.

But when they turned the corner of the Turk's store, the group of tents was deserted and the fire was cold. Matthieu went to Rahman's door and knocked, then knocked hard, but there was no light and no reply. He felt sure that the Turk and his family were there inside; he could sense them.

Two hundred yards away, a fire burned. He saw the gouts of smoke, and silhouettes of men passing in front of the flames, but it was impossible to perceive them clearly. In every way, his information was weak.

'All over there at the pen, maybe.'

Matthieu and Silke gazed towards the confrontation waiting for them: it would be so easy not to go on. No one would know, unless Rahman was watching through a crack in his wooden wall. In the darkness, Silke felt for Matthieu's hand.

He said, 'You should go home.'

'No.'

So they walked forward, stumbling over the stones. As they advanced, the thorns of the Dove's compound were black against the moonlit grey of the distant hills. Curious, that something as permeable and impermanent as a thorn fence should appear blacker than the old rocks.

They came nearer, and saw the firelight playing among the complex surfaces of the entanglement, saw the mobile shadows it made. The colours – even the flame orange – were grey-tinged and dulled. Matthieu and Silke were increasingly chilled; the prospect of fire made their backs feel cold. Matthieu could see now four or five figures standing by the heat. All held rifles and all faced in the same direction, save for one who watched their backs, and who peered into the blackness though he could not have seen more than twenty paces.

Then Matthieu noticed other men: two seated on the ground by the fire, and a third in shadow nearby. These were distinguished by their dress: they did not have the fur capes and ponchos, but long sea coats.

They were drinking from mugs: steaming coffee with plentiful rum against the wind. One wore an officer's peaked cap.

Matthieu pressed Silke's hand.

'He is here. Surely you will go back now? You don't wish to meet him.'

'He's of no interest to me,' she replied. 'If you can come here, so can I.'

They were spotted. One of the men, perched on a stone by the fire, reached up and prodded a rifleman in a poncho. There was a weedy but penetrating shout.

'Aha, the good doctor! Welcome, and Miss Silke too, my Lord!'

The group opened for them, though one man stood his ground: First Officer Schultz treated Silke Kahn to a taunting stare which she returned with complete indifference, walking right past him so that Schultz was left frowning.

Still most of the men faced into the darkness together, holding their rifles in readiness. Matthieu peered that way and glimpsed, some sixty paces off, a shadowy cluster among the tussock grass, waiting, watching, with helpless stubbornness. They were parents on a vigil.

'Delighted to see you, Doctor,' insisted Lovell in that piping voice so devoid of warmth. 'To what do we owe...'

'Where are the children?' said Matthieu.

'Can you not be a tad civil, after I welcome you...'

Silke said: 'Where are the children?'

'Good Lord, they sing in unison.' Lovell laughed aloud, his jovial mockery ringing around the fire. 'You know very well where they are.' Behind him, the thorn fence appeared impenetrable, an unpleasant mass of grey spines.

'I'd like to see them,' said Matthieu, feeling for a mid-way between courtesy and demand.

'Ho, it's an inspection, gents!'

Around the fire, the gauchos and sailors smirked.

'Go on, take a keek,' said Lovell, lifting one podgy little hand off his rifle to wave in the direction of the gateway.

Matthieu, Silke following, passed around the fire. He was acutely aware that, from the gloom, the Indians were watching. One of the gauchos – big Merryweather, on guard – stepped aside with a little nod, allowing them into the enclosure.

They could not at first see any children. In the moonlight, the long wings of the Dove curved out and back on either side, and through the pale fabric stiff with cellulose, the moon gleamed. It filled the hollow wings, revealing the delicate structure like the cartilage of some earthbound and redundant angel.

As their eyes adjusted, they at last saw the children: beneath the aircraft, six small shapes squatted on the ground. They were huddled by one of the wheels as though that might protect them, or as though the Dove might miraculously lift them clear. In the half-light, Matthieu attempted to recognise the tiny faces, but he could not. There came a whimper; one small thing rose and teetered straight into Silke's arms. Another was clawing at Matthieu and quietly keening; he gave the girl an awkward hug. The remaining four were all edging towards Silke, as though to tuck themselves under her plumage. Matthieu heard Silke whispering, but could not tell what. He himself murmured: *It's all right, it's all right.* Which was so grossly untrue.

'We'll bring you food,' he said, as they clung tighter.

He eased himself free; the children subsided onto the cold, stony ground. Looking down at them, Matthieu was terribly aware of the cold; the chill washed straight through the thorn fence and across the enclosure. He took off his heavy woollen coat, and beckoned the children into a huddle, draping it around as many as he could.

Matthieu and Silke came out of the enclosure. Lovell was jollier than ever.

'All well with the bairns?' he chirped. 'Oh, you're without your coat.'

'You have to let them go,' said Matthieu, feeling absurd.

'Must I? Doctor's orders?'

'They'll freeze. They've no food, no water.'

'Och, tough little buggers, these savages. You're best not to think of them as...'

'For pity's sake, Lovell – where's your humanity? These are small children!'

'And there's me thinking they were rodents. Don't push me, Doctor, or my natural generosity might fail me. Certain creatures turn my stomach, and savages turn it inside out.'

Around the fire, the men smirked again, while the wind gusted and pushed the flames flat along the ground.

'Lovell…' Matthieu tried again.

'Be quiet, will you!' The piping voice was capable of glassy hardness. 'The matter will all be settled in the morning. Until then, hold your tongue.'

'I cannot!'

'Oh? Is that a disease, or are you the voice of God now? Michty me, what a lot you think of yourself.'

'I may not remain silent while you mistreat these innocents.'

But the high moral tone did Matthieu no good. Even Silke looked unconvinced, while the gauchos and sailors scoffed.

'You're sounding like a man of the cloth,' laughed Lovell. 'Innocents, my backside. The Good Lord would take one keek at this bunch and spew up. They're disgusting, quite disgusting in their habits. Now, I see Brother Ferenc from time to time, Doctor: we pass in the street. There's a true scholar – though, mind, not every man as studies passes the exams, do they?'

'That's of no relevance,' Matthieu muttered.

'I'd say it is,' retorted Lovell, cuddling his rifle. 'If a man preaches at me from the high ground, I like to know which hillock he's standing on, and how he shinned up there.'

'That has nothing to do with now,' Matthieu said. But Lovell began to skip about, a gleeful frisk in front of the flames.

'Oh, it does, though! Are you a man that I should listen to? Do we know what sort of a man you are, Doctor Macanan, or do we not?'

Silke stepped forward, hissing at him.

'You let those little ones go, or my goodness!'

There came a derisive *Oooh!* from Lovell and the gauchos, and a laugh from Schultz, while the sailors grinned like a pack of mongrels. But only for an instant, for they must constantly check the whereabouts of the parents in the darkness, who would be watching for any opening, and therefore the gauchos fingered their rifles, the sailors by the fire their carbines.

'Don't threaten me, Mrs Kahn. You don't know the half of your

French paramour.'

'I know he is twice the man you are!'

Lovell snickered.

'Is he? And twice the man of Herr Schultz? Or were your researches incomplete in that quarter?'

'Hold your filth!' cried Matthieu. The fire billowed acrid smoke at him, so that his eyes stung and watered just when he wished to appear masterful. Lovell near choked with laughing at his own wit, crying:

'Our Doctor quacks louder than a duck!'

'You spout nonsense,' snapped Silke.

'We did not come to discuss doctoring,' shouted Matthieu. 'We came to tell you that those children…'

'Always the damn bairns. Speak of something else, can't you? I don't care for bairns. If their elders and betters don't do as I ask, I'm going to burn them.'

Matthieu started or made some move – and Lovell raised the rifle one-handed and sighted straight at him.

'Monsieur, you so much as touch that revolver at your belt, and I'll blow your face back to Tierra del Fuego.'

Silke blenched; she'd not seen the revolver. Matthieu leaned towards Lovell, as though to push him back by pressure on the intervening air.

'Lovell, this is not Tierra del Fuego. These Tehuelche are not poor starving animals. There is trade here, there is respect…'

'Leave it be!' cried Lovell, howling with laughter. 'What do you say, Schultz? Did they respect you when they booted you in the privates?'

Schultz smiled pure frost.

Matthieu burst out: 'There is civilization here!'

More laughter blew back at him.

But Lovell had had enough of Matthieu Macanan. He marched forward, poking at Matthieu with his rifle, gesturing him to get out of the way, to leave. When Matthieu attempted to turn the gun aside, Lovell placed it across his chest and pushed. Matthieu stumbled on the stones; he staggered against Silke, then fell at her feet, grazing and twisting his hands, his kneecap striking a pebble even as Silke reached down to him.

'Go away,' jeered Lovell. 'Go away, Monsieur. I don't care for your medicine and I don't care for your hectoring. Run away to your Indian friends, look, they're watching for you in the dark. Run away – you're so very good at that!'

Sprawled there, with his knee bleeding and stinging, Matthieu heard an incongruously gentle voice:

'Come, then, dearest.'

She pulled him to his feet, hauling at his wrist. He felt, as he straightened, all the wounds and hurts inflicted on him, all at once, and they made him very sore. He looked back and saw Lovell mocking, and his gauchos leering, while by the fire the sailors laughed more restrainedly and Schultz watched, biding his time.

'Boo!' jeered Lovell, making as though to stab Matthieu with an imaginary bayonet. Before Matthieu could think of reacting, Silke dragged him away from the firelight and towards the dark, towards the Indians' vigil.

They saw Matthieu coming, but had nothing spare for him. They looked straight past Silke also, and did not take their eyes off those people who held their children. Only when Matthieu was right by them did one of the fathers with the barest gesture signal that he and Silke should follow. Coromín and friends were there, camped in the Spanish ruins, but there was no greeting for Matthieu, only a muted: *Miss Silke.*

'They have been in the compound,' said someone.

This changed matters; at once the Indians clustered about Silke: *Are the children hurt, are they harmed?*

Matthieu hung outside this discussion, cut out of it. The Indians were avoiding him; if they sneaked a glance, it was with disappointment.

There was a stir; he realised that certain men were making preparations, but that others were objecting. He heard arguments, saw how some men stalked about with expressions of resolve. Others were pleading, and Matthieu heard: *We can't risk that! They will be killed!* But resolve was winning: there was a faction who would throw themselves on Lovell and his allies. There was new activity; the men were gathering around something wrapped in sacking or hides, something that made a dull chinking like a heap of coin being poured. He saw an Indian straighten, holding up what appeared to be a shirt that clinked and glinted: it was a coat of chain mail.

There were two, in fact; these were opened out, fingered respectfully, and laced onto men who then picked up the few firearms the Indians had: one pistol, three muskets, colonial detritus perhaps dug up from these Spanish ruins. They were putting on armour; they were going into battle with muskets and chain mail.

Matthieu looked around for the *cacique*.

'Coromín, what are they thinking of?'

The old *cacique* studied Matthieu as an aged puma might look at a troublesome skunk. Then he began to help a young man strap on the mail.

'Coromín,' Matthieu began again.

'Leave us, Makan. We know what to do.'

'You cannot take on the guns,' cried Matthieu. 'Chain mail won't help!'

'Your advice has not been so good recently. Go to your home, please.'

'No, for pity's sake…'

But Coromín snapped:

'Go right now. Miss Silke, go with Makan now. We will not listen to his opinion now.'

'It's not opinion!'

'No, it is our children. We cannot stand aside. You can, when we ask you to go to Buenos Aires, you say no to your friends. But the children are crying, and we shall go to them. Miss Silke, take him home.'

Matthieu peered at Coromín, not knowing where to start to defend himself. Silke placed a hand on his arm, lightly.

'Dearest, come.'

So he was turned aside, with Silke, going from the ruins back to the river and his own house silhouetted against the moon's glow off the sea.

*

'Will you tell me?' she whispered.

'I can tell you, certainly: I shall leave here.'

'No!'

'Before I do more harm.'

She rested on his bed of furs, leaning back against the timbers. One candle burned. She felt the chill; Matthieu had not re-lit the fire. He sat islanded on the bench by the table. He was bolt upright, searching for the last of his dignity, a last shred of self-esteem. He was closely observed by Silke from among the furs.

'Tell me,' she tried again, 'about what happened, long ago.'

'What?' He pretended not to know.

'Matthieu,' she leaned forward, 'many people have tried to make you small and dismayed, but they are ignorant. Tell me everything, and I shall not be dismayed.'

He remained still, colder and colder.

'If you wish,' she added.

She saw that he was struggling to commence. His hands made small, abortive gestures. He peered into the lifeless fireplace.

'I am not,' he said, 'a doctor. Not in the accepted way.'

He stopped. After some long seconds, she prompted:

'Does it matter, this accepted way?'

'People like Lovell make it matter. He uses it as a stick to beat me. He's done so before.'

'You knew him where?'

But Matthieu of a sudden changed tack:

'Shall I tell you what happened to me, when I was a student? You will see what results from foolish offers of help.'

'Tell me what you like,' she answered, 'but it would be nice if you would light the fire also.'

'Forgive me, I wasn't thinking,' he mumbled.

'Dearest, let us at least be warm.'

He knelt at the little fireplace, snapping and striking. On the fur covers, Silke watched and waited. She saw him order his tale in his mind, clearing the mental throat. He needed formality.

'I did study medicine.'

He stopped. Perhaps he could not do this.

'Tell me, dear.'

Matthieu breathed deeply, then blew out through pursed lips as though expelling a pain. She was about to prompt him again, but he held up both hands, begging her patience.

He tried once more.

'My father was a small town pharmacist. For me to become a physician, a man of standing: that would be a great thing. My parents scraped and saved for me to attend Montpelier. I lived on bread, haricots and onions, I wore my eyes out, but I was the best, I was earning respect from our teachers... You must understand how far I fell.

I had a friend, Lucian. He was always funny and charming even when we were hungry and overworked. But Lucian was lazy, and he couldn't charm the professors.

We had to present a discourse on a subject that the professor would give us the night before: a limb amputation, treatment of neurasthenia – anything. There were many of us, so this was spread over three days. Lucian's turn came before mine. He had the evening to prepare, and in the morning would speak from the lectern. He was terrified.

Lucian, I said, calm down: what's the topic? Well, it was syphilis and its treatment with mercury vapour. Lucian had spent most of his year partying. He might have caught syphilis but he'd no notion of mercury vapour treatment; he'd no idea that this was the speciality of Professor Colbert, because he'd missed most of the lectures.

I told him: you've two chances at the exam. But he broke down: no, he had one chance only. Why? Because his girl – her name was Jeanne – she was pregnant. Lucian was decent, and he meant to marry her, but he must qualify now: his family couldn't pay the fees any further. If he failed first time, he and Jeanne were ruined.'

Matthieu prodded the fire, jabbing it angrily, jamming on more fuel. Silke watched the scraps of brush and driftwood catch, saw the flames light the room, and saw Matthieu flushed and defiant.

'I knew all about syphilis. I was rather prurient, and I'd taken a special interest. I could help Lucian, and I was flattered to think it.

So, next morning, Lucian stood before the Faculty of Medicine, and gave a discourse on mercury vapour therapy that was entirely my work. He read fluently enough (I'd been coaching him) but his terror and uncertainty were obvious. There was the usual ripple of applause – then, disaster. It was rare for the professors to interrogate candidates deeply: there were too many of us. But this was Professor Colbert's pet subject. Colbert paced up and down firing questions at Lucian. Not one was simple. I might have answered, but poor Lucian was lost. He mumbled, sweated, stammered – and gave up. Colbert stopped pacing, and glared at him.

"Nothing to say? Have you learned this by rote, like a schoolboy?"

Lucian was in trouble, but we'd no idea what would happen next.

Colbert held out his hand: "Give me your notes."

Lucian froze.

"Your discourse!" barked Colbert. Lucian handed it over. Colbert rapidly turned the sheets.

"Is this your handwriting?"

Lucian went white, while I broke into a sweat, for the handwriting was mine. Colbert said:

"Well? This question at least is not beyond you, surely. Open your satchel. Give me your notebooks."

Lucian came down the steps trembling so much that he stumbled and almost fell on top of the professor. He opened his satchel and offered the whole thing. Colbert gave him a withering look and held out a hand.

"Notebooks."

Lucian took out a bundle of books tied with a leather thong. Colbert scanned the handwriting, glanced again at the discourse, then dropped everything on the floor. He turned to the audience.

"This student's discourse was not his own work. *Ergo,* it is by someone else, and that means one of you."

I felt cold and sick.

"Why?" said Colbert. "Why has one of you written the discourse for him? The answer must be: you have received money. In doing so, you have compromised your own honour, the integrity of this school, the worth of the qualification it bestows, and the safety of the public."

Lucian shrivelled into a pew looking as though he'd vanish in a foul-smelling puff. But Colbert wasn't interested in Lucian. He studied us one by one, like a surgeon hunting a tumour.

"Whoever took that money, I regard in a worse light than I do the candidate. He at least had the excuse of desperation: you have been purely mercenary. So, whose is the handwriting?"

He continued to scrutinise us, lips pursed.

"No confessions? Very well. Gentlemen, if the true author of this piece does not identify himself within one minute, I shall declare the entire examination null and void – for all of you."

This catastrophe took a moment to digest. Not only Lucian's family would be devastated: we'd all have to wait to try again – a full year! With all the fees to be found. It was too much. Lucian could have spoken out, but he was dumbstruck. So I stood up – and this was the end of my medical degree.'

Matthieu fell silent, his hands in his lap, peering into the now busy little fire. Silke gazed at him, and wondered how many years he'd been rehearsing this recital. It was curious: although she believed the story entirely, she felt something not quite true in the tone of it. It was too measured, too well groomed. It was like the tableau of a disaster, made of plaster figures in the shadow of which those actually involved could hide. Now that Matthieu was done, she sensed no release, no throwing open of shutters to admit the day, no loosing of the chains that bound him. She watched him closely, hoping to see those chains fall away. But Matthieu did not move, and she was struck by a horrible idea of failure: that, instead of unshackling him, she had merely made him uncover the locks and re-examine their weight. Matthieu could stare at the past, and re-live it, and recall ever more detail, but could not escape.

So this was critical: if she was to penetrate his reserve, it must be now, but she could not see a way in: he sat there in a defensive shell. She searched him with her eyes, but found no chink. The moment was slipping away. She had been laughably vain about her own powers. Perhaps Matthieu was beyond reach; he'd not responded to her. She wondered, as she watched him hunched before the fire, whether she was mistaken in him. Perhaps, after all, he was closed to her love.

But she'd not believe it; she'd not allow that she was wrong. She thought of him at work: the tender generosity, the impartial sympathy, the tireless care. He *was* tender, he *was* generous, he *had* love – she was sure! If only she kept driving this moment forward, if only she didn't lose touch with him. But she could not see how, and he was drifting from her.

The only thing left was to keep talking.

'You tried,' she said, 'to help your friend, and you were both punished.'

He grimaced.

'Why did I offer that help? I wished to play the benefactor, the superior intelligence, with Lucian's future in my hands. But who paid for my pride? My parents: their son was disgraced, their savings gone for nothing. My father was destroyed. He closed his business.'

'What became of Lucian?'

Matthieu did not respond. She saw a mask of ice descend.

'Or Jehanne?'

He was fighting with something, she could see.

'Matthieu? Tell me what...'

'She died,' he said, suddenly brusque. 'She went to some vile back alley to be rid of the baby.'

Matthieu had grown pale – and Silke thought that the blood would never come back to his face until everything was said. But now he turned his look on her, and he was begging her to stop.

'Lucian left Montpelier,' he whispered.

They stared at the fire, whose heat seemed to be failing though the flames rose ever brighter.

'Where did he go?' she persisted. 'Matthieu, tell me. Did you ever hear from him...'

'He shot himself,' said Matthieu. Gazing straight at Silke, with his head cocked slightly to one side, he said:

'Lucian went to his parents' home. He found a shotgun.'

They sat in helpless silence a moment.

'So much,' Matthieu murmured at last, 'for assisting my friend. There can be a terrible arrogance, don't you think, in our presuming to help.'

She said wearily: 'I'm sorry I pressed you.'

'And yet, you see, I had a talent for medicine. Everyone said so, and it was true. One has to make something of it...'

It hung on him, that albatross, that gift. He shrugged.

'One moves on, finds somewhere else. One tries to compensate for the previous débâcle. I came to Punta Arenas. I set up as a doctor in that fine town.'

'There is a real need, in Patagonia.'

'There is every need in Patagonia. But I specialised in just those diseases which ruined me, to get even with them.'

'Did you perhaps think of changing your name?'

'No: no more dishonesty. My name is my name.' He gave a huffing little laugh. 'Also, perhaps, a part of me courted disaster, as though I should give scandal a chance to catch up with me, like a soldier who can't resist showing himself to the enemy.'

Silke felt glad: this was not quite the same steely recital as before. She wanted to come off the fur bed and wrap herself about him, but instinct told her to be still. Matthieu threw more wood on the fire, which sparked at them.

'You've been,' she said, 'candid with me.' At least, in part; she sensed that this was not over. 'What more?'

Matthieu breathed deeply and exhaled to clear toxins from his lungs. He began to tap one finger on the edge of the bench, as though to bring himself back into the present.

'Coromín asked me to travel to Buenos Aires, to represent the Tehuelche in some grazing dispute; I never heard exactly what, but you saw Margall, the land agent, out to defraud them. I could not go. Coromín is furious with me, but I've changed my mind, I shall go, I was about to tell him.'

'Why did you refuse?'

'Because I'd be recognised. Those people are legion in Buenos Aires, people like Lovell and Margall. They're all out to make fortunes from Patagonian land; if someone like me stands in their way, they'll dig until they find dirt. There's plenty of French there; someone would recognise me. I know it – because two years ago I tried. I went there on *Luisa Menendez*. I wanted... oh, you can imagine! I wanted to see a city again, buy shoes, take a tram, hear violins. I wanted to visit the book dealer myself: what a simple thing. Then I noticed some people eyeing me, as though trying to place me – and I left in a hurry.'

He sighed despondently.

'That's what would happen, I was sure. Someone would have heard the tale from Montpelier, and would make the most of it. They would learn that I am hiding in Sanlúcar. Patagonia is an astonishingly small place. My privacy here is like a china vase in a house by a railway: with each passing train, the vase shakes a little towards the edge of the shelf. Coromín does not understand this.'

'After all that you have done for them?'

'The past never lets you off. It only makes you more vulnerable to the future. The past shows Coromín that I *could* help if I wanted; if I refuse now, it must be because I no longer wish them well. It's the bitterest thing: I had decided, I'm ready to go – but I've not had a chance to tell them.'

Silke saw him trapped; every manoeuvre that he made merely loaded onto him another crime.

'You are torturing yourself,' she said. 'You're kind, and resolute, and skillful – I've seen it. The rest is paper certificates, far-away colleges. That is not the truth about you!'

She came creeping across the bed and reached out to him; he tipped his neck back to meet her touch. She shuffled to the edge, and sat beside him.

'In all this,' she breathed, 'what have you done selfishly? Not a thing.'

She took his hand, studying him with her guileless intelligence, flame-lit and framed by her cloud of floatingly light hair.

'No,' she said, outraged by the injustice, 'not a thing.'

She peered into his eyes and saw that they were narrowed and tense, full of pain that he could not shake off, a profound pain that packed every corner of his skull, a pain that she recognised.

And seeing this, she knew what to do.

'Matthieu, my dearest, may I ask you to prepare another injection?'

He was startled; now he must scramble back into his trade. She seemed so radiant; it was difficult to think of migraines.

'Of course,' he blurted out. 'I had no idea…'

He managed to collect himself, to recall what was needed, to reach for the bottle of *Heroin*, to prepare the brass and crystal syringe. He fumbled, and hoped she'd not notice how his hands shook. He returned with the injection, and nodded to the bed behind her.

'Will you lay down?'

She smiled, and put a hand on his.

'It's for you,' she said.

He looked at her nonplussed.

'I think,' continued Silke, 'that you have never tried this on yourself; believe me, it is remarkable. It gives a calm, a well-being, like slipping the mind into a warm bath. I have felt nothing like it. It gives courage, it gives ease. Doubts fall away, fear and hesitation fall away. I see your poor face so tight, so twisted, so miserable – I am sure this is what you need. Tomorrow you will be able to face anything. *We* shall face it.'

Matthieu peered at the syringe in its small wooden bowl.

'I am sure!' she breathed.

He was too weary to resist.

'I've never had to…'

'You've never injected yourself? I shall do it.'

'You?'

'Why not? I have had training. Let me do this for you, and then you for me!' She took his hand again, stroking it tenderly. 'Lie down.'

Afterwards, they lay together, gazing at each other in astonishment. As the drug took its sweet hold on them both, he gave way entirely as she smoothed his face, her hands cool and superbly light. He felt her caress to be infinitely benign and life-saving, and he recalled how, helpless in a cave, he had lain under such a caress of hands and was saved.

There were, he now understood, moments of unqualified goodness in our lives. He turned to her, kissed her, pulled her towards him while his hands slipped without guilt under her clothes and felt her trembling. She closed her eyes, blissful, and the drug set them free.

*

Later, with Silke Kahn sleeping naked in the furs at his side, he lay listening to the darkness and to the tinkling of the fading fire. Then he heard, from below, a gentle slithering under the floorboards – two such sounds, perhaps even three, that slipped over each other, interspersed with an amused dialogue of hisses. He welcomed it; he would willingly have reached a hand among the vipers to caress them. He was brimming with tenderness.

He thought of the day's events.

Tomorrow, without question, he would stand and speak.

Eight
DAFNE & THE DOVE

But at dawn, as Matthieu Macanan again crossed the stone-littered ground through a buffeting wind towards the *Taube* pen, with a leather bag over his shoulder and a head full of determination, he became aware of commotion by the still-burning fire. Tension he had expected: what else, with six children captive, and the parents beside themselves with rage? He had been prepared to find a battle in progress, or butchery. But things had changed. The German sailors were gone. Lovell was locked in a shouting match with a man who quite ignored the gauchos' firepower, a man hugely excited by the situation inside the thorn pen, and incensed to be told by Lovell to clear off. The newcomer roared, gesticulated, and tried to push his way past the imposing Merryweather and into the enclosure. When he was repulsed, he merely came on again, haranguing the guards in the gateway, waving his arms like a demented semaphorist, stabbing a finger and thrusting his chin at Lovell. The man was lean and wiry, wore a stout woollen jacket, was fair-haired, was awash with outrage, and Matthieu knew him.

It was Theo Kahn.

'Doctor!' shouted Theo, pointing at Lovell. 'Doctor, can you talk some sense into this lunatic, this drunk? There's aviation spirit in the pen, the thorn will burn and there will be an explosion I am sure, and the *Taube,* my God, if any harm comes to the *Taube,* I will tear him limb from limb, what does he think he is doing, is he mad? He is a cretin, he is a…'

Matthieu saw an ugly heaviness in Lovell's face. Lovell had not slept, and had surely been drinking. He looked sullen, dangerously annoyed by this intrusion. Theo Kahn was not some savage that Lovell could cheerfully knock over with a bullet, but a European, educated, perhaps well-connected – in Patagonia, you never knew. Theo might be the scion of a mighty trading house who would drive Lovell from these shores if any harm occurred. But the blood was up in Lovell – the blood, the drink, the bile. He gibbered at Theo, his face purple, his anger on the cusp of tipping into something uncontrolled. Matthieu prayed that, in the stream of mutual insults, Theo would not call Lovell a savage or a primitive; there were some words that Lovell would never tolerate.

But Matthieu misjudged the situation, for Lovell was not in the least interested in Theo, who was nothing more than a nuisance getting between him, the Tehuelche, and *Dafne*. When Lovell saw Matthieu, he forgot about Theo.

'Talk some sense into your damn savages, Monsieur,' he spat at Matthieu. 'Smack their heads together till they hear reason, will you! They appear not to understand a word I'm saying. The thing is simple if they'll listen, but they won't. If they'll do what I say, they can have their verminous brats straight off. Are they half-wits, what is it they don't understand? Tell them!'

But Matthieu could not tell them. The Tehuelche had no reason when it came to their children; they simply must have them back. There could be no deal, but Lovell would never see it; he had no notion of love.

As Lovell spoke, Theo was hopping about with impatience. Matthieu thought again: I must stop him provoking Lovell.

'How are the children?' Matthieu tried. 'Have they had anything to…'

But he only unleashed another tirade from Theo.

'Children should not be in there! What if they clamber onto the *Taube*? She could be hurt, her wings ripped – anything could happen!'

Matthieu shifted the leather bag on his shoulder, and scanned the pale morning horizon, expecting to see a charge of Indian horses over the hillside.

'Where are the Indians? And the Germans?'

'Germans?' blinked Theo. 'What Germans?'

'There are sailors…'

'Oh, the ship! They were here a while back, but someone came with a message and they went scampering off.'

'And *Luisa Menendez*, where is she? When did you arrive…'

'I didn't come by ship.' Theo stamped with irritation. 'Ships are not to be trusted, Macanan! *Luisa Menendez* is stuck at Rivadavia, and God rust the stupid hulk and that idiot Welshman. She hit a rock, her rudder or propeller is jammed or cracked or fallen off, what do I care? We had to be tugged into Rivadavia, and there she sits. I rode overland with some sheep men. They are camping two hours back, but I could not wait. I've got the valve rubber, I've got everything! Give me just ten minutes with the *Taube*, get those children out from under the wheels, my God, and she will fly again – ten minutes!'

Theo paced about in agitation – then stopped and fell silent. He eyed Matthieu as though something had occurred to him, and he came sidling up. They stood side by side, neither looking at anything much, except perhaps the small stones at their feet.

'What is in your bag?' asked Theo.

'Bread and water for the children. I don't believe Lovell has given them anything.'

'I wouldn't know,' murmured Theo. 'How is Silke?'

Matthieu, shivering in the dawn wind, peered sideways at Theo. The man had ridden hard to get to his aircraft at the first possible moment. His wife was an afterthought.

Matthieu said: 'She is quite well.'

He received a smile that was complicit, and shifty.

'It's not that I don't care,' said Theo. 'Don't think that. But there are things that I cannot do, and things that I can.'

Theo glanced back towards the thorn enclosure.

'Please get the children out. Something terrible could happen.'

Lovell was in discussion with his men, eyeing Theo, eyeing the doctor, eyeing the *Taube* pen, eyeing the distance. Matthieu believed he detected hesitation among the gauchos; they frowned at Lovell in distaste, glancing at each other, while their leader prowled up and down growling at them. Matthieu saw the men edging away, and he thought: they're scared of him. They were not scared of him yesterday; they were with him. Now he has got them frightened, and these are not men alarmed merely by poor odds; something about Lovell has them rattled.

Only the huge figure of Merryweather seemed unperturbed, a sea-rock around which others swirled.

Matthieu stood close to Theo, trying to stop shivering and to think. For all this morning's resolve, he had no plan; he would simply demand the children's release. He would demand it louder. He would walk into the thorn pen and release them with his own hands, and probably he would be shot in the process, by Lovell or Merryweather. That was quite clear.

But the situation was so elusive; events slipped and mutated, and he was constantly having to readjust his understanding: who was who, what did they want, why was this happening? He tried to clarify this: Lovell and the Germans all wanted the ship afloat because it carried gold and they intended to sail away. They were trying to force the Indians to help, to unload coal or haul her off the sandbar with horses; this was the point of holding the children hostage. That, at least, had been his understanding – but now he felt less certain. Even the ship's name was debatable; he had heard some men refer to *Dafne*, then correct themselves and say *Chloe*, then shrug, as though the very identity of the boat was in doubt. Sometimes the sailors had been in uniform, at other times not. Who was in authority? Who was allied to whom? Why had the Germans (or Chileans) gone back on board without taking further part in the matter of the hostages? What were the Indians doing, or planning? He was sure they were nearby, on the hillside, creeping up some gully with revenge in their hearts. And the children? Were they still unharmed?

He kicked himself for havering; he had set out from home clear about what must be done. Now, in the strengthening daylight, he should be strong. The children, nothing else…

'Lovell!' He moved towards the knot of men who seemed to be debating amongst themselves. 'Lovell, I have food and water for the children. I must see them.'

Lovell paid Matthieu no attention whatever, but began poking a stubby finger at the face of one of his own gauchos. The man tipped his head back taking his eyes out of range, but otherwise stood his ground. Matthieu thought he heard the gaucho say: 'It's not working, Señor, don't you see?' But Lovell took no notice, and now Matthieu realised what was wrong – what, above all, was appallingly wrong: Lovell did not care. He no longer cared about the gold, or his own plans, or anything as rational as fabulous stolen wealth. What Lovell cared about – what had filled the man with overwhelming rage – was that the Tehuelche should do his bidding. They were nothing but savages, they were weak, contemptible vermin, but they would not do what Lovell demanded, and Lovell could not bear it.

'Lovell,' Matthieu called again, 'I insist that you allow me to see the children.'

Hearing this, the gaucho turned and came towards Matthieu. He was a young man, with bandy legs and weak-looking ankles that wobbled in his battered boots (childhood rickets, thought the doctor). His expression was open, almost friendly, and he was raising a hand to indicate the *Taube* pen, to suggest that Matthieu bring his satchel of bread...

But then the young gaucho lurched and staggered. Matthieu thought: he has stumbled, he has caught his foot on stones. The gaucho teetered two more steps, and fell hard, face down on the stones, without putting his hands out to save himself. At which point, Matthieu realised that he had heard a shot.

Behind him, Lovell held a rifle at hip height, holding it more like a pike than a firearm. His companions were staring in disbelief, backing away in an attempt to get a perspective on something incomprehensible. Nearby, Theo craned forwards at the corpse as though short-sighted.

Matthieu looked again at Lovell, who was watching him. Still he must go to the children. He shifted the satchel further up his shoulder, and walked towards the *Taube* pen.

'Keep away from there, Doctor!' shouted Lovell. 'I warned that fool, and I warn you.'

It was just thirty yards to the entrance. Theo was drawn to follow him, turning into Matthieu's slipstream.

'Doctor, I warn...!'

There was movement: not Lovell, but the enormous Merryweather who put a big restraining paw to Lovell's rifle, turning it aside, saying something to his boss, striding over to Matthieu, reaching for his shoulder with a massive hand that could doubtless dislocate bones with a flick.

Merryweather was propelling Matthieu forward towards the pen.

'Keep walking, Doctor.'

Matthieu expected a bullet to knock him down. But Merryweather shouted back to Lovell:

'All right, Mr Lovell, sir, we'll keep them together, keep them tidy.'

He shoved Matthieu past the smouldering fire and into the entrance. The gaucho on guard stepped aside in deference to Merryweather. There was no shot.

'Quickly, damn you. He's gone mad, and no fault of mine.'

Merryweather pushed Matthieu inside, with Theo scampering after.

Within the enclosure, it was oddly peaceful. The thorn did not stop the wind, but broke its rush, reducing the buffeting to a chilly draught. The *Taube* stood as immobile as ever, lifeless and useless thought Matthieu, who saw that the machine had acquired a thick coating of dust. It could not even adequately shelter the six children, who cowered near one wheel in exactly the position that Matthieu had left them, still under his coat but evermore shrunken, a little heap on the dirt.

He went straight to them, pulling the coat from their faces, searching the dull eyes. Two were asleep. The others gazed at him with no understanding.

Matthieu dropped the satchel off his shoulder. He brought out two canteens of water, some heavy bread, and a pan of cold boiled potatoes, oiled and salted. The children reached out before they had fully registered what these things were. They devoured, and gulped, and a spark of life returned. Matthieu shook the two sleepers awake lest they miss out.

Where – this question was in his head all the time – where on earth were their parents? Where were the Tehuelche? Even the vigil had gone.

He heard a curious hollow drumming: Theo was standing on

the makeshift ladder, patting in a sorrowful way at his Dove's wing, sending up clouds of dust, then caressing the Mercedes motor as if needing to feel 99 horsepower this minute, grieving at its silence, huffing at the grit on valves and crank-casings.

'What are they scheming out there, Doctor?' called Theo, astonished that Lovell had no feeling for air travel. From his ladder, Theo peeped over the top of the thorn enclosure.

'What's Lovell doing?' asked Matthieu.

'He's staring about like a mad thing. He's ignoring that dead fellow. Is he going to leave him lying there? The others don't like it; they are mooching around, keeping their distance. They see it too: Lovell is mad.'

At Matthieu's feet, the children were nibbling cold potato and bread, sipping at the water. Some appeared to have little strength even for that, and gazed into mid-air. He wanted to comfort them, but was dismayed to discover how remote the children now seemed. He knew all of them; he had treated their little sicknesses, but in this distress they had retreated into a private world, a Tehuelche world where he could not speak with them. How easily they had submitted, how cowed they were, how little they had attempted. He thought: surely even little ones like this could have found a way out from some dark corner, under the heaped thorn; it was hardly formidable, with no one to watch them. But the children had scarcely moved. One of them, a pinched grey face that might have been boy or girl, looked up at him and began a thin wailing so insubstantial one might have taken it for wind through telegraph wires.

There was something standing on the dirt near the thorn entrance-way. It was a tin – no, two tins, of lamp oil. Matthieu felt sure the *Taube* could not run on lamp oil, so they must be Lovell's. Lovell was very mad. It did not bear thinking of.

'Doctor,' called Theo, 'someone is coming.'

Matthieu hurried to the entrance from where he could glimpse Lovell through a corner of the thorn, but believed Lovell could not see him.

There was a cluster of men approaching from the settlement half a mile distant. They were on foot, sometimes breaking into a jog over the rough ground: Matthieu recognised a mix of Indians and Germans. As they drew near, they began waving and calling, but what they called was caught by the wind and thrown out to sea.

Lovell shouted, 'Ricardo, see what the hell they want.'

One of the gauchos began to walk that way.

'Run!' shrilled Lovell.

The man Ricardo called something over his shoulder – at which Lovell lifted his rifle and fired one shot that smacked into a boulder at Ricardo's side. The gaucho twirled about in panic, yelled some appeasement, then sprinted towards the newcomers who waved and gestured in the direction of the settlement and the bay.

Matthieu glanced at Theo on his ladder, then at the children. Some were on their feet, chewing at their fingers, peeking at Theo and edging towards him, as though – high as he was – he offered protection.

Matthieu heard shouts, the oncoming sailors and Tehuelche all shouting together:

'...floating...! Off the sand! Afloat!'

Matthieu cried to Theo:

'The ship is off! A high tide, or the engines repaired, maybe. She's off! This is all over.'

'But why?' bleated Theo, who could not comprehend a ship mattering at all. 'Why such excitement, I don't...'

'Because,' cried Matthieu, 'all this was about getting that ship off the sand. If she's afloat, there's no reason for Lovell...'

But nothing was over; reason carried no weight here. Neither ship nor cargo fired Lovell's soul. The newcomers were close, and Matthieu saw that the sailors were just two, while around them the ecstatic Tehuelche agreed that the business was over...

'Get back!' screeched Lovell, puce with outrage. 'Merryweather, stop them right there. Get back!'

Lovell strode towards the enclosure, brandishing his rifle like a stave. Then he fired a shot over their heads.

The group stopped fifty yards off, islanded on the sea of stones. The sailors, Bagan and Sahler, could not decide what to do, nor understand why they were being shot at. They'd brought news...

'Herr Lovell,' shouted Bagan, 'there's no need now.'

'What do you know, you half-Dago-Hun. Button your lip!'

Astonished, Bagan dithered among the pebbles. Sahler attempted to speak with more military bearing, stepping forward.

'First Officer Schultz has instructed us to tell you, he thanks you but he does not need your assis...'

To confirm this, there came a startling steam-blasted hooting: *Dafne* was celebrating her release from captivity.

'Tell Schultz to go hang,' shouted Lovell. 'Tell Schultz he's a scoundrel. Don't you come near me, you damn vermin!'

He fired again, cracking a stone by an Indian who had started forward. The man halted; his friends muttered caution.

'Lovell!'

The firm call confused Matthieu until he realised that it had come from himself. He was close to Lovell, moving forward; the moment must be seized.

'Lovell, it's all different now; you've no call to keep the children now. That's all over. You go with the ship, and let me take the chi...'

But Lovell lifted his gun again. He swung the rifle with one hand, and the butt caught Matthieu on the side of the face with a smack that sang through his skull and sent him reeling to the ground, grazing the palms of his hands, tearing his knee open on stones. He crouched, stunned, his left ear and temple bleeding profusely down his cheek.

Lovell called, 'Merryweather, bring one of the children out here.'

'What are you proposing, Mr Lovell?' The deep dark voice of the mountainous Merryweather.

'Merryweather,' retorted Lovell, as though to a fool, 'bring *two* of the children here.'

Blinking up through his bloodied hands, Matthieu saw a moment of hesitation in Merryweather – who nonetheless passed into the enclosure.

'You stand right where you are!' Lovell squawked at the Tehuelche and the two Germans. 'You try anything, and you'll see what happens. Merryweather!'

Merryweather returned. He led by the hand a small child, a boy of no more than seven or eight, and a girl the same. They were shivering, and their noses ran with terror. Merryweather was about to speak...

'Give me that,' snapped Lovell, and he seized the girl's forearm, jerking her round in front of him. Matthieu saw the Indian men flinch. One was about to rush forward, to seize her back or be shot trying – but still was restrained by his companions.

'Lovell!'

Matthieu, his voice thick, his head pounding, had organised his legs and cranked himself to his knees.

'Lovell, that is enough, I'll not let you do...'

'You still here, Doctor?' jeered Lovell. 'You here for the savages again? I don't like savages at all, and I don't like people who like savages. Don't get between me and savages. I know what there is to be done, you see? I know what's to be done.'

Lovell turned to the German sailors.

'Where's Schultz? You!' Lovell gestured at Sahler. 'Come here. I've a message for your Herr Schultz. Now come here so I can give it you.'

Sahler hesitated, then walked forward. His fair hair was tugged to and fro by the wind and, as he came, a silly grin spread across his face.

'What do I tell Herr Schultz?' said Sahler, drawing near.

'You don't tell him a damn thing,' replied Lovell, pointing at Bagan. 'He does.'

'So why...?' began Sahler.

'You're staying here,' said Lovell – and, lowering the rifle slightly, he shot Sahler in the knee.

The German dropped, shrieking, grabbing at his leg.

'Shut up,' commanded Lovell, 'shut your bloody mouth or I'll give the other leg the same, you hear? You there!'

Terrified and alone, Bagan was trembling.

'Yes, you!' shouted Lovell. 'Tell your Herr Schultz that he can have this one back in exchange for two bags of his cargo. I'm a modest man; one bag of gold will do me fine. He's to bring just enough, you understand? A bag for me and a bag for my colleagues. Just enough will do but not enough's no good. Then he can sail away on his precious damn ship. Where is he just now? Speak up, man: where is Schultz right now?'

'He's taking provisions,' Bagan replied, piping with fear, 'from the Turk.'

'I hope he's not paying that nasty little olive pip. You run along and tell him: his man's right here and bleeding. And if Schultz isn't quick about it, I'm going to start shooting the children, you understand? That'll be his fault too. I might start anyway, to hurry you along, so you can share the odium.'

'No,' grimaced Matthieu with what was left of his willpower, his voice gurgling with the blood swilling down his cheek. He was trying to look at Lovell. The left side of Matthieu's face was gashed and swelling so rapidly that the eye had all but disappeared, while the right side was smeared with a gritty paste of blood and sweat. Matthieu saw, through this crimson mud, the figure of Lovell with the little girl's arm clamped in his hand. He saw also that the muzzle of Lovell's rifle was against the base of the child's skull.

Giddy and sick, Matthieu nonetheless attempted to stand.

'I won't let you,' he intended to say, though this came out as a bubble and a cough. He staggered forward, holding out a hand towards the girl.

'Don't waste my time,' spat Lovell – and he swung his heavy boot in an arc, knocking Matthieu's legs from under him.

'Goodness me, Macanan, you're a pitiful sight. It's time you went home. Merryweather, put Doctor Charlatan on Luna's horse.'

So Merryweather reached down and with one powerful hand hoiked Matthieu to his feet, dragging him thirty yards to where the horses stood in a cluster, saddled and ready, not far from the dead gaucho Luna. As though placing a small parcel on a table, Merryweather deposited Matthieu onto a red-roan pony.

The animal shifted and stomped under him; Matthieu groped for reins, for ears – for anything he might cling to. Panicking and near-blind, he swayed forward thinking to lean along the neck. But there was no neck. He felt about in confusion: he found ropes and saddle-bags, he found leather straps he could not understand, and a set of stone *bolas,* and finally believed that he had taken a handful of the horse's mane. But this mane was attached incorrectly. At last he understood why: it was the tail. He was facing backwards.

Matthieu heard a squawk from Lovell – *Very good! That's very good!* – followed by a nervous puff of laughter from the others.

'He's frightened of horses!' he heard Theo object. 'Doctor Matthieu does not ride, he is very scared.'

'Oh, then bravo! Giddy-up, Doctor, giddy-up!'

Lovell's laugh sounded quite deranged. Matthieu heard him call:

'Where's that other brat? You, boy, lead the doctor home. You can keep Luna's horse, Doctor, you look fine on it, ha ha! Lead on!'

But the boy was frozen in fright, and would not move. The fretful horse, freed of its hobble by Merryweather, started to drift.

'Boy!' yelled Lovell, incensed by anyone not doing as he ordered. 'Lead the damn animal!'

The horse shuffled and stamped and stared.

'Damn you all!' squealed Lovell. 'Who do I have to shoot to get things done? You see this girl? You see her?'

He was hauling viciously at the child in his grip; she cried out in pain and her father prepared to rush.

'Don't you bloody dare!' screamed Lovell, jabbing the rifle into the girl's neck. 'You stand steady, you damn primitive, or I'll blow her head off, you hear? I expect I'll blow it off anyway, but my God, don't push me so bloody fast. Who's that bloody whining? You, Sahler, stop your noise. Your pal's half way to Schultz, and when he's back with some gold, we all go home. You can be patched up by Dr Charlatan if you like, ha ha! Where in hell is everyone?'

Lovell was rotating on the spot, pulling the helpless Indian child around after him, while Merryweather and his remaining gauchos gazed at them. The red-roan pony ambled uncertainly towards Lovell, while, swaying backwards in the saddle, Matthieu fumbled with the knotted cords. He was trying to untie something, hardly a clever way to keep himself upright on a horse.

'Ha ha! Hang on there, Doctor, hang on while I blow this scrap of vermin to kingdom come. Turn your steed about and ride home, Doctor!'

But Matthieu did not turn the horse about, and did not go home. His pony came on right past Lovell, albeit with Matthieu riding in reverse. He straightened in the saddle, and he had something in his hand; Lovell did perhaps register three stone *bolas* in their hide casings, and the plaited hide ropes in Matthieu's fist. Lovell had time to appreciate that Matthieu was now upright, and had lifted the *bolas* behind his left shoulder. Lovell saw the heaving effort from Matthieu that brought the three balls in a high swing over the horse's rump. Lovell glimpsed, for half a second, Matthieu's one clear eye that swivelled and stared at him out of that bloodied face.

'Blast you...' Lovell began, as he noted a leather-wrapped stone hurtling towards his own forehead.

But that was the last Lovell ever said, or ever saw.

*

When the Tehuelche witnessed the fall of Lovell, they rushed his remaining companions. One attempted to fight, and lost. Ricardo made a run for his horse, but collided with Coromín. Bewildered, he staggered and stood looking round; as the savages hurtled towards him, Ricardo merely shrugged and smiled at them, as though hoping to escape notice or to dissociate himself from what had happened – but they killed him anyway.

Merryweather was surrounded. He turned this way and that, eyeing the five or six men circling him. They had long knives only, while he had a rifle in his hands, but he did not shoot. He frowned defiance as in all honour he must, but they sensed his failing will. They moved closer, some fingering their machetes and shuffling, some affecting a low spring – but in the event Merryweather merely lowered the rifle and let them come.

'Wait!' Matthieu shouted, 'he tried to help...'

It was too late. When at last Matthieu was able to approach, Merryweather lay on his side, coughing. Blinking through his own pain and swollen face, Matthieu tried to see where Merryweather had been cut, but Merryweather was not helping. He was punctured all over. He gave Matthieu a long stare, as though the doctor's future was more interesting than his own, then lay his head down.

Now the Indians became simple family men gathering up their children who had emerged from the thorn enclosure, burst into floods and teetered to their fathers and mothers who came running. The sailor Bagan still stood fifty paces apart, staring at his colleague

Sahler sprawled on the ground and clutching at his knee, but they were ignored. The Tehuelche gathered up Matthieu. They patted him, gripped his hand, growled manly praise, and were about to lift him onto yet another pony and send him home – with an Indian taking the lead rein – when there was a further arrival.

Silke Kahn saw the figures strewn on the dirt near the *Taube* enclosure, put her hand to her mouth and ran forward. She went straight to Matthieu and embraced him, crooning over his wounds.

He was awkward.

'Silke, my dear…'

She was about to shush him, when she glanced across his shoulder and saw her husband. Theo Kahn stood with his scant weight on one skinny leg and his hands clasped in front of him, as though waiting to be introduced.

'How,' she whispered, 'did he come here?'

She released Matthieu, and studied Theo. She walked towards him, stopping where they could both examine the ground at their feet.

'Good morning, Theo.' She was hardly audible because the wind was rising. Out at sea, there was a liverish light and a sickly white flicker on the water.

Theo gestured with his head to the enclosure.

'I've brought the membrane for the fuel valve. Ten minutes, and she can be flying.'

Silke Kahn regarded him.

'Is that all you have to say to me, Theo?'

He half-opened his mouth, either to laugh or protest, while still looking in any other direction. The wind pulled at his hair and his words.

'There are many things,' he declared, 'but this is what I can say.'

And he looked towards his aircraft once more.

'I shall take the doctor home,' she said. 'He needs some care. You may visit us later.'

She returned to Matthieu who had averted his one good eye. His knee had bled profusely, but he could walk.

'We can manage,' Silke said to the Tehuelche who proposed to accompany them. 'Thank you.'

They set off walking the half-mile to the clinic on the river bluff, Silke steering and supporting Matthieu. When she glanced back, she saw Theo standing just where she'd left him, watching her. He was also paying some attention to an Indian who spoke with great animation, indicating Silke, indicating also the German sailors, telling him something that stirred him at last.

*

Theo Kahn came to them soon after, at the house. Matthieu was seated at the table, and Silke was bathing his face with a wash of permanganate that made him wince and stained his cheek and temple a ridiculous purple. Theo flung open the door without knocking. He was very agitated.

'They told me what happened with that damned Prussian!'

'Please calm yourself,' said Silke. 'What happened, and to whom?'

'To you!' bawled Theo, 'to you, and I believe here, right here...'

He surveyed Matthieu's home as though for evidence.

'Very little happened to me,' said Silke, 'and what happened is my concern only. Do not trouble yourself.'

'You are my wife,' continued Theo, still loud but with less conviction, like a student.

'Oh, yes?' She did not look at Theo as she dabbed Matthieu's wounds.

Theo was incredulous.

'Do you make light of it?'

'Make light of what, Theo? Our marriage, or what happened?' Silke stopped wiping and dabbing, and returned his gaze. 'Of neither – but the significance of both is past.'

They faced each other. He began to mouth fragments of phrases, as though to test them on this bizarre situation; he seemed to find none adequate. Silke did not move, but Matthieu slowly turned his swollen face to regard Theo, stranded in the doorway with the cold skies of Patagonia behind him. Slowly, Matthieu stood and the two men confronted each other, though the one could hardly see or move for pain, and the other was jigging about in humiliation. There was almost as much grit and grime on Theo's face as there was on Matthieu's, and the Austrian's fair hair was so full of it that a comb would bring out a small landslip. Matthieu was about to speak...

Silke forestalled them.

'Be quiet, both of you.'

She spoke to them as though to schoolboys.

'It is for me to decide what outrage has or has not been committed against me. You will both kindly mind your own business.'

There was a deflated silence.

'Then,' breathed Theo at last, 'that is your choice.'

'That is my choice,' she returned.

'But I cannot accept that!' he howled. He turned, stepped outside and strode from their view.

*

Matthieu sat with Silke on the bench in front of his house, overlooking the bay. Under the shelter of a broad-brimmed hat, his face was washed and bandaged; the bandage circled his skull, sweeping above his left eye and covering a gash to the orbital bone of the right eye, ear and temple. The day was chill; they had shrouded themselves in furs, while the bench was sheltered from the wind by a wattle screen. The sun sprang from cloud to cloud like a child jumping rocks in a mountain torrent. From time to time, a shiver ran through Matthieu, but he had no desire to move; the cold soothed his aching face, and he wanted to witness the last scene: to see *Dafne* and her crew depart. Beyond the estuary's protective promontory, out at sea the spume twirled over the water; the wind was winding itself up into yet another gale, though it had not struck Bahía Sanlúcar as yet. The vessel now at anchor beyond the bar was riding a significant swell.

There was an urgency about her. Somewhere on board, Matthieu supposed, was the decent Captain Hase – but whether locked up or now freed he had no idea. Her funnel steamed and smoked with impatience. At the stern, three seamen waited with a scrambling net and davits, waving encouragement to the rowing boat that was setting out from the foaming gravel in front of the settlement. In the skiff, two sailors rowed while First Officer Schultz stood in the stern, hand on the tiller, staring seaward commandingly. The skiff bobbed and bashed its way out from the beach.

'I wonder,' said Silke Kahn, taking Matthieu's hand, 'that you never mind, seeing vessels come and go. Do you not wish to sail with them? Do you never wish for great ports and society?'

He did not reply at once. Did *she* want ports and society? Without them, might she despair or tire of him? He stared out at the rowing boat, now almost half-way to the steamer and with Schultz imperious in the stern, urging on his oarsmen.

'I've no need of society,' he said, 'intruding with all its obscenities.' He pressed her hand.

She was staring at the little boat that bumped its way through the swell, and at the tall man who stood in the stern not looking back.

Matthieu said:

'There is, of course, *Luisa Menendez* passing regularly. One need not remain in Bahía Sanlúcar all year round.' He was being as careful as he could. 'You need not feel trapped. You could come and go.'

She squeezed his hand, laughing.

'You forget: I am from Carlsfelden. How could I feel trapped here?'

'But how,' he began, 'shall you resolve...'

It was so complex.

'My marriage? Does it need to be resolved? Theo and I may remain as colleagues. I am part of his vision.'

But she was not certain, Matthieu could tell.

'My husband and his vision!'

She laughed again, and raised her almost invisibly pale eyebrows in irony. The sun darted out to light them both.

'Anyway...'

Matthieu held up his hand.

'Listen.'

There was a new sound: a note that came and went on the wind, harsh then smooth then harsh again: the snarling note of a 99 hp Mercedes engine, the best in the world.

Silke Kahn stood up as though electrically jolted; the fur cloak fell from her and lay ignored. She was staring in the direction of the settlement, and the thorn enclosure...

'Look!'

A scrap of white – as slight as waste paper on a breeze – fluttered up from behind the settlement. The wind found it, and tossed it into the sky where it wobbled on the gusts so wildly that Silke gasped and Matthieu, who understood nothing of this, thought that the *Taube* had been torn apart. But it was sailing above Bahía Sanlúcar in a broad sweep, out to sea and back over the bone dry pampas as it climbed.

'What is he doing?' she demanded.

Matthieu thought: Theo is displaying to us, showing us his splendour.

The aircraft swung towards them, the note of the Mercedes growing, the pilot sometimes visible as a black dot above the white of the fuselage. As the machine straightened, the shape of the extraordinary wings was exhibited: the lovely bird-like swept-back tips, the long fan tail. Then it came overhead. The sun was still cloud-skipping, but it burst out just as the Dove turned seaward directly over them. Momentarily there was full sunlight pouring into the plane which seemed to fill with pale fire. Light flooded the tightly stretched cellulosed fabric; the Dove was incandescent in a flare of white. It became translucent, and for an instant the aircraft melted into the sky.

But a cloud hid the sun; the aircraft reverted to silhouette. It was heading out towards *Dafne* where the handful of crew could be seen on the stern waving and shouting encouragement to the rowing boat.

Matthieu and Silke understood what Theo was doing. They could see how he was tipping the Dove into a plunge, a *paloma sagrada* falling upon Schultz. In the skiff, Schultz looked up and saw the aircraft coming straight at him. He would hardly credit this; he perhaps thought it a joke, a fly-past, a skimming and buzzing – what else could it be? Not even an Austrian could hate a German that much. But the plane did not pull up, did not level off; Theo had pushed it into a dive directly at the little boat. Schultz yelled at his oarsmen who pulled frantically but no rowing could take them clear. There was a shot, then another: someone on *Dafne* had a rifle, and fired repeatedly, but it made no difference; the Dove was committed to its plunge, pulled unstoppably down by the power and weight of the Mercedes.

Dafne's funnel belched fumes, offering concealment; the scrambling net and davits offered sanctuary. Matthieu saw one of the oarsmen leap clear of the skiff and start to swim through the swell towards *Dafne.* The second sailor grabbed both oars and tried to continue, but it was too much for him. Schultz seized one from him, and Matthieu thought he would row – but he did not sit. In the last second, Schultz brandished the oar over his head at the plunging aircraft, to swat it away.

The Dove struck.

In the last instant of its fall it seemed to slow, to hesitate. There was a plunge, a smacking impact, but the tail of the Dove still stuck into the air above the water, and only slowly did it topple and flop onto the sea, upside down. Of the skiff, there was nothing. There had been no sound of impact, only the cease of the Mercedes' note. The water was spread with white wreckage – until the heavy motor dropped to the seabed, dragging everything under, as though gathered through a funnel and vanishing.

Epilogue taken from

SKETCHES OF THE PATAGONIAN SEABOARD
by
Huw Asbury Prothero

It was all over long before I arrived. I'd been delayed a fortnight at
Comodoro Rivadavia, mortified by the damage to my propeller and
shaft. Our passenger Kahn, the impetuous Austrian aviator, had left
us with bad grace and derogatory remarks about steam navigation. He
had chummed up with a pack of gauchos, and had ridden south to
Bahía Sanlúcar and his death.

All was quiet when I at last brought *Luisa Menendez* inshore and
dropped anchor. We found Lovell and his associates dead and buried
in stony ground – it was all stony ground there – half a mile up the
coast, where two German sailors had been buried beforehand. I'd
met Lovell often enough in my days with the Tierra del Fuego packet,
and had sometimes given him passage. He was usually civil, though
seldom without a bottle; he could become ugly when the wine told
him so. But there were rumours even then; few at Punta Arenas or
along the Strait of Magellan had much good to say about the Fuegian
natives, but fewer still were comfortable with open talk of massacre.
On the whole, the likes of Lovell were kept at arm's length, even by
fellow Caledonians.

Anyway, he was now in a shallow grave heaped with rocks, among
the tussock grasses and guanaco bones.

Theo Kahn's grave was a watery one; his body was not found,
but wooden spars, fabric, and other splintered remnants from his

aircraft washed ashore – though not, of course, the motor. The thorn enclosure he'd built soon fell apart. It was all dragged into a heap and set ablaze by the local tribes who were not good with death and suffering, and always destroyed the memory as soon as possible. This seems curious in people who lived a harsh and perilous life, but they were sensitive.

What of *Dafne*? The end of that little ship is not certain. Her captain, the worthy Gunther Hase, was restored to his command immediately after the destruction of First Officer Schultz; I daresay the few hands remaining on board decided that their one chance of survival lay in the hands of a competent master. But now Hase, by reputation such a sensible and shrewd fellow, took a decision that perhaps cost all their lives: he set sail. With his people reduced to five, with a ship that had received only the hastiest of repairs to her damaged engines, Hase weighed anchor and sallied out into the teeth of a ferocious storm that was building before everyone's eyes. What was he thinking of: Kaiser Bill's gold? His country's need for howitzers? Duty and honour? No one has ever had the opportunity to ask him, for *Dafne* has never been seen since – unless, of course, you give credence to tales of a tramp steamer with an unusual turn of speed reported now in the Azores, now at Kowloon, now at Batavia, and under differing names: *Aureus,* or *Chrysos,* or sometimes *Dorado.* But I don't buy it.

And Dr Macanan and Mrs Kahn: what of them? When I finally reached Bahía Sanlúcar, two weeks after the fracas, Dr Macanan extended his usual courtesy and hospitality, with a dinner cooked by Mrs Kahn. I offered to take them off then and there, south to Punta Arenas or – on my return run – north to Bahía Blanca and the connection to Buenos Aires. I believed them to have been much disturbed by events. But they declined, saying that they were determined to continue serving the interests of the Tehuelche community. I saw nothing of any natives at the time; they seemed to be keeping clear of the Bahía Sanlúcar settlement, and I wondered if there was perhaps a cooling of relations. However, not long after, I was asked by Dr Macanan for a passage both for himself and for Coromín, the *cacique* or native chief of that district. They were travelling together to Buenos

Aires to make representations regarding Indian lands. I do not know what came of their efforts; I suspect not much, since the last of the Tehuelche are now gone from the vicinity of Bahía Sanlúcar.

I saw Dr Macanan and Mrs Kahn often enough, in the course of my regular calls in *Luisa Menendez*. On one such, Dr Macanan contrived yet again to surprise me: he requested me, in my capacity as ship's Master, to marry them. I think it likely that my own example in wedding Miss Dinah Morris (at that time a landlady in Comodoro Rivadavia) may have persuaded the doctor to regularise his position. Dr Macanan had taken a keen interest in my wife's business career, and had urged me to persuade Dinah to retire, citing the risks to her health.

I soon noticed a gentler aspect to the Macanans' own domestic arrangements, with small but significant concessions to comfort. Meals had less of the gaucho about them (less of the stewed nettles, less of that curd cheese found in the young guanaco's stomach) and rather more of the Austrian: she once produced for me a Linzer torte – a considerable triumph in Bahía Sanlúcar! At Madame Macanan's request, I was able to deliver such items as a dinner service, a set of crystal, a mantle clock and some Vienna chintz for curtains. I continued to keep the Doctor supplied with medical necessaries, although some of his requests became more difficult to furnish. There was in particular a painkilling injection that he ordered in large quantities, but the Argentine authorities had forbidden its import, so that I was obliged to obtain Dr Macanan's requirements from private addresses in Bahía Blanca that he provided.

He and Madame Macanan did not enjoy good health; I noticed the decline in both. The rigours of the environment and their chosen way of life had begun to tell, and on subsequent visits I was saddened to see them grown thin and lethargic, with poor complexions and an increasingly nervous disposition. They seemed, nonetheless, a very devoted couple, uncommonly happy in each other. I would encounter them walking hand in hand along the bluff near their home. There was one great joy in their lives, which was the birth of a baby daughter whom they charmingly named Luisa.

Madame Macanan died in 1919 of a fever, while her husband perished in an unaccompanied riding accident only weeks later. Both were buried at Bahía Sanlúcar. When the news reached Punta Arenas, a missionary of that town – Brother Ferenc Zsolt – asked if he could accompany me to Sanlúcar; together we went through Dr Macanan's papers, and in the course of this there came to light a collection of verses translated by the Doctor from their primitive originals, which has since been issued. The Sanlúcar house was briefly occupied by an agent named Margall employed in the acquisition of pampas land. But Margall was found dead on the floor of the house one day; he had been bitten by a poisonous snake, a lancehead viper that had gained entry. Thereafter, the surgery was abandoned and fell into disrepair. Little Luisa was for a short while lodged with a trader called Rahman, until at last my wife Dinah urged me to bring the child in under our wing – so I fetched Luisa to our colony on the Chubut River, and a better life among the Welsh.

FINIS